LAWS OF PHYSICS BOOK 1: MOTION

PENNY REID

HTTP://WWW.PENNYREID.NINJA/NEWSLETTER/

Caped Publishing

Made in the United States of America

1st Edition, February 2019

PRINT EDITION

DEDICATION

For nerds who aren't a Bohr.

AUTHOR'S NOTE

If you have read the Elements of Chemistry trilogy (Hypothesis Trilogies #1), the action of this book (*Laws of Physics: MOTION*) occurs one year prior to the action of *Elements of Chemistry: CAPTURE*

If you have read Knitting in the City series, the action of this book occurs the summer between *Love Hacked* and *Beauty and the Mustache* (and one year prior to the action of *Dating-ish*)

If you have read the Dear Professor series, the action of this book occurs two years prior to *Kissing Tolstoy*

If you have read none of these books, ignore this note.

[1]
PHYSICS IN A PERSONAL AND SOCIAL CONTEXT

"Y ou are receiving a collect call from *ACCEPT THE CHARGES, MONA!* at Cretin County Jail. If you accept the charges, press one. If not, disconnect," the robot—apparently the love child between Alexa and Baymax—announced via my cell phone, the sound an odd amalgamation of her voice and his cadence.

No. Strike that. Inaccurate.

Most of the words were announced by the robot. But the words "ACCEPT THE CHARGES, MONA!" and the voice that whisper-shouted them belonged to my twin sister, Lisa. I didn't press one and I didn't disconnect. But I did stare at nothing, probably making my about-to-sneeze face, and attempted to parse through what I'd just heard.

"Is everything okay?"

Dr. Payton's perfectly reasonable question hijacked my attention and reminded me that I wasn't alone. I was in a restaurant. The planetary astrophysicist's eyebrows inched upward as we stared at each other, his last bite of steak left forgotten on the tip of his fork.

Fraught and feeling illogically harassed, I sputtered, "I don't know."

This was one of the very few times in my nineteen years that I'd said *I don't know*. I didn't like not knowing. I preferred *I'll find out, I'll figure it out*, or *I'll know soon*.

If he'd asked me the same question just thirty seconds ago, I would've known how to answer. Prior to my cell ringing seconds ago, today had been a great day. I'd meditated as soon as I'd awoken. I'd journaled. I'd located and eaten a perfectly ripe avocado for breakfast. The best. Avocados in Chicago and Cambridge, Mass were so seldom perfectly ripe, or they were ripe for only 4.4 seconds. Whereas California had all the ripe avocados.

Traffic on the I-5 had been light while my driver transported me from the Pasadena Marriott to the Palomar Observatory. I'd spent most of my day elbows deep with my best friends: the gorgeous symmetry and chaos of relativistic equations, infrared array imaging, spectroscopy data.

Late afternoon, I'd gone to the dentist for a teeth cleaning, X-rays, and exam where I'd been told that my home regimen of flossing and brushing was exemplary. Praise from the dentist always put me in a good mood.

Presently, I was having dinner with Dr. Poe Payton, a second-year fellow in planetary astrophysics who was as intelligent as he was handsome and charming, which was considerably. Not that his handsomeness or ability to charm was relevant. As with all my prospective colleagues, nothing was relevant about Dr. Payton other than his ability to keep up.

Afterward, my plans included swimming in the hotel pool, showering, and finally an hour of scheduled fiction reading before bed. Although, now that I was living on my own, and finally free of Dr. Steward's daily oversight, I sometimes read for an hour and a half.

"You are receiving a collect call from *ACCEPT THE CHARGES, MONA!* at Cretin County Jail. If you accept the charges, press one. If not, disconnect," the Alexa-Baymax hybrid announced again, startling me a second time.

Flustered, I pressed one and brought the phone back to my ear. "Uh, hello? Hello?"

"Thank God!" My twin sounded far away, like the connection was bad or she was speaking in a tunnel.

"Lisa?" I whisper-asked, my eyes darting to Dr. Payton's curious and concerned expression.

"First, don't freak out. Second, I don't have a lot of time, so don't ask questions. Just do what I say, okay? I've been arrested."

Arrested.

Oh God. Oh my God! Okay . . . OH MY GOD!

Clutching my forehead, heart racing, I dropped my gaze to the napkin on my lap. "Are you okay? I- what? Where are—"

"Listen," she said firmly, "I need you to listen to me."

"Should I call—"

"No! Don't call anyone. I already have a lawyer, and—if everything goes according to plan—I should be released by next week."

What? "What?"

My eyes darted up, snagging on Dr. Payton, who was now looking at me with some alarm.

He asked, "What can I do?" But this time he mouthed his question.

I didn't answer, I couldn't. Lisa was still talking in my ear, my mind accelerating to a million miles per second.

". . . so I need you to go home and pretend to be me. Otherwise, they'll know what happened and I'll be so, so screwed."

I lifted a finger, motioning for Dr. Payton to give me a minute, and turned my body toward the window on my right. "Uh, pardon?"

"Mona, focus." My typically imperturbable sister's voice trembled. "You have to get to Chicago—*tonight* if possible—and be me."

Go to Chicago? Impossible. But one thing at a time.

Taking a deep breath, I closed my eyes and asked the most pertinent question. "First, tell me if you're okay. Are you hurt?"

Lisa heaved a watery-sounding sigh. "I'm not hurt. But, no. I'm not okay."

Lisa. My lungs constricted, I rubbed my sternum with my fingertips. We weren't particularly close, not anymore, but right now that didn't matter. This was my sister, my twin. There'd been a time when

I'd thought we shared one-half of the same heart. Our brother Leo used to tell us this story and we'd believed him.

No. Strike that. Inaccurate. I'd believed him. Lisa had never been as naïve or gullible or susceptible to fictions and romanticism as me.

"What can I do?" I asked, opening my eyes.

"Get to Chicago. Pretend to be me for a week. And—"

"I can't. I'm in California for my visit with Caltech. I'm interviewing for their PhD program."

"Oh please. You mean *you're* interviewing *them.* Everyone wants you. They wouldn't care if you left, they wouldn't care if you did a striptease on the dean's desk while snorting coke off his letter opener. Hell, he'd probably love it."

"The dean is a heterosexual female."

Lisa grunted. "Whatever! Please, please, please listen, Mona. This is serious. This is life and death for me. You have to wear my clothes, my makeup, sleep in my room, act like me. Mom and Dad can't know I'm in . . . shit. I can't believe this happened."

I shook my head. "Lisa, no. No. Listen to yourself. This is crazy, even for you. Mom and Dad will know I'm me."

"Obviously, Mona!" she whispered harshly. "But you don't have to fool Mom and Dad. They're still in Greece. Abram is watching the house. You just have to fool him until I get there."

She was talking so fast, I was having trouble keeping up. "Who is Abram?"

"Abram. You know, Abram, Leo's friend? You don't know Abram? Oh, good"—she sounded relieved—"in fact, that's great! I've only sorta met Abram once, so this'll be super easy. Pretend like you don't remember him or anything about the night we met, which is actually pretty accurate, because I don't remember much. We'll switch places before your BFF Dr. Steward arrives, and no one will know about this nightmare."

Overwhelmed by my confusion and her sense of urgency, I couldn't organize my thoughts into any logical order, asking questions as they occurred to me. "Wait, Dr. Steward is coming?" Dr. Steward had lived with me and served as my guardian for most of my undergrad; this arrangement had lasted until I'd turned eighteen. "And why do I have to go to Chicago if Mom and Dad are in Greece? Shouldn't I come to where you are and—"

She made a short growling sound. "They're planning to cut me off, okay? They said if I wasn't home by tomorrow, and if I didn't hand over my phone to Abram when I got there, *and* if I don't cut off all contact with Tyler, then they'd close my bank accounts and credit cards and that's it."

I struggled anew with this information, mostly because I thought Lisa had already ended all contact with Tyler. Our family had been living the last few months under the assumption that she was safe from his influence, that they were finally over-*over*. She'd sworn it was over. She'd promised.

"You're still with Tyler?"

An epic scoff-snort sounded from the other end of the call. "Not anymore. God, never again. Not after this. I am so done with that lying, cheating, massive piece of shit!"

I had to press the cell closer to my ear to hear her. Unlike most people, both Lisa and I became quieter when we were angry rather than louder.

"Lisa, this is crazy. I can't be you." I kept my voice low, turning in the chair as far from Dr. Payton as I could. "No one will buy it." We hadn't been raised together past the age of eleven. Both my older brother and I had stayed home with private tutors—he studied music, I concentrated on math and science—while Lisa had been sent to boarding school.

"They will buy it. We're physically identical. All you need is a makeover."

I struggled with how to phrase my next objection, but ultimately decided I didn't have time to be tactful. "Lisa, I love you, but I wouldn't know the first thing about acting like you. I don't know you." Most of what I knew about my sister's life was deduced from chance encounters with the gossip sections of newspapers and magazines.

Exotica and DJ Tang's youngest daughter spotted at New York hot spot

Exotica and DJ Tang's youngest daughter in trouble again

Exotica and DJ Tang's youngest daughter rumored to be dating Pirate Orgy's front man, Tyler

Exotica and DJ Tang's youngest daughter partying at fashion week

Exotica and DJ Tang's youngest daughter wrecks Tesla

"That's not true." She sounded exasperated rather than hurt.

"I call you once a week, you never pick up. And when you respond it's with a text message."

"Mona, you never returned my letters when I was sent to boarding school, so what's the big deal?"

What? Why was she bringing this up? Again! Lisa had been bringing this up to excuse treating me poorly for *years*. It's how she justified her jokes and pranks, none of which were funny.

"I did return your letters. How many times—"

"I'm not going to argue with you about this again. You didn't return my letters, which is why I stopped sending them. So, again, why does it matter if I text you back?"

"Because when we do talk on the phone, it's for less than five minutes. You think my life is boring and we have nothing in common." I tried—and succeeded—to keep emotion out of my voice. This was my superpower, a skill I'd honed as a fifteen-year-old girl, entering a field dominated by not fifteen-year-old girls. "You were right. We have nothing in common. And now you want me to pretend to be you? It won't work."

For better or worse, I had more in common with my musician older brother than I did with my twin.

"Yes. It will. Like I said, Abram has only met me once, and he didn't seem impressed, and I hardly remember it. So as long as you're wearing my clothes and your impersonation is passable, he'll leave you alone and we'll be golden. I've already set everything up with Gabby. She's expecting your call. She'll meet you in Chicago, dress you to look like me before you go to the house."

Gabby. My nostrils flexed, flared with annoyance (I hated it when they did that).

Gabby was Lisa's best friend and used to be mine, once upon a time. The three of us had been inseparable as kids. We used to pretend we were triplets, with Gabby being our long-lost sister. Noteworthy, Gabby and Lisa had always been more interested in pretty dresses and painting their nails than I had; and I loved reading in a way they both eschewed; but our differences hadn't seemed to matter at the time. I would paint my nails right along with them, and they indulged my love of stories by listening to me read out loud.

Things started to change around the age of nine. Gabby and Lisa's interests moved firmly from imaginary games involving being dragon tamers—or being astronauts, or being stranded on a desert island—to imaginary games involving being famous and important in the *real* world, calling the games I wanted to play "baby stuff."

But pretending within the confines of "the real world" made no sense to me. It's like they were speaking a different language, one I couldn't understand, and one that seemed horribly . . . well, *boring.*

Anyway.

Our official friendship separation (Gabby and Lisa versus Mona) could be traced to one night when we were eleven. I'd alerted our nanny that my sister and our friend had snuck some whiskey from the liquor cabinet after asking them repeatedly to put it back. Lisa had been sent to boarding school not long after, but when she was home, I'd played on my own and they'd been virtually inseparable.

Fascinatingly, eight years later, Gabby still held a grudge—let me repeat, for *eight years*—related to my snitching on her when we were eleven. I'd never snitched again. On anyone. For anything. Ever.

Understatement: I'd learned my lesson about snitching.

I'd tried (and failed) to get in their good graces for years after the whiskey-snitching incident until Gabby introduced Lisa to Tyler. Now Gabby's dislike of me was entirely mutual. I didn't know how to forgive her for introducing my twin to that scumbag.

Conclusion: At this point, I worked under the assumption that Gabby was quite possibly mentally unhinged and strongly disliked—if not outright hated—me.

But back to now and Lisa being in jail and me being shocked and awed and making my about-to-sneeze face.

Lisa continued, "When you get there, all you have to do is wear designer clothes, eyeliner, and make terrible life decisions." She laughed, the sound both hysterical and sad. "Plus, you have to do this for me. You don't have a choice. Unless you plan to do nothing—*again*—and let Mom and Dad to disown me."

What the what?

"Doing nothing? What are you—"

"Forget it, Mona. Now isn't the time. If you care about me at all, go to Chicago and pretend for Abram until I get there."

"But who is Abram? Why is he at the house? Why would Mom and Dad trust him to do this? And how can I—"

"God! Look, I don't have time to argue with you about this." Her tone was tired, strained, frazzled. "Are you going to help me or not?"

I wanted to say, *This will never work!* But when I opened my mouth, no words came out.

"Call Gabby, she's expecting your call. Go to Chicago. Get a ticket for tonight, okay? My cell phone has been mailed to Chicago and should arrive tomorrow or the next day. If Abram asks you for my phone when you get there, just tell him you left it behind and are having it mailed to you. Sit tight and let your inhibitions go—for once—until I get there."

"Lisa—"

"Promise me, Mona. Promise me. I swear, I'll be so good. I'll be so fucking good. I'll go back and finish high school, I'll never touch drugs again, I'll never see Tyler again, I'll be the best sister and daughter, I'll forgive you for everything, we'll create a special handshake for when the next NASA thing lands on Jupiter or whatever, I will never call physics boring, and I will make this up to you. I will never, ever lie. But if you don't do this for me, I'm dead. I'm so, so dead." Her voice caught on the last sentence, adopting a decidedly watery edge, and that sobered me more than anything else would have.

My sister didn't cry. Ever. What a messy mess.

"You don't have to worry about paparazzi or anything like that." Her breath hitched, and that told me she was now unable to stem the tears. "Gabby hooked me up with the best lawyer, she specializes in this kind of stuff, keeping it out of the papers. This won't make it out to the press. And you know they only care about the over-achievers in the family."

I resisted the urge to huff and remind her that she was the lucky one, the one the press didn't follow at all, the one who was able to live her life out of the spotlight. But every time I told her this it just seemed to piss her off.

"They don't care about me unless I fuck up . . ." she added quietly.

"Lisa—"

But then she said, "Please."

The single word sounded so desperate, so broken, it struck a chord deep within me, a bond I'd assumed had dissolved, but now understood had merely been dormant. She hadn't asked me for anything since we were kids. How could I say no?

I couldn't.

"Of course. Yes." Even though it was complete madness.

"Thank you, thank you. And when I see you, I'll tell you everything, don't worry. You won't be sorry. You are the best sister in the world. I love you!" she said just before the line went dead.

Removing the cell from my ear, I stared at the blank screen, my mind in chaos. I was unsure what to do, or on which problem I should focus.

Am I really going to do this?

Hastily, I made a list of the most basic action items. Getting a ticket to Chicago shouldn't be a big deal. If I left directly from the restaurant, I could probably catch something tonight, stay in a hotel by O'Hare. I'd call Gabby on the way. Assuming my parents didn't insist on speaking to me—well, "to me" meaning Lisa—then I might be back in Pasadena by the end of the week.

Am I really going to do this?

"Hey." Dr. Payton's soft voice cut through my list making. His wide brown eyes moved over my face, concern etched between his eyebrows. "Hey, is everything okay?"

"I'm sorry. That was rude. I should have left the table," I said on autopilot, my brain still working through next steps. I felt his eyes on me as I returned my phone to my backpack. His stare felt assessing, but not in the usual way. Usually, when people stared, I knew exactly what they were thinking.

Depending on the person and context, it was either, *Isn't that the girl whose research on Bose-Einstein condensates improved the reliability and power of infrared arrays? Wasn't she twelve when that happened?* Or the person was thinking, *Isn't that one of Exotica and DJ Tang's daughters? Is that the cool crazy one or the weirdo math prodigy?*

"Don't apologize," Dr. Payton said unexpectedly, drawing my gaze back to his as he reached a hand across the table and covered mine.

I pulled my fingers away. Immediately. On instinct.

Tangentially, I noted his skin had been warm and that this was the first time he'd touched me other than a handshake. In fact, other than my one friend, Allyn, this was the first time someone had touched me to offer comfort since . . . well, since longer than I could remember.

"What's wrong?" he asked, his voice gentle and interested. "How can I help?"

"Wrong? Help?" *What?*

"All the color left your face." Dr. Payton paused to study me, the intensity of his frown increasing. "Mona, what happened? Who was that?"

Mona? The informality was a bucket of ice water, cutting through the haze of confusion. I blinked at him and the use of my first name. For these last two weeks he'd been Dr. Payton and I'd been Ms. DaVinci, which was how interactions within my world worked. Always.

As the youngest person by far in any given room—and the room was typically full of men with PhDs fighting for prestige, tenure, and grant dollars—I'd learned early and often that informality meant being taken advantage of. It meant being the second or third author instead of the first on a scholarly article of my own original ideas. It meant opening a door to borrowing (i.e. stealing) my work and intellectual property.

Nothing was more sacred or worth protecting in academia than intellectual property, and everyone wanted to take credit for mine.

"Dr. Payton, I'm very sorry to cut our meeting short." When I stood, he stood, giving me the impression his good manners were ingrained. "I hope we can continue our discussion on Illustris soon, but I have to go." Once again, I flexed my superpower, removing all emotion from my voice.

Clearly surprised by my coolness, Dr. Payton rocked back on his heels and stuffed his hands in his pockets. "Absolutely. I understand," he said, though it was obvious he didn't understand.

Placing my backpack on the chair, I furtively studied him as I zipped and unzipped it, searching for my wallet. I noted the cautious yet concerned way he continued to examine me, at the tense set of his jaw, like he was engaging in an internal debate. I had to swat away a pang of guilt and doubt.

Dr. Payton—Poe—had been nothing but gracious since I'd arrived, but not overbearingly so. Overbearing and overly solicitous faculty had been my experience at the other institutions I'd visited during my quest to find the right PhD program. Even his willingness to collaborate and share, discuss and troubleshoot had been unpretentious. Poe's ideas and approach were unique and refreshing.

The man was certainly brilliant, seemed to be a genuinely good guy, and I was curious about his thoughts on Illustris, the universe-scale simulation project, which was why I'd agreed to dinner. Yet, tempted as I might be to soften my rules about informality and friendly fraternization with colleagues, I wouldn't.

"Do you need a ride anywhere?" he asked stiffly, quickly adding, "No pressure. It's just, my mother would be appalled if I didn't offer."

His slight confession, and how he referred to his mother with deference, made me pause my furious zipping. "Thank you. I have a driver."

He cleared his throat and nodded, seemed to stand straighter. My gaze flickered to his then away and I dug for my wallet. Finding it, I placed a fifty-dollar bill on the table to cover the cost of my dinner.

"You don't need to do that." He frowned, reaching for the money and offering it back to me.

I shook my head and swung my backpack into place on my right shoulder. "My advisor told me I should pay for my own meals during the recruitment process so as to not unduly influence my final decision."

He flinched subtly, like I'd surprised him again. "I see," he said, then huffed a little laugh. It was amused, but also sounded a tad incredulous. I got the sense I'd offended him somehow . . .

A renewed wave of flustered urgency crashed over me. I didn't have time to think about Dr. Payton. I had to call Gabby, get to Chicago, and figure out how to behave like Lisa and not like me.

"I'll be gone for a few days," I said, not understanding why I felt the need to explain anything. "There's an unexpected emergency. I'll email Dr. Clarence and the team to let them know."

"Fine." He pressed his lips together, a flat line, his expression now neutral.

I hesitated for a split second, knowing I was doing something wrong yet unable to put my finger on what. But exigency—for my sister's sake —spurred me to move. Giving him a final head nod, I left the restaurant.

With any luck, I'd be in Chicago before midnight.

* * *

"We're going to have to get you a blowout." Gabby pursed her lips at the sight of my single braid, sighed dramatically, and marched past me into my hotel room. "And Lisa's hair is a little shorter I think, so we'll also need a cut. But the color is fine, she went back to her natural dark brown too, like, I don't know, a few months ago, when she pretended to split from Tyler. Do you own any makeup at all?"

Turning, I allowed the hotel door to shut behind me and faced my former friend. "Hello, and yes I own makeup."

Of note, Gabby's real name was Lyndsay. Gabby was a nickname she'd earned because she talked too much and had no filter, always saying whatever popped into her head. This worked for her because her parents were massively wealthy movie stars and had no problem bailing her out of whatever trouble she—and her mouth—found herself in.

Ignoring my greeting, she set a bag on the bed. "I bet it's the wrong kind of makeup. Whatever. There's a Sephora on the way to your house, we'll go there. Lisa said you don't know how to do your eyes, so they can teach you there. Lisa *never* shows her face without mascara and liner, so make sure you do that every day. And here"—she gestured to the bag—"I brought some of Lisa's clothes from the last time she spent the night at my house. We got *soooo* drunk. And it was tequila drunk, not vodka tonic drunk, you know what I mean?" Gabby laughed and gave me a commiserating look.

I didn't know what she meant, but I could extrapolate. Regardless, I did not return her look.

Her amusement vanished.

"Anyway." She paired the single word with an eyebrow lift, a sure sign of exasperation. "This should have everything you need for now. Feel free to thank me at any point here."

No thanks was forthcoming, but she already knew that.

I hadn't returned to my hotel in Los Angeles last night. There was no point in packing clothes before leaving via LAX. Other than underwear and socks, I was supposed to wear Lisa's clothes anyway.

Everything I needed was in my backpack—my laptop, my research notes, my journal—so I sent a text to Gabby and hopped on the next plane to Chicago. We touched down just after 1:00 AM and I spent the night at the Westin near O'Hare, wearing the same clothes to sleep that I'd worn to the dentist.

There's something liberating about sleeping in clothes instead of pajamas, I'd mused the next morning as I brushed my teeth with supplies hastily purchased from the lobby store. The thought felt rebellious, so I pushed it aside and waited for Gabby to show up.

Which brings us to now.

Am I really doing this?

Not for the first or the thousandth time since hanging up with Lisa yesterday, I took stock of this messy mess and how I'd arrived at this moment, peaking inside a bag brought by Gabby. Speaking of the Gabster, she was staring at my profile as I peered in the bag.

Abruptly, apropos of nothing, she said, "You're boring."

My eyes lifted to hers. "Okay."

"You look boring, I mean. Like, I know you and Lisa are supposed to be identical, but if you were in a club you'd be invisible. You'd be wallpaper. Doesn't that bother you?" Though the words might've been interpreted as harsh, the question sounded honestly curious.

Nevertheless, it aggravated me. This was my chance to find out why Lisa had been arrested and Gabby was already getting under my skin before I could ask any questions.

"No," I answered, just as honestly, withholding all emotion from my voice and expression.

"Haven't you ever wanted to be noticed? Be . . . interesting?"

"Not really." I turned my attention back to the clothes and spotted a black lace bra tucked to one side.

. . . Am I really doing this?

"How is it possible you are still such a Mary Sue?" She poked my shoulder. "Haven't you heard? Nowadays, being nice is unlikable. It's all about the rebel. You should do something unexpected, mean, self-ish, and don't apologize for it. Be bad for once and tell everyone to fuck off."

I sent her a quick glare. "I just ditched a PhD program interview. I'm about to lie and impersonate my twin sister for several days so my parents won't disown her. Maybe save that question for later, when it might be more accurate."

"Well, you kind of owe her, don't you?"

"Owe her? Owe her for what?"

"For getting her sent off to boarding school? For ratting us out to your nanny? Ring any bells?"

I was so proud of myself for not punching her in the face, and even more proud for keeping my voice level and calm. "We both know Lisa wasn't sent to boarding school because I told our nanny that you had taken whiskey from the cabinet."

"Oh? Really? That's not how I remember it."

"Yes. Really. The only reason Leo and I stayed with Mom and Dad was because of his music and my research."

"Whatever you need to tell yourself so you can sleep at night." Gabby studied her nails. "And you know what I mean about being a Mary Sue. Helping Lisa is just part of the same saintly shit, different day."

Why was she giving me grief about being helpful? *Oh. That's right. Because she's unhinged.*

"While you're standing here telling me to be bad, Lisa is in jail. Aren't you at all concerned about her?" As much as I despised interacting with Gabby these days, we were both here for one reason: to help Lisa because we loved and cared about her.

Gabby rolled her eyes. "Of course I'm concerned about her. I'm terrified for her, okay? And I'm doing everything I can to get her out and save her ass, including putting up with you."

"Putting up with me?" Arg! She was so irritating, all my questions fled my brain.

"You heard me." Talking to her was like arguing with a flat-earther. *Ignorance plus arrogance is why we can't have nice things!*

Best just to get straight to the point. "Why was Lisa arrested?"

Gabby's flippancy morphed into a severe scowl. "Does it matter? She needs your help. What? Now you don't want to help her?"

"I didn't say that."

"Then help her, and put on these clothes, and stop making this about you."

"I just want to know why—"

"Classic Mary Sue behavior. Even when you're being bad, you're still looking for a way to be the do-gooder center of attention. Where is the fun in always being the good one when it means you have no friends? Why must you ruin fun for everyone else?"

"Oh, you know, I think the fun is in not being arrested for doing something stupid and selfishly forcing your sister to clean up your giant mess." Despite my best efforts, a hint of bitterness entered my voice, and that flustered me.

Rattled by my uncontrollable, unexpected, and uncharacteristic show of feelings, I cleared my throat and dropped my eyes. Apparently, my ability to speak truth without emotion was on the fritz. Best not to speak to her at all. Pulling out the black bra and shirt Gabby had brought, I held the top up to me. Scowling, I wondered where the other half was, it seemed to be missing the section that covered the stomach.

Gabby snorted and rolled her eyes. "None of Lisa's clothes are boring. You're going to be noticed."

Reaching for a bunched-up pile of black leather in the bottom of the bag and realizing it was pants, I heaved a sigh. "Whether or not I'm boring is irrelevant. Whether or not I'm likable or nice or good or a Mary Sue is irrelevant. The fact is, I am boring and unlikable by your standards. That's never going to change because I don't subscribe to your standards. So, moving on, is there anything else I can wear other than these two items?"

Gabby turned her grumpy expression to the scrap of the shirt, black lace bra, and the black leather pants. "What's wrong with these?"

"Nothing," I mumbled, resigned, and scooped them up before turning for the bathroom. "I'll go change."

"Too bad you can't actually change," she called after me. "Too bad putting on Lisa's clothes doesn't also give you some of her badass mojo and rebel spirit."

Unable to help myself, I mumbled, "You belong on Venus, Gabby."

"You mean, because it's, like, the planet of love?" she asked with fake sweetness.

"No. Because it's, *like,* our solar system's analog to hell." And with that, I closed the door to the bathroom and changed. Into my sister.

[2]
INTRODUCTION TO ONE-DIMENSIONAL KINEMATICS

"You actually look . . ." Gabby snorted, as though she couldn't believe what she was about to say, and then said, "You're fucking gorgeous."

We'd left the Westin near O'Hare via taxi and were now downtown in the Old Town Triangle area of Chicago, near my parents' brownstone. We'd already visited the hair salon and were now finishing up at the makeup store, during which I'd said less than ten words total. I didn't want to fight with Gabby. Even though we only saw each other about once a year, I was *so tired* of fighting with her.

But now the moment was imminently upon us. Soon we'd be walking the few short blocks home. Time flies when one is fretting about impersonating one's twin sister.

While I'd been getting my "blowout" as Gabby called it, I'd received a call from someone who identified herself as Lisa's lawyer. She'd left a voice message, detailing her strategy for getting Lisa released, the projected timeline—still one week—and that Lisa's phone had been sent via priority to the Chicago house.

What she didn't reveal was why Lisa had been arrested in the first place. I'd tried calling her back, but it went straight to voicemail.

Currently, I was staring at my reflection; at the copious waves of dark brown hair falling over my shoulders, how wearing it down brought out the olive tone in my skin more than wearing it back; at the red stain and gloss accentuating the fullness of my lips; at the dark liner and mascara and eye shadow emphasizing the thickness of my lashes and honey color of my eyes. Paired with the half shirt and leather pants, the entirety of everything together made me look . . .

I look hot.

With a resigned sigh, I accepted that Gabby was correct. "I look like Lisa." Which meant I also looked like our mother. Even at fifty-two, our mother and Lisa were often confused by the press.

"Exactly." She grinned. "Like I said, you're gorgeous. You work out, right?"

I gave her a noncommittal shrug. I swam daily and used a standing desk, which probably didn't meet her definition of working out. Lisa and Gabby, I was pretty sure, both had personal trainers. Theoretically, I wanted a personal trainer—because wouldn't that be nice? Someone to plan my workout, keep it interesting, keep me engaged, think about my health so I didn't have to—but in reality, I didn't want one.

I'd tried it once. The guy touched my arm to reposition it without asking me first. I flinched, which caused me to drop the dumbbell on his foot. I never went back, but I did pay his doctor's bills and sent him a year's supply of protein bars.

She walked to the other side of the chair, and the Sephora external aesthetic-modifier technician (which is what I decided they ought to be called) stepped back, giving Gabby room to inspect my face from a new angle. "Wow—" her eyes swept over me, from the black and white Converse on my feet, up to the leather pants, to my bare midriff, chest, collarbone, neck, "—you really do look like her." She sounded surprised.

I bit my tongue so I wouldn't point out the obvious, that we were identical twins. Of course I looked like her. But Gabby wasn't being insulting for once and I had enough on my mind. No need to pick another fight. Hopefully, merely looking like Lisa would be enough to convince Leo's friend that I was Lisa, because I had no idea how to act like a normal person, let alone like my sister.

Gabby cocked her head to the side, her gaze growing thoughtful. "Why don't you wear your hair down ever? Or do your eyes. You're beautiful, or would be if you put in the effort."

"We already talked about this."

"Because you want to be a nerd-girl stereotype, Mary Sue?"

"Human beauty is irrelevant in physics," I mumbled. Not wanting to get into it, but beauty was more than irrelevant. It was a liability.

"Okay, Borg." She lifted that eyebrow. "It doesn't matter."

"Then it has no mass," I said automatically.

"What?"

"If it has no matter, it has no mass."

Her stare was blank. "What are you talking about?"

"It's a physics joke. If something has no matter, then—never mind." I pressed my lips together.

"No more physics jokes!" Gabby stabbed a finger at my shoulder.

Leaning away, I lifted my hands in a show of surrender.

She administered one final exasperated eyebrow lift before turning and giving the external aesthetic-modifier technician instructions on what items we were going to purchase.

Meanwhile, I stood from the chair and tried not to lick my lips. The lip stain wasn't flavored, but the gloss the employee had applied over it tasted like bubble gum. In a word, delicious. I'd had a minor addiction to cherry flavored Chapstick at one point and it had taken a year to break the habit. Thus, I vowed to throw away the bubble gum gloss as soon as I left Chicago.

Or as soon as I landed at LAX.

Or, at the very latest, as soon as I made it back to the hotel in Los Angeles.

Maybe I'd keep it for a week, *what's the harm in that?*

"Let's go, Mona Lisa." Gabby nudged my arm, pushing me toward the door as she handed over the bag with all the makeup. I gave her the side-eye, accepted the products, but said nothing.

Once outside, she nudged me again. "Get it? *Mona Lisa?*"

"Yes." Hil-AR-ious.

My parents had decided naming my brother Leonardo, me Mona,

my sister Lisa, and giving us the last name of DaVinci was a really great idea. It could have been worse. They could have named my brother "Michel," me "Ang," and Lisa "Elo," which had been their original plan. Over the course of my life, I'd come to understand that my parents had named their children as a reflection of themselves rather than as a reflection of their hopes for us. Based on my informal sampling of celebrity children, it was always thus for superstars.

I glanced at my watch, it was only 1:00 PM. I considered calling the lawyer to check on the status of Lisa's release even though she'd just touched base a few hours ago and I'd left her a voice message already.

"Your backpack." Gabby flicked my bag. "What are you doing with that? Where will you put it?"

"Um." My steps faltered. "I hadn't thought about that." I was bad at this. *What other lying logistics had I not considered?*

She continued to eye it. "What's inside? Clothes?"

"My computer, research notes, wallet, phone."

Gabby started shaking her head before I'd finished speaking. "Ah, no. You can't bring that to the house. Lisa said Abram was supposed to take her phone as soon as she got there, right? Well then, he'll definitely take—and probably search—your backpack. If he searches your backpack, he'll know you're you and not Lisa. Plus, he'll find your phone, and you're supposed to pretend like you left it behind."

I scowled even though she was right. None of her valid points had occurred to me. "I guess I could go back to O'Hare, bag check it at the Westin, and pick it up on my way out of town next week." I didn't like the thought of being separated from my research or my journal.

She inspected me. "When we get to your block, give it to me. I'll carry it the rest of the way and say it's mine if he asks."

I shifted away from her, distrustful. "What will you do with it?"

She made another of her give-me-a-break faces. "I'll put it in your room—in *Mona's* room—when we go upstairs. By the way, don't forget, your room is Lisa's room. Because you are Lisa and you don't tell physics jokes. You tell peen and poop jokes like all self-respecting feminists."

"You're not going to take it?" I lifted my chin, scrutinizing her dependability in this particular situation. "If you try to take my backpack out of the house, I'll break character right there and tell Abraham the truth."

"You have trust issues. Don't worry, I won't take your precious backpack. It doesn't match my ensemble. And it's Abram, not Abraham."

Speaking of not-Abraham. "Have you met him?"

Gabby gave me a meaningful look and kept on walking. Unfortunately, I'd never been gifted at deciphering meaningful looks.

I tried again. "So you do know him? Or what?"

"Abram?" Gabby blinked, once, hard. "Lisa didn't tell you about Abram?"

I shook my head.

"Leo didn't introduce you? They're, like, best friends."

"No. Leo never mentioned him." When Leo and I talked, it was once every six months and typically focused on him telling me about his upcoming gigs as well as questioning me about girls—how they thought, why they did certain things, etc. He rarely mentioned his friend group, if at all. I'd tried to explain that I didn't understand girls. Or people. He persisted. As such, I did my best to offer generalizable theories about female behavior.

Gabby stopped, blinking several times as though her brain was having difficulty accepting my words. "Oh, Mona. You are in for a *treat.*" Flipping her braids over her shoulder, she'd placed special emphasis on the word *treat.*

I glanced from side to side. "Why? Does he abhor superstring theory?"

She made another face of distaste, or at least tried to. I caught the tail end of a suppressed smile as she said, "I know him a lot better than Lisa does, because sometimes I hang with Leo when he's in town. Abram can be uptight, for sure, but he's also a big flirt. And woman, he's so gorgeous it hurts. I mean, it physically hurts my hoo-hah to look at him in the best, hoo-hah happiest way. He's so gorgeous, I've already forgiven him for being mean to our girl. And he's a musician."

She paused here to bite her bottom lip and look at the sky. "Writes his own music," she moaned, "plays the bass guitar, and the piano, and every other instrument, and he sings. And when he sings, it makes my panties want to melt right off my body. Just *whoop*"—she made a swooping motion with her hand, gesturing from her crotch to the side-walk—"they want to melt right off."

"Is he smart?"

"Uh, what?" Her gaze flickered over me, leaving me with the impression I'd disappointed her. "Here I am talking about his fineness, and you have to rain on my parade by asking about his brains?"

"Is he smart?" I repeated.

"Does it matter?"

Don't make another physics joke about matter! "It's relevant if his level of intelligence means he'll deduce I'm not Lisa."

"Okay, first of all"—she lifted a finger between us—"you can't speak like that."

"Like what?"

"Don't use words like *deduce* or *relevant*." Gabby over-pronounced the offending words, obviously attempting an impression of me.

"Fine." A flutter of disquiet hit my stomach, which I hid. "Maybe I won't speak at all."

"That works. Don't speak. Or, just give one-word answers. For example: no, yes, what, who, when, whatever. If in doubt, saying *whatever* usually works." Gabby turned back to the sidewalk and we both began walking again.

While interacting with people about non-academic topics, I'd experienced my fair share of difficulty knowing how to segue into a new subject, or how to end a conversation, or knowing what to say when people over-shared. When I was fifteen, I stumbled across a list of phrases that mostly worked for any occasion, and I'd put them into practice with varying levels of success.

Phrases like *But at what cost?*

Or *In this economy?*

Or *So . . . it has come to this.*

Or *So let it be written, so let it be done.*

Or my personal favorite for when I didn't know how to end a sentence or complete a thought . . . *And then the wolves came.*

These phrases seemed to work best when attempting to diffuse a tense situation or confuse the other person long enough for me to make my escape. Regardless, in the same spirit, I appreciated Gabby's tip. I could default to saying *whatever.* That would be fine.

"Just don't say anything obviously Mona-like," she continued. "You look so much like Lisa, I don't think the possibility that you're Mona will even occur to him."

"But he's met Lisa."

"Yes, but for like five minutes. He doesn't really know her. Lisa only met him the one time, when we crashed one of your brother's parties." She paused here, sighing wistfully, as though remembering the encounter, and then added, "And even though they barely inter-acted, he was kind of a dick to Lisa."

He'd been "a dick" to her? That triggered the ingrained protective-sister sonar. Regardless of how close (or not) we were, sister-sonar meant I would automatically dislike anyone who'd been "a dick" to Lisa, no matter how much hoo-hah happiness he inspired. Hoo-hah happiness was irrelevant.

"What did he say to her?"

"They didn't really, uh, talk."

Even with my paltry conversation-nuance detection skills, I picked up on the weird way she said *talk.* "Expand on that, please."

Gabby waved her hand in the air, dismissing my question. "Whatever, it's not important. Getting back to your original question, Abram might be smart, I don't know. But he doesn't know Lisa well enough to tell the difference between the two of you *as long as* you don't go around telling physics jokes and asking him to deduce or expand on things."

"Fine." I turned and continued walking toward the house, wondering if Gabby would fly off the handle again if I asked about Lisa's arrest. Not wanting to inspire another round of insults, I tried a different—but related—topic. "So, why Abram? Why did my parents choose Abram to keep an eye on Lisa?"

"Uh, I don't really know. According to Lisa, when I talked to her yesterday on the phone and we discussed the plan, she made it sound like he just happened to be in the right place at the wrong time."

"Was she okay? When you talked to her?"

Gabby sent me a sharp, irritated glare. "How do you think she was?"

Okay, fine. *Don't ask Gabby about Lisa.* Got it.

"Anyway—" Gabby flipped her braids, her tone growing lofty "—Lisa said that your brother was supposed to be at the house this summer, but that he went down to Florida for a thing."

"I think he has work in Miami." The last time I spoke to Leo, he'd mentioned spending part of the summer in south Florida, playing a few clubs.

"Yeah, something like that. So, I guess your guardian lady was supposed to step in and watch the house. What's her name?"

"You mean Dr. Steward? She can't, I think she's in China." I was nineteen now, but the day after I'd turned eighteen, Dr. Steward had taken off to travel the world. She'd been planning the trip for as long as I'd known her.

"That's right. So, until Dr. Steward comes back, your brother suggested Abram keep an eye on the house. I think he's being paid to house-sit. So when your parents issued the ultimatum that Lisa had to go home and wait for their return, they asked Leo to ask Abram to keep an eye on her."

"Do they even know Abram? Why do they trust him?" I felt like I already knew my parents well enough to know the answers to these questions. But I also felt like they needed to be asked, just in case this would be the one time my parents surprised me.

"I don't know." Gabby shrugged. "I guess they figure, if your brother trusts the guy . . ."

I released an irritated puff of a breath, shaking my head, now absorbed in secondhand anger on my sister's behalf. "That's great."

So, not surprised.

It had been the same way with Dr. Steward. The woman was a friend of a friend, an adjunct professor at a college in the Northeast.

They hadn't even interviewed her in person before sending me to the Northeast to live with her full time as a teenager. She'd been . . . fine. Strict and considerably more interested in the money she was banking than in me as a person, but fine.

"What?" Gabby poked me lightly, presumably to get my attention. "Leo wouldn't recommend someone to watch the house who isn't trustworthy, would he? Plus, like I said, they're best friends. *Plus*, like I said, Abram is super uptight."

"And uptight is trustworthy?"

"Exactly. Just look at you."

I grumbled but said nothing to that.

Earlier, Gabby had said, *He was kind of a dick to Lisa,* and yet she saw nothing wrong with this guy keeping an eye on Lisa?

Nothing about Abram, or spending the next week in the same house as him, sounded treat-like to me. Another almost-stranger my parents trusted with one of their daughters. Granted, this guy was Leo's good friend, and Leo did seem to have better judgment about people than either me or Lisa.

Am I really going to do this?

Yes. Yes, I was. We were about two blocks away now, I wasn't a snitch, my sister needed help, and I'd promised. There was only one logical path forward.

But mostly, I refused to be another person in Lisa's life who let her down. Gripping my bag's strap tighter, I imagined the moment I'd have to hand it over to Gabby. Just the thought of trusting her with my backpack for any length of time was making my hands sweat.

"What?" She bumped me with her shoulder.

I shrugged, irritated I couldn't wipe my hands on my pants. Wiping sweaty hands on leather just made for visibly wet leather and still sweaty hands, and wet leather was never a good idea. Never.

"What is that face you're making?" She pointed to my face with her index finger, moving it in a circle.

"I don't know, I can't see myself." There was just something about Gabby that grated, brought my emotions closer to the surface. Or perhaps it was this entire situation. Whatever it was, I couldn't wait for this week to be over and return to the world I understood.

"Here, I'll make the face you're making." Gabby caught my arm and I immediately maneuvered out of her grip. My reflexive reaction didn't seem to bother her, or she didn't notice. Regardless, she cleared her features of all expression except her eyes. She'd narrowed them subtly, and seemed to peer at the world with a hypercritical coolness. "This is the face," she said robotically.

Trying to stuff my fingers into my pockets and failing—because the pockets were sewn shut—I scratched the elbow she'd grabbed and started walking again. "It's just my face."

"Well don't make that face around Abram. Lisa doesn't make that face."

"Okay." *How the hell am I going to do this for a week?* I pasted on a big, fake smile. "Is this better?"

"God, no. Don't do that either." She looked horrified. "What the hell was that? Was that a smile? Was that you smiling?"

I neither confirmed nor denied her speculation, keeping my attention forward as I twisted my lips to the side, trying not to smile for real. Gabby was a nebulous assemblage of unscrupulousness and exasperating nonsense, and we'd likely never be friends again, but she was undoubtedly charming when she wanted to be. There'd always been something about her timing, her delivery, that veered into the territory of funny.

"Okay, hand it over." She touched my arm again, stopping me, and this time I had the wherewithal to not yank out of her grip. Instead, I removed my backpack with *extreme reluctance*, which elicited an eye roll from Gabby. "Oh, give it a break, Mona. Just hurry up. I have other things to do today."

With continued *extreme reluctance*, I eventually handed her the backpack. She carried it the rest of the way to our brownstone while I continued to carry the makeup bag. Every so often, she'd pretend like she was going to toss my backpack in the road, snickering when I tensed.

"Relax, *Lisa.* I wouldn't do anything to jeopardize the happiness and well-being of my BFF."

Gabby batted her eyelashes as I punched in the gate code, all nerves and thumbs. Our brownstone had a tall cast-iron fence facing the sidewalk. I wasn't surprised by the lack of paparazzi. Everyone assumed the DaVinci family members people cared to gossip about—my parents and my brother mostly, me sometimes, Lisa only when she did something crazy—were elsewhere.

After three attempts, I finally got the code right and opened the gate for her. She preceded me up the stairs while I glared at the back of her head. When we reached the door, I reached for my backpack. She twisted away.

"What are you doing?" she hissed.

"I need my keys to open the door."

"No. Your keys aren't in my ugly backpack, *Lisa.*" Gabby sent yet another meaningful look to the house.

Oh. That's right.

Giving my backpack one more longing look, I stepped away from Gabby and rang the doorbell.

"Good." She moved closer to me as we waited for this Abram person to open the door. "That face you're making is very Lisa. Pouty. I approve."

Before I could respond, the door swung open, revealing . . . well, revealing an extremely handsome guy. Upon my initial cursory inspection, I noted that he was tall, had brown hair and eyes, was both startlingly attractive and visibly displeased. One might go so far as to call him irked.

The guy—dressed in a faded black T-shirt and worn blue jeans—pushed a hand into a fall of shiny hair, lifting the long strands away from his forehead. Most men look sloppy in faded T's and worn jeans. But he did not. He looked hot.

Oooohhhh. Okay, I get it.

Yep. I understood at once what Gabby had meant. Abram had won the genetics lottery. Or Powerball. Or whatever. The point was, this guy probably received congratulations cards for his face. *Noted.*

"Lisa," he said to me. A muscle at his defined jaw jumped, visible even beneath the few days of stubble covering the lower half of his face.

"You're Abram," I said, because who else could he be? This statement was made to his distracting chin. His chin—like the rest of him—was pleasingly formed, but his stubble was remarkable. A shade lighter than the hair on his head, it was just as thick. If he ignored it, he'd likely have a hell of a wizard beard in a matter of months. The only thing I truly envied men was their ability to grow wizard beards.

Lifting my hand for a shake, Gabby intercepted it before I could bring my fingers parallel to the ground. "As always, a real pleasure to look at you, Abram. What do you have to eat? Lisa left all her stuff behind—including her wallet—so we're starving." Using my mistakenly offered hand, she pulled me inside the house, brushing past Abram.

Oh, right. Why would Lisa shake his hand? I sent Gabby a glance of gratitude and wondered again how in the helium I was going to fake being not-me for a week.

"There's leftover Chinese food and pizza in the fridge." His tone blatantly hostile, providing additional proof that he wasn't happy to see us.

Gabby steered me into the kitchen and sat me on a stool, giving me a hard look before turning for the fridge and pulling out a box of pizza. I placed the Sephora bag on the counter and waited, unsure what to do. If I'd been me—Mona, not Lisa—I'd have made myself mint tea. But I had no idea if drinking mint tea was in character for Lisa. *Maybe I should pour myself a glass of whiskey?*

While I was stuck debating my beverage choice, Abram appeared in the doorway. He opted to hover by the entrance to the kitchen, leaning his back against the doorframe and shifting his irked glare from me to Gabby. Even scowling and visibly inimical, he was hot.

"Where's your phone?" he asked, his attention coming back to me, lifting his chin as his eyelids drooped.

"Like I said, gorgeous—" Gabby walked into his line of sight, blocking me from view "—she left all her shit behind, even her phone."

"How'd she board a plane if she left everything behind?"

I was used to people talking about me in the third person, like I was a calculator. *These numbers make no sense, how did she arrive at these values? Did she do this part in her head?*

It didn't bother me.

"Well, if you'd let me finish, I would tell you. She left it all at security. She was almost late for the plane and had to run to the gate," Gabby lied smoothly, making me envious. "We'd already arranged to have me pick her up from O'Hare. Don't fret, though. My mother's secretary called the airport and they're sending her phone and stuff. It should get here tomorrow or the day after."

Gabby's lies were so persuasive, spoken with such artlessness, I almost believed her.

Conclusion: I required lying lessons.

Abram leaned to the side to peer around my sister's friend, his eyelids still droopy, his gaze still irritated and distrustful. "You don't have your phone?"

One-word answers. One-word answers. One-word answers.

"Nope," I said, both proud and disgusted with myself for the lie. Needing a distraction, I picked through the fruit bowl in the center of the island, hunting for the perfect apple.

In my peripheral vision, I watched as Abram stepped away from the door, walked around Gabby, and stopped four feet from me just as I took a bite from the apple. *Honeycrisp.* I chewed and he studied my face. Meeting his inspection directly, I concentrated on the taste of the apple and hoped I was making a Lisa-face.

Lifting his chin toward the Sephora bag, he asked, "You had money for makeup but not for food?"

"Priorities, Abram," Gabby spoke for me.

He ignored her. "You don't mind if I search you for it?"

Before I could catch it, I felt my eyes squint and my lips curve into an unfriendly sneer. *Like hell* he was putting his hands on me. I didn't care who he was, whether or not he was Leo's best friend, or whether my parents trusted him, I didn't like being touched by *anyone*.

Abram's glare sharpened, as though my reaction surprised him, or he found it confusing.

But Gabby laughed, taking the stool next to mine. "Yeah, sure. Go for it, handsome. Where is she going to hide a cell phone in that outfit? But, okay. I'm sure you'll both probably enjoy it, so go ahead."

I glanced down at myself, at my boobs on display in the tank top and black lace bra, my bare stomach, and the second skin of Lisa's leather pants. Once again, Gabby made a good point. There was nowhere to hide anything in these clothes, the pockets were sewn shut for Bohr's sake.

Returning my attention to Abram, it was my turn to be surprised. An expression of mild repugnance passed over his features as he looked me over, like the thought of giving "Lisa" a pat down was just as distasteful to him as it was to me.

Well, okay then. Maybe nineteen-year-old, olive-skinned, heavily makeupped, athletic with big boobs, long black hair, and brown eyes wasn't his type.

Crossing his arms, Abram leveled me with a severe stare. "As soon as your stuff arrives, you give me the phone."

"Fine." I shrugged and took another bite of the apple while Gabby selected a piece of pizza from the box.

My calm capitulation seemed to increase his irritation. "No drinking. No drugs. No parties. No sneaking out. No one comes over until your parents get home in two weeks, or Dr. Steward arrives, whichever comes first. And no leaving the house without me. Anywhere you go, I go."

I stared at him evenly, because—other than having him escort me out of the house—he was basically reading my Christmas list. Total seclusion and quiet for the next week? Where did I sign up?

But staring evenly with no reaction must've been the wrong thing to do, because the force of his eye-squint escalated, his gaze flickering over me with suspicion. "Did you hear me?"

"Yep," I said, wishing I'd thought ahead and brought books to read.

I'd already read all the ones here. *Maybe I can go to the library? Wait, no. Shoot! No card. Bookstore?*

Abram continued to examine me, his frown intensifying, his suspicion now edged with confusion. "Are you . . . feeling okay?"

I sensed Gabby's restlessness before she stood from her stool and stepped in front of me again. "Okay, Dad. What are you, like only three or four years older than us?" She huffed, rolled her eyes. "Whatever. We got it. No fun."

Successfully disguising my disapproval at the petulance in her tone and the instinct to distance myself from her puerile response, I continued to give him my very best blank-face. To be clear, I'm not against sass or sarcasm. Both definitely have their place. But Gabby's dramatics felt immature and superfluous.

Given the situation, the fact that Lisa was currently in jail and had been lying about being with Tyler for months, this Abram guy's rules made complete sense. If I'd been left in charge, I would have set similar limitations.

"We'll just be upstairs." She pulled me from the stool, and I had to consciously force myself to allow Gabby to lead me toward the back stairs. "And just so we're clear, we'll be doing absolutely *nothing*," Gabby spat, the venom in her voice—again—striking me as childish.

"No." Abram shook his head, moving quickly to block our path. "No, Gabby. You're not staying."

I was relieved to see the earlier suspicion and confusion pointed at me had faded, replaced with a hard look for Lisa's friend.

"What?" she screeched, her mouth falling open. "What the hell, Abram? You're cute, but you're not *that* cute. Stop being such an asshole."

Abram rubbed his face tiredly, his jaw ticking again, his eyes now almost black. "Do you think I want to spend the next few weeks babysitting Lisa? No. I'm doing this as a favor to Leo." He said this last part to me, his animosity a palpable thing. "So, if you could just, you know, not do anything stupid or crazy for the next two weeks, that would be really great."

"Wanting to talk to her best friend is neither stupid or crazy." Gabby inched us closer to the back stairs.

He moved to counter our progress, a big wall of lean muscle and unyielding determination. "Gabby, time for you to go."

"Lisa isn't a prisoner!"

I tried not to smirk at the irony of Gabby's statement.

"Gabby," he said, the single word a warning.

"This is such bullshit!" she continued to protest, but it was evident Abram wasn't going to bend.

Turning my arm, I encircled Gabby's wrist with my fingers and tugged her lightly, encouraging her to face me. "You should go. I'll be fine."

Her moss-green eyes moved between mine, hot with anger, but also tempered with worry. She made a frustrated sound in the back of her throat, like a grunt, and pulled me into a hug.

I stiffened in her embrace, baffled by the action and feeling a familiar reflexive suffocation, but then she whispered, "The backpack is under the stool I was sitting on. Don't let him see it or we're all dead."

Gabby released me and leaned away to administer one of her meaningful looks. This one I read perfectly.

Nodding once, she turned back to Abram, looked him over, and promptly walked to the kitchen exit. "You're still hot, Abram, even if you are an uptight asshole."

"I'll walk her out, you stay here." He exhaled a harassed-sounding breath, turned, and followed Gabby from the kitchen.

I watched them go. As soon as they were out of sight, I dashed to my backpack, grabbed it, and . . . hesitated. Would I have enough time to run up to my room, deposit it within, and be back in the kitchen before Abram returned?

Probably not.

Which meant I needed to hide it before he returned. There were many, many options as the kitchen was expansive. Did I hide it in the pantry? Or beneath the double oven? Or above the fridge? The unmistakable sound of the front door shutting made my decision for me. The pantry was closest, so that would be its home for the time being.

Rushing, I shoved the bag behind baking supplies on the bottom shelf. Unless Abraham—*Abram? Abraham? Damn. Which one was it?*—was secretly a pastry chef, I felt like it was the safest place.

"Lisa?"

He'd returned.

Panicking, I reached blindly for a bag of something on the snack shelf and poked my head out of the walk-in pantry.

Following Gabby's advice, I said, "What?"

The guy's gaze found me, his slashing dark eyebrows pulled low, giving him an air of being thoroughly . . . *I'm going to go with the word* irked *again.* "What are you doing?"

"Getting—" I held out the bag of whatever I'd grabbed in front of me, reading the package "—prunes."

Ah jeez. Prunes. Why'd it have to be prunes?

He blinked. Some of the severity in his glare seemed to dissolve into confusion as he looked between me and the bag. "Prunes."

I nodded. What else could I do? I was holding a package of prunes, now I just had to *commit* to the package of prunes.

"Yes. Prunes. As you see." Tearing it open and walking out of the pantry, I reached into the bag. Slimy, larger versions of raisins were waiting for me inside.

"You're going to eat . . . prunes?"

I nodded, struggling to find a lie that sounded as plausible as Gabby's had been. "You don't know anyone who eats prunes?"

"My grandpa," he said flatly, still splitting his attention between me and the bag.

"Smart man. They're high in fiber."

"Fiber."

"Yes." I lifted the bag to scan the nutritional information, hoping they were actually high in fiber. Though I had a suspicion, I wasn't 100 percent certain. After reading the package, I released a relieved breath. "Twelve grams of fiber per serving. It says so right here. That's a lot. And I need my fiber."

"Why do you need fiber?"

"Flying makes me"—*oh God, don't say it!*—"makes me"—*oh noes, here it comes*—"constipated." I nodded at my own assertion, quickly stuffing my mouth with three prunes so I wouldn't be able to speak.

His confusion persisted, but he said nothing. Holding perfectly still, he watched me with a frown that teetered on dismayed.

Meanwhile, I had to stop chewing. Each prune had a pit. *Shit.* There existed no graceful way to remove a pit from one's mouth. I would have to spit the pit.

Holding his gaze, which now seemed to be fascinated in addition to dismayed, I spit the pits into my palm. I then gave him a tight-lipped smile while I continued to chew, because that's what I did when people stared at me. *I wonder what Lisa does when people stare at her?*

One of his eyebrows lifted and he gave his head a subtle shake. "Okay. Right." He glanced at the ceiling and then around the kitchen, as though trying to figure out where he was. "I'm going to have to call your parents' assistant, Dr. Steward, right? And let her know you don't have your phone."

Luckily, I was still chewing the prunes, which gave me a few moments to think about how to respond to this statement. As an aside, carrying around a bag of food and stuffing my face whenever he asked me a question was a solid plan. It would give me an opportunity to stall, to think.

Stating that Dr. Steward was my parents' assistant wasn't entirely accurate. More like, she had incidentally become one of the various team of people my parents called upon when they needed a problem handled. But I didn't need to clarify that with Abram. Trying to explain the complexities of staff and their unofficial roles to people who didn't understand celebrity was time-consuming and typically yielded even more confusion.

Moving on.

Even though I dreaded the possibility of speaking to either of my parents while pretending to be Lisa, his logic made sense. I couldn't see any way of talking him out of calling Dr. Steward as I could form no compelling—i.e. logical—argument against it.

Therefore, after swallowing, I said, "Whatever, Abe."

I'd decided to say *whatever* since Gabby had indicated it would always be a safe choice, and I'd called him Abe since it was short for both Abram and Abraham. For the life of me, I couldn't remember which was correct. I'd never been good at remembering names. Or remembering faces. Or people.

This must've been precisely the right thing to say—and by that, I mean it was the wrong thing to say but in the right way—because his eyelids lowered again to half-mast and his mouth flattened. He looked perturbed, which was good. Perturbed was much better than suspicious or confused. Perturbed meant he saw me as Lisa and not as a potential imposter. So, in summary, *woot woot!*

"Forget it," he grumbled, turning from me and running a hand through his longish brown hair. "Just, hand over the phone when it arrives, okay? I'll be in the basement. Let me know if you need to go out for anything. Otherwise just . . ." his gaze flickered to me and I spotted that same hint of repugnance as before, like he found my presence unsavory. "Just don't do anything stupid."

I wanted to respond with *In this economy?* But instead, and without thinking too much about it, I saluted, still gripping the pits in my hand. Why I did this, I had no idea. Luckily, the action didn't faze him. With one last irked look, Abe walked out of the kitchen, leaving me with my prunes, their pits, and an immediate sense of relief.

[3]
DISPLACEMENT

Prunes would be my constant companion for the next week, the means by which I delayed answering or speaking to Abe. *Good plan.* The fiber consumed would be a bonus.

Tossing the pits in the garbage and rinsing my hand, I zipped closed the bag, tucked it under my arm, and glanced at the pantry. The backpack would stay put for now. Abe didn't trust Lisa. Best to move the bag in the middle of the night, or at some point when I could be 97 percent certain we wouldn't cross paths.

So, what did I do now? Read? Exercise? Going for a walk was out of the question. Watch a movie in the theater downstairs? I hadn't seen a movie or TV in months, but Abe said he'd be in the basement, so that was a no-go . . . *How about a* s*hower?*

Yes. Shower. A shower was the answer. I hadn't showered since yesterday. Plane rides didn't make me constipated, they made me feel grimy. A shower sounded divine. Hydra environments were deeply within my wheelhouse.

And yet, I was faced with a quandary: I wanted a shower, yet I couldn't get any part of my head wet. Gabby had been adamant about not allowing Abe to see me without Lisa's hair and makeup. Protecting my hair and face from the shower spray was necessary.

A waterproof implement was in order, one that allowed me to see and breathe, and ideally large enough to cover my entire head. A shower cap wouldn't cut it, I had too much hair and by design it left the face exposed. The more I thought the issue over, the more I realized I would need something reusable. I didn't want to have to reapply makeup all the time, or redo my hair.

Conclusion: What I needed was a shower helmet. I was fairly certain a shower helmet didn't exist. I'd have to make one.

Biting the inside of my bottom lip, I searched the kitchen drawers closest to the gas range and found what I sought: aluminum foil, parchment paper, tape, scissors, and plastic wrap. Laying my materials on the kitchen island, I used the aluminum foil to make a mold of my entire head. I lined the inside with parchment paper, cut away spaces for my eyes and mouth, and finally covered the outside with several layers of plastic wrap.

I did have to make a few minor tweaks: air holes, increasing the size of the eye area for better range of vision, expanding the crown section so that I could wear my hair up and out of the way. Once I was satisfied, I carried my shower helmet and bag of new makeup to the bathroom, making a pit stop in my room first to grab underwear.

When the house was remodeled before we moved in, my parents had installed an elevator. Since my room was only one flight up, I typically took the stairs. Lisa and I shared the bathroom off the main hall on the second floor.

Leo's room was on the third floor, he shared his bathroom with the two guest rooms on that level. My parents had their own bathroom and living space on the fourth floor, a giant master suite that took up the entire level.

Stripping out of the tank top and leather pants, I twisted my hair into a bun and fitted the waterproof helmet into place. Three minutes into my shower, I was generally pleased with the results of my efforts. The helmet succeeded in its purpose. My hair and face were dry. The only downside was the interior acoustics, which seemed to amplify the sound of the shower tenfold. Ah well. I would have to make notes for a second prototype, should the need arise.

Toweling off, I studied my image in the mirror as best I could given the limitations of the helmet, and debated how to best dry the contraption. Leaving it outside was the obvious choice, just not in direct sunlight. I didn't want the plastic to melt. The small balcony off my room should work and had the added bonus of giving me an excuse to access "Mona's room" whenever I wanted.

Decision made, I pulled on my underwear. I left the helmet on—enjoying the novelty of feeling like a Storm Trooper, or perhaps a member of Daft Punk—wrapped an oversized towel around myself, and opened the bathroom door just in time to almost collide with Abe. But we didn't collide, thanks to my eyeholes and his veering to the left at the last minute.

"What the hell?" he said, staring at me aghast. "What are you doing?"

Bah! I forgot my prunes.

Lifting the towel closer to my neck, I met his stunned gaze through the plastic sheeting of my helmet, and debated how best to answer. In the end, I decided the truth would have to do. "I'm walking to my room. What are you doing?"

"No, I mean, what are you wearing?"

I glanced down at myself. "A towel and underwear."

"No. On your head." He touched his temple and I mimicked the movement, my fingers coming in contact with the plastic outer layer. "What's that thing on your head? Is that aluminum foil?"

"Oh. It's for the shower. To keep my hair dry and, you know, my face also." An image of me, of what I looked like in the helmet, flashed into my brain. I guess I looked silly. Removing it, I gave him another of my tight smiles. "Is that better?"

I could see him more clearly now. His forehead was scrunched, like I, or my shower helmet, or both of us together were inconceivable.

"That's actually . . ." His expression cleared and he blinked, shifting back a step as though to get a better look at me. "That's actually really smart."

Now I frowned at him. The way he'd said *smart* irritated me on my sister's behalf, as though the mere idea of me—Lisa—doing anything smart was outside his understanding of reality.

So I lifted my chin and said, "Well, *you* would know."

He must've detected the undercurrent of sarcasm in my tone because his head moved back an inch on his neck, his gaze flickering over me. "What?"

"Clearly, you're a foremost expert on what qualifies as 'smart.'" I tugged my towel higher.

"Are you"—his eyes narrowed—"are you giving me shit for complimenting your—your—"

"Shower helmet."

Abe pressed his lips together in an obvious attempt to curb a smile, but the presence of faint indents on either side of his mouth, the beginning of dimples, betrayed him. "Shower helmet," he said, eyes—which I'd just this second realized were the color of amber when he wasn't irked—glinted with amusement.

"Yes, I'm giving you shit regarding your paltry compliment about my shower helmet, because it was wholly eclipsed by your incredulity that I am capable of doing something 'smart.'"

He gave up the fight against his grin. "Oh? Really?"

"Yes. Really."

Abe huffed a disbelieving laugh, looking at me like I was a puzzle. "Well then, you know what would've been *actually* smart?"

"Please enlighten me."

"Taking a bath."

I opened my mouth to volley a new sarcasm, but then promptly snapped it shut, blinking in astonishment. He was right. Taking a bath would have been the simplest and smartest course of action. But taking a bath hadn't occurred to me. I hadn't taken a bath since Lisa and I'd taken them together as children.

"Unless you don't like baths." Abe's left eyebrow tilted upward a hint, as did his mouth.

Scowling, because I wasn't going to admit that taking a bath hadn't occurred to me, I deflected by asking, "Why are you here? I thought you were in the basement."

"I'm staying in one of the guest rooms on the third floor, I'm on my way up."

"Oh. That makes . . . sense."

We traded stares for several seconds, neither of us moving. I debated what to do or say while I watched all the good humor slowly leach from his features, leaving a mantle of renewed hostility. My stomach fluttered, startling me, and I pressed a hand against it.

You're having butterflies because he's pretty, I told myself. But the hurried explanation felt woefully inadequate.

Let the record show, Abe really was extremely attractive in a cool, aloof, tall, dark, and handsome kind of way—if you go for that. For some strange reason, I couldn't help but compare him to Dr. Poe Payton, who was also extremely attractive. But although Poe was tall, dark, and handsome—objectively, perhaps even more handsome than Abe—he wasn't aloof. He was friendly and brilliant.

That's the problem, a voice inside my head informed me, *has anyone brilliant ever been nice to you without having an ulterior motive?*

Releasing a silent sigh, I wallowed for a split second in the sudden cold nausea curdling my stomach, fighting a duel with the flutters. It might have been the hastily eaten prunes, but I didn't think so. More likely, it was the realization that I was more inclined to trust someone who disliked me than someone who liked me.

Which was probably why despite Abe's apparent dislike for all things Lisa (and therefore me) in that moment, while standing so close to his handsomeness, I felt a small kinship with Gabby and her hoo-hah. Abe openly disliked me/Lisa, and I found him and his dislike attractive as evidenced by the increasing fluttery activity in my abdomen. How messed up was that?

Needing to break the moment, I considered saying one of my anytime phrases.

My first instinct was to use *Is this why fate brought us together?* but immediately dismissed it as an option. I usually employed this one when I spotted something I wanted, like chocolate gelato or fingerless gloves. So, nah.

Perhaps, *Be that as it may, still may it be as it may be?* Eh. No. Too random and too much time had passed with us just staring at each other.

Eventually, I channeled Lisa and flicked my wrist, moving my hand in a dismissive out-of-the-way motion I'd seen her use the last time we were together.

"Move. You're in my way."

His lips curved, definitely more of a smirk than a smile. Hinted at dimples made an appearance, deeper on the left side than on the right. But that might've been because his mouth hitched higher on that side. Licking his lips, his eyes dropped to the ground, the radiant amber irises now hidden by his long black lashes. He stepped to the side, lifting his arm in a go-right-ahead gesture.

So I did. I walked to my room. I opened the door. And then I closed it.

Not three seconds later, he knocked.

Gritting my teeth, I opened it, once again coming face-to-face with his smirking smile, dimples, and amber eyes, which—for the record—held no amusement.

"What do you want?"

"Isn't this your sister's room?" Abe crossed his arms and lifted a dark, challenging, irked eyebrow.

Ah! I was in my room! But that was okay because of my shower helmet plan. Which meant I didn't even need to lie.

"This is Mona's room." *Truth.* "This room also has a balcony, which I plan to use to dry my shower helmet." *Also truth.* Turning from him, I walked to the single French door leading to the small balcony and unlocked it, opened it, and placed the helmet under the small table so it wouldn't get direct sunlight.

Shutting the door to the balcony, I was surprised to see that Abe had followed me into my room. His gaze moved over the interior of the space, seemingly taking in or cataloguing the objects within. His unexpected inspection made me look around as well. I attempted to view my sanctuary from his perspective. What must it look like to a stranger?

The walls were white. I liked rooms painted white, especially if I spent any period of time within the room. Books. Lots of books on four giant shelves lining the wall closest to the door. Two floor-to-ceiling windows on either side of the French door dominated the far side and flooded the space with light. The bed was twin-sized with a night-sky print comforter and one white pillow. I preferred the small footprint of a twin over surrendering valuable floor space to a larger bed. A drafting table that served as my desk sat against the fourth wall. Books and papers were stacked beneath.

"'Heisenberg may have slept here,'" Abe read the sign over my bed, his tone thoughtful. "What does that mean?"

Since I didn't have my prunes, I didn't pause to think before asking, "You're *uncertain* who Heisenberg is?" and then immediately grimaced, because *no physics jokes.*

Abe's gaze moved to mine. "The name sounds familiar."

"Have you ever taken chemistry? Or physics?"

"Yeah. In high school."

It was on the tip of my tongue to explain who Heisenberg was, and that the Heisenberg Uncertainty Principle related to the fact that everything in the universe behaves like both a particle and a wave at the same time, which meant no one can ever simultaneously know the exact position and the exact speed of an object at any given time. Furthermore, just the act of measuring anything—or attempting to measure—changes the object being measured.

But then I remembered I was Lisa. I was Lisa, not Mona. And Lisa had never understood or cared why the sign over my bed was funny.

Taking a breath, I swallowed and shrugged. "It probably has to do with something like that. Mona likes, uh, physics. A lot."

"Leo said she went to some big deal, Ivy League school."

I cleared my throat and nodded once. "Correct."

"When she was fourteen?" Abe's gaze moved back to the sign.

"Fifteen." The fine hairs on the back of my neck prickled, probably because I was still standing around wearing nothing but a towel and undies. But maybe also because I was discussing myself like I wasn't me.

He made a dismissive, scoffing sound and moved to leave. "That would suck."

I scowled at the back of his head, following him into the hall and catching myself before saying *Pardon?*

Instead I said, "What?"

He glanced at me, his expression one of clear aversion to the direction of his thoughts. "Going to college at *fifteen*? Never getting to experience high school? That would have sucked."

My throat felt oddly tight and a bizarre restlessness stirred in my chest. "Some people say that high school sucks." I didn't know why I was arguing with him about this. I should have been avoiding him. And getting dressed.

"High school does suck." Abe nodded, tilting his head to the side, his eyes growing fuzzy as though he was recalling a specific memory. "But fifteen-year-olds are still kids. High school is your last chance to make mistakes without huge adult consequences. Missing out on that chance would suck. That's like losing four years of your childhood."

His gaze returned to mine and seemed to be guileless, as though we were just two random people having a random conversation about a random topic where neither of us had an emotional investment. It was the first time since I'd arrived an hour ago that he'd looked at me without being irritated, or confused, or—as he'd done just moments ago upon finding me with my shower helmet—freaked out with a hint of good humor.

Meanwhile, I was still scowling.

Abe blinked, apparently what he saw on my face confused him. But then his expression cleared, as though he'd just realized something significant.

"You dropped out of high school." He said this with no malice, but rather as though this fact—Lisa dropping out of high school—explained my persistent scowl.

"Yes," I said stiffly. And just for good measure, I added, "Whatever." *So . . . it has come to this.*

His gaze moved over me, assessing and yet surprisingly free of judgment. These amber eyes of his were making me tremendously self-conscious as I sensed something new behind his inspection. Something like interest, but not quite. Whatever the something was, it also made me acutely cognizant that I was wearing just a towel and underwear.

I gathered a deep breath, about to walk around him to Lisa's room, when he said quietly, "So did I."

"What?"

"I dropped out of high school."

I flinched, astonished. "You- you did?"

He nodded, biting his lower lip, a faint smile in his eyes. "That surprises you?"

"Why would you do that?" I asked this as myself, as Mona, because dropping out of school made no sense to me. To have access to knowledge and to reject it made no logical sense.

Abe's left dimple appeared, his pretty eyes—yes, they were pretty, but *alluring* might have been a more fitting word—seemed to glow.

Instead of answering, he countered, "Why did you drop out?"

"My parents couldn't find a high school that would take- take me. I was kicked out of ten schools by my junior year." I thought everyone knew this story. It had been in all the papers.

He made a low whistling sound. "Ten?"

I nodded, remembering the phone call I'd had with Lisa after number ten. She'd seemed proud, like it had been an accomplishment. I didn't understand her.

"So, technically, I didn't drop out," I said, repeating what she'd said to me at the time.

"Right." He looked less than impressed, which echoed how I'd felt about Lisa's statement.

Before I could catch the impulse, I rolled my eyes, a small smile tugging at my lips, forgetting for a moment that we weren't commiserating over Lisa's recklessness because, you know, I *was* Lisa.

Abe looked at me like I'd again surprised him.

Oh. Oh no. He thinks I'm being self-deprecating. Yikes.

"Yeah. Well. I'm the funniest person I know, and then the wolves came." I forced a light laugh, knowing I'd messed up. Lisa was many things, but I'd never known her to be self-deprecating. If there was one thing my sister took too seriously in this world, it was herself.

"Wolves?" His gaze traveled over my face, a smile lingering even though his eyebrows had pulled together. The dichotomy of his expression had me wondering whether he was enjoying our conversation, or if perhaps he was confused about the fact that he was enjoying our conversation.

"Anyway." I took a step to the side, and then another. I needed to extract myself. I needed the prunes to chew on before I could be trusted to speak. "I'm cold. I need clothes. Goodbye."

With that, I crossed to Lisa's room, stepped inside, and shut the door behind me. I counted the seven seconds until I heard footsteps on the stairway leading up. Shaking my head at how incompetent I was at lying, I moved to Lisa's dresser.

As I searched for something to wear, I admitted to myself that I failed at pretending to be someone else. Everything that had just happened—except for me saying *whatever* and flicking my wrist at him—had been completely out of character for my sister.

Avoiding Abe was the only way to salvage this week and allow Lisa to slip back into the house without raising suspicion.

Avoidance. I would avoid him.

Complete avoidance.

Yep.

[4]
VECTORS, SCALARS, AND COORDINATE SYSTEMS

W hen someone asks where I'm from, I say Chicago. I'd spent less than one sixty-fourth of my life here and yet, of all my parents' houses all over the world, the Chicago house was the one I considered home. Perhaps because my parents were both born on the outskirts of Chicago, or maybe because it was also the only house without permanent live-in caretakers. As a kid, I'd thought the other houses belonged to the caretakers and we were merely their guests.

Which is all to say, I knew where the best hide-and-seek places were in the house.

Upon waking, I checked my hair—as far as I could tell, it still looked fine—reapplied the makeup as faithfully as I could, and crept from Lisa's room early in the morning. The questions I'd been asking myself since hopping on a plane thirty-six hours ago still whispering between my ears, *Are you really doing this? Are you really going to impersonate Lisa for up to a week? Are you really okay with pretending to be her?*

I had no answers. Furthermore, I was frustrated that the questions persisted. The decision had been made. Lisa was in trouble and probably scared out of her mind. As much as the situation gave me a sour stomach, I was more worried for her than for me.

And anyway, allowing myself to be swept up and along by momentum was normal for me. Momentum was good. It made sense. It existed for a reason. It helped people stay on the right path.

Second-guessing my decisions was not normal. It, the impersonation of my sister and the lies, was already happening. I was already doing this. I'd promised my sister. I'd *promised*. And I never snitched.

So, defeating the impulse to check my phone and call the lawyer, I hid.

My hiding spot was the mudroom off the back door. The light was excellent for reading, and it housed a cozy cushioned cubby built into the wall, a space that had likely been a small closet at one point. There was no chance of being happened upon as no one used the back door.

I read my book, *Moby Dick*, while ignoring the whispers of doubt until they faded. I also listened for Abe. Once he was up and about, I'd make an appearance in the kitchen just after he finished his breakfast/when he was on his way out. That way he would see me, but there'd be no loitering and or making of further chitchat.

Maybe I'd pretend to be on my way to the bathroom.

A while later—a long while later—I came up for breath and glanced at my surroundings. The earlier post-dawn diffused glow now felt like midmorning sunlight. I frowned, worried that Abe had grabbed breakfast at some point, I hadn't heard him, and I'd neglected to check in. Chewing the inside of my bottom lip, I set my book to the side and tiptoed to the kitchen, searching for any sign of life and checking the clock mounted above the wood-fired pizza oven.

I experienced a shock. It was now past 1:00 PM. I then experienced a spike of alarm, hoping Ahab hadn't gone looking for Lisa, given up, and called my parents.

"Doom, doom, doom!" I murmured, dashing toward the back stairs. I would have to find Ahab and convince him I'd been home all morning, and then I'd—

"Did you just say 'doom doom doom,' or 'zoom, zoom, zoom'?"

I stopped short and was forced to take several steps backward. Ahab was walking down the stairs, his longish hair in messy disarray, his voice roughened with sleep, and his eyes squinted like the room was too bright.

"I . . ." Incredulous, I inspected his rumpled attire. He was still wearing the same T-shirt and jeans he'd been wearing yesterday. "Did —did you just wake up?" *And he slept in his clothes?*

Yawning, his gaze moving down and up my person, he nodded. "What time is it? I think I left my phone down here."

My eyes bugged. Wasn't he supposed to be watching Lisa? Wasn't he supposed to take her phone and ensure she didn't call Tyler and didn't leave and didn't do anything stupid? And he was just now waking up? I could have been out all morning. *I could have met with and had sex with and dropped acid with Tyler ten times by now!*

To be fair, I didn't know how long it took to drop acid, but based on various data sources and movies I'd watched, I could extrapolate.

"You—did you—your—" I couldn't figure out which question I wanted to ask first.

"Is there still pizza?" he asked, walking past me and making a straight line for the fridge.

Confounded, certain I was missing something critical, I stumbled after him. "I can't believe you're just waking up."

I'd never slept until 1:00 PM. Never. Not after a long international flight, not on the weekend after pulling several all-nighters the week prior, not even when I'd been sick with the flu. Never ever, ever.

Sending me a quick, small, sleepy smile, Ahab opened the fridge. "Why? When did you wake up?"

Crossing my arms, I wished for my bag of prunes or something else to chew. I suspected this was one of those situations where telling the truth would make a negative impact to my Lisa-credibility. It was a safe bet to assume my sister didn't often wake up at 6:30 AM.

Rather than outright lie, I decided vague was just as good. "A while ago. When did you go to sleep?"

"Around five."

I started, blinking several times. "Five? AM?"

"Yep." He pulled the pizza from the fridge and placed it on the island, flipping open the box.

"That's insane, Ahab. What were you doing until five AM?"

He'd been lifting a slice of cold pizza—*COLD PIZZA!*—when I spoke, but his hand halted midway to his mouth and he glared at me.

"What did you just say?"

"I said, that's insane." Frowning at him and the slice of cold pizza in turn, I had to ask, "Do you want me to heat that up for you?"

He returned the pizza to the box, staring at me like I was a curiosity. "My name is Abram."

Dammit. Abram!! Why didn't I just call him Abe?

I blinked some more. "Uh, I don't mind heating up the pizza." Maybe if I ignored the slipup, he'd let it drop?

"You just called me Ahab."

Oh noes! He wasn't going to let it drop.

"Pardon? I mean, what? I mean, no I didn't." I laughed, backing away, stuffing my hands into the back pockets of Lisa's only pair of semi-tight jeans instead of boa-constrictor-tight jeans.

"Yes, you did." His eyes narrowed, moving over me.

I tossed my thumb over my shoulder. "Would you believe that I was just reading *Moby Dick?*"

He shook his head, and I didn't know how to feel, because that was good, right? I mean, it wasn't good that I'd messed up his name, but it was good that he didn't believe I'd been reading *Moby Dick.* I felt a level of certainty that Lisa wouldn't read *Moby Dick,* so he must've still believed I was Lisa . . . right?

"Ahab?" His voice dripped with irritation.

"Why would I call you Ahab? I don't think that happened. Your name is Abram. You heard wrong. You're an unreliable witness." I glanced behind me, not knowing where I was going. I only had three feet until my back hit the wall, so I pivoted, still walking backward but aiming for the arched doorway.

"Unreliable witness?" His left dimple reappeared followed by the right, and he was doing that smile-frown thing again. It was cute. How irksome.

"Yes. You just woke up. You're muddled. Go eat your disgusting cold pizza. Whatever!" I was almost to the arched doorway, which would lead me to the back stairs, which meant I could hide for the rest of the afternoon. It would probably take all afternoon for my heart rate to return to normal.

"Fine, I will." He lifted the pizza to his mouth and added, "And then we're going out, *Liza*."

That had my feet coming to a halt. "Pardon?"

"Your name is Liza, isn't it?" He said this with a sardonic twist to his lips.

But I didn't care what he called me as long as it wasn't Mona. I was more concerned with the first part of this statement. "We're going out? Where?"

Abram didn't respond right away, instead he took a bite of pizza and chewed. My attention dropped to his jaw and neck and, for some inexplicable reason, I was entranced by the sight of his jaw working, flexing, and the action of his Adam's apple as he swallowed. I can honestly say, I'd never noticed the way someone chewed before, because why would I? But in his case, I don't know. . . It was just all extraordinarily man-like.

"I'm looking at a guitar, the guy is holding it for me until three."

"Why do I need to go?" I forced my eyes back to his and crossed my arms, bewildered by my preoccupation with his chewing. *So weird.*

"I can't leave you here by yourself." He said this like it was obvious.

I regathered the threads of the conversation just in time to find critical fault in his logic. "But you'll sleep until after noon? What if I'd gone out this morning?"

"Did you go out this morning?" He asked this like he already knew the answer.

"That's not the point. I could have."

"But you didn't."

"But I could have. You trusted me to stay put this morning, but not this afternoon?"

"This morning is in the past, this afternoon is now. You're coming."

I glared at him and his stunning lack of sense. "You make no sense."

"I don't have to make sense." He stalked around the kitchen island holding two pieces of pizza, his grin smug, slowly regaining the steps I'd placed between us. "I just have to keep you from doing anything stupid until your parents' assistant shows up. You're coming, *Liza*."

Giving me another second of his smug grin, he walked around me, bumping my shoulder with his arm as he did so, and walked up the stairs.

Once I was fairly certain he was out of earshot, I mumbled darkly to myself, "So . . . it has come to this."

Full-out avoidance was now no longer an option. At least not for the next few hours. Since I had no choice but to accompany Abram on his errand, my new plan was to avoid conversation. I would do this by taking Gabby's advice regarding single word answers.

While Abram showered and changed on the third floor, I crept to the kitchen pantry, pulled my phone from the hidden backpack, and checked for messages from Lisa or her lawyer. There were none.

But my good friend Allyn had messaged, and so had Gabby. I ignored the Gabster for now and opened Allyn's thread.

Allyn: *How's it going in CA? Remember, you're eating avocados for two. I am living vicariously through you. Also, send pictures of the avocados before you eat them.*

Allyn: *PS I love you for more than just your avocado pics!*

I grinned, because she was so weird and cool. We'd met my senior year, which happened to be her freshman year, and we'd clicked instantly. I'd begun to doubt clicking with anyone in any sort of situation was ever going to happen. And then I'd met Allyn, in the cafeteria, picking through sad avocado flesh. We'd shared a sigh over the substandard options and she'd taken that as an open invitation to become my best friend. I had no objections, because she was everything I was not—funny, open, engaging, comfortable in her own skin—but definitely wanted to be.

I sent her a quick text, promising to send her photos when possible —probably next week—and, with *extreme reluctance*, navigated to

Gabby's texts, a series of messages beginning last night and through this afternoon.

Gabby: *I will be over tomorrow evening to check on you. Stay strong, nerdy grasshopper.*

Gabby: *Don't forget to apply makeup in the morning. Heavy on the liner.*

Gabby: *And do your hair.*

Gabby: *Good morning, sunshine. How are things?*

Gabby: *Since you haven't responded, I'm assuming you're sitting on Abram's face and I totally applaud this development.*

I stopped here, sucking in a small, startled breath as a lurid flash of an underwearless me sitting on Abram's face suffused every millimeter of my consciousness and sent pinpricks of tingling awareness racing beneath my skin. It was like being assaulted with hot honey, leaving me flushed and sticky and confused, because why would someone assault another person with hot honey? That would be strange.

"Jeez, Gabby," I murmured to my phone, fanning my shirt and blinking away the vivid image, though the visceral effects lingered. I endeavored to not dwell on the fact that none of my initial, secondary, or tertiary reactions to the thought had been displeasure or disgust.

No. Best not to dwell on that.

But I did dwell on it, how could I not? Thankfully, my brain rescued me, reminding me that my last quasi-sexual encounter with another person had been several months ago, after which I'd definitively determined that sexual partners were optional—often superfluous—to the sex act.

Abram had an attractive exterior and therefore I was attracted to it, and that was normal. My body had physical urges that I'd neglected, and that was also normal.

Yet being attracted to someone's exterior and having neglected urges did not mean taking action with that exterior was a foregone conclusion. I wasn't a slave to my physical urges and attractive exteriors. I could, and would, simply ignore the attraction and attend to myself when convenient. Maybe tomorrow. Perhaps even tonight.

But where . . . ?

Plugging my phone into the portable USB charger I always carried in my bag, I stuffed both into the backpack, and stuffed the backpack back into place. I'd taken too much time already, I'd have to call the lawyer to check on Lisa another time.

Wiping clammy hands on my pants, I stood and searched the snack shelf for something quick to eat. Granola bars seemed like the best choice, given my options, but I did note that there were four more bags of unopened prunes near the edge.

The discovery made me feel a modicum better about grabbing one of the bags earlier. Of all the snacks, prunes were in the greatest abundance. Statistically speaking, I'd been more likely to grab prunes than anything else on the shelf. But as I left the pantry, granola bars in hand, I couldn't help wondering why we had so many prunes, and who had bought them.

I made quick work of the granola bar and washed it down with water, setting the glass by the sink for later use. Checking the time, I meandered to the front door and searched the shoe cubby for footwear. I found some of my old Birkenstocks and a pair of Lisa's flip-flops—Vera Wang, black soles with bejeweled straps. Gazing longingly at the Birkenstocks, I pulled on the Vera Wang sandals.

But then, when I stood and tested them, I was *shook*. Fantastic arch support, supple leather straps, soft soles. They were the most comfortable sandals I'd ever worn.

"Huh," I said to my feet's reflection in the mirror as I rocked back and forth, testing their flexibility. "Nice." Maybe I'd have to invest in some fancy Vera Wang sandals.

"Is that what you're wearing?"

Abram's question pulled my attention away from my feet to his approach. I noted his hair was wet and his clothes were different.

"Yes." Glancing down at myself, at the semi-tight jeans and plain black tank top I'd been wearing all day, and then back to him, I asked, "Why?"

Abram lowered a pair of aviator sunglasses into place, blocking his eyes. "No reason."

"Should I change?" I tossed my thumb toward the kitchen stairs. "Is this a rococo guitar shop? Is there a dress code?"

"What's *rococo*?" Abram walked to the front door, stopping directly in front of me.

His approach and proximity made me tense, so I believe I can be excused for not thinking before responding, "Rococo is characterized by an elaborately ornamental late baroque style of decor prevalent in 18th-century Continental Europe, with asymmetrical patterns involving motifs and scrollwork."

His left dimple made a brief appearance, a very brief appearance, but I almost didn't notice because, just then, I caught a whiff of soap and shaving cream and something else I couldn't identify. It—he—smelled *SUPER* amazing. Wet and fresh and warm and clean. It smelled so good the tension in my body dissipated, leaving goose bumps and a languid kind of stunned relaxation instead. From a smell.

"No. Not rococo. Let's go," he said flatly, opening the door and motioning for me to exit.

I didn't move. I lowered my eyes to scan his clothes while also maybe inhaling deeply. I told myself I was comparing his clothes to mine to determine if I were dressed appropriately while also breathing normally. I was not sniffing.

Upon completing my perusal and inhaling the glorious scent of him —but not sniffing—a few more times, I could see no deficit in my outfit. In fact, after his shower he'd changed and now we were similarly attired: jeans, black shirt, he was in dark sneakers, I was in dark sandals. One might even say we matched.

Lifting my chin to peer up at him, I found him gazing down at me. Right there. Super close. Still smelling super good. My breath caught and any comments I had about the similarity between our attire scattered. I could feel the heat from his body.

Time seemed to slow as my mind sluggishly wondered how I'd arrived at this moment. I could mostly make out his eyes behind the dark lenses. They were lowered, focused somewhere on my face. I didn't think it was my eyes.

Did he move? Or were we always standing this close? And why wasn't I cringing away? Goodness, his face would be nice to sit on.

AAHHHH!

"Um." I flinched, startled by the direction of my thoughts, and stepped back, scratching my cheek. Frowning, flustered by how flustered and hot I suddenly felt—*flustered squared*—I sputtered, "I, uh, yeah. I go. Out. The door." Unnecessarily, I pointed to the open door, and then dashed through it, my heart swooping between my throat and cervix.

Shading my face from the afternoon sun, I took two large breaths and endeavored to regain my dismantled composure. It was hot, even for August. I replaced the lingering exquisite smell of him with the city air, a heady aroma of pavement and steadily rising temperature. Pushing open the gate, I darted through it and began speed walking up the street.

"Where are you going? That's the wrong way," Abram's voice called after me.

I turned, rubbing my forehead. I had no idea where we were going.

"There's no escape from destiny," I mumbled one of my anytime-occasion phrases to myself, jogging back, and keeping my attention pointed at the sidewalk behind him. "I'll follow you."

He didn't move, and I felt his scrutinizing gaze travel over me. I thought about tossing out *whatever* while also actively biting back the urge to say another of my anytime-phrases, such as, *As the prophesy foretold* or *So . . . it has come to this.*

The less I spoke at this point, the better. Clearly, Gabby's text had lit a spark, and that spark had flared, and now oxidation of a nearby fuel source had occurred. I needed to keep my head down, be quiet, and stop thinking about sitting on his face. The flames must not be fanned!

Damn Gabby and the power of suggestion!

Perhaps this was something odd about me, but when my physical urges were like this, sometimes they made concentrating difficult. I'd discovered that a tangible, present partner wasn't necessary for satisfying these urges, yet space, quiet, relaxation, and time to think of fantasy situations were essential. But for right now, and likely for the next week, I could do nothing about it. Satiating measures would have to wait until I returned to California.

Ignore him. That's the only logical course of action. Good, solid plan.

[5]
TIME, VELOCITY, AND SPEED

I gnoring Abram proved difficult.
 On the way to the shop, I walked slightly behind him. This made sense since he knew the way. I distracted myself by counting the number of houses we passed instead of staring at his ass, and I deserved a medal for this because he had a super great ass. Super. Great.

I also distracted myself by cursing out Gabby in my head. I rarely noticed man parts, and usually only as a *Well, look at that nice thing. Huh. Moving on.* Presently, however, I was on the precipice of full-on man-part appreciation. Frustrating.

Once the houses gave way to shops, I counted the bus stops, but continued to curse out Gabby.

Overall, my coping strategies kept me from fixating on his very attractive form, backside, confident stride, and how he stopped at every intersection to walk adjacent to me, as though he were a gentleman from a bygone age of lusty ankles and jaunty carriage rides. Afterward, he would motion that I should precede him. I refused with a tight shake of my head, a flat smile, and no eye contact. With a sigh, he would lead the way once more until the next intersection.

It was just after the fifth intersection that he attempted conversation. Not allowing me to resume my position behind him, he slowed his steps such that we were shoulder to shoulder.

"Do you play?" he asked.

I knew what he meant and I had no reason to lie. Both Lisa and I had taken piano, oboe, singing, and violin lessons. I nodded.

"What do you play?"

"Several instruments."

Out of the corner of my eye, I saw him tilt his head to one side, as though leaning closer so he could hear better. "Like what?"

"Violin."

"Do you still?"

"No."

He was quiet for a moment, perhaps contemplating this information, before asking, "You don't like to play?"

"No time."

Abram made a small grunt that sounded both derisive and amused. "Too busy managing Pirate Orgy's social calendar?"

Pirate Orgy was Tyler's band and Tyler was the grossest human ever. Unthinkingly, I glanced at Abram's sunglasses and caught my reflection. I might as well have had a marquee on my forehead that read *INTENSE DISGUST.*

Get control of your facial expressions, Mona!

His eyebrows shot high on his forehead. "You split from Tyler?"

Nodding, I wiped at the beading sweat on my forehead with the back of my wrist. "Yes."

"Huh."

I felt his eyes on me, so I glanced at him again. "What?"

"I'm surprised. When Leo asked me to watch you for the week, until that Steward lady gets here, he said one of the reasons your parents were so pissed was because you kept seeing Tyler behind their backs."

I nodded even as my wheels turned, realizing that this conversation had presented me with a unique opportunity. "What else did Leo say?"

"About Tyler?"

As I studied Abram, the curiosity floodgate I'd sealed shut hours ago sprung a leak. Due to the urgency of Lisa's predicament, I'd agreed to lie for her. And though I'd been playing along and doing my best, justifying my role as sisterly duty and worry for her and *Whatcha gonna do? Decision has already been made*, nothing about this hatched plan sat well with me.

The whispers of doubt I'd suppressed this morning were now asking different questions: What had Lisa done that made my parents so angry? Knowing my parents, it had to be something that had the potential to make them look bad or damage their carefully constructed images of having it all: a happy, well-adjusted family; beautiful houses and clothes and art and things; cultural relevance; respect of the industry; living their best life of ethical hedonism.

She'd done a ton to make them vaguely annoyed, but what could have possibly galvanized them into acting? It couldn't be just Tyler. And why was she in jail?

Up to now, I'd endeavored to ignore my curiosity about the subject, reasoning that curiosity with no source of reliable information was pointless. Gabby had been either unsurprisingly vague or outright hostile when I'd asked her. I couldn't question Lisa or Leo or my parents, and I had no idea when I'd be able to get in touch with Lisa's lawyer.

But Abram? . . . *Possibly.*

Choosing my words carefully, I asked, "What else did Leo say about my parents and why they were—or are—upset?"

"Trying to find out how much they know?" He seemed to be scrutinizing me. I couldn't see his eyes, but I could feel them.

Rolling my lips between my teeth, I said nothing, hoping he'd fill in the answer for himself.

Abram watched me for a bit longer, and then released a short laugh. He shook his head. He sighed. "Um—" he sighed again "—according to Leo, it was the drugs that really freaked them out."

"Hmm." They were upset about drugs? That made no sense.

My parents' attitude toward illegal substances was that nothing should be illegal. To say they were progressive would be an understatement. They'd always done a variety of drugs, even when we were little, making no secret of partaking in what they called "creativity enhancers," like ecstasy, marijuana, and mushrooms. They'd even talked about it openly in interviews.

That said, my dad had "the drug talk" with me and Lisa when we were eight. The message had been: wait until your brain is fully developed, and then consider them like a rich dessert: fine on birthdays, bat mitzvahs, Christmas, and when you want a rare treat, but avoid more than one serving at a time.

I'd never touched anything—not cigarettes, not alcohol, not marijuana—mostly because any curiosity I might've experienced ended after I took a series of MIT OpenCourseWare classes on the brain and cognitive sciences, including neurochemistry. I'd subsequently decided that if I was going to put chemicals in my body, then they better be pharmaceutical grade, produced in a lab overseen by the FDA, and prescribed by a medical professional.

While I was still pondering the puzzle of his response, Abram added, "I guess they didn't want their baby girl selling cocaine to sixteen-year-olds at concerts." And that's when I choked on air. Hard.

What. The. HELL?

LISA!

Oh man. Oh man oh man oh man. Cocaine? To *SIXTEEN-YEAR-OLDS?*

I had to stop walking or risk falling over. Standing in the middle of the sidewalk, I was coughing so hard, tears formed in the corners of my eyes and I wheezed when I inhaled.

Cocaine was right up there with opiates as the most addictive, life destroying substances. When I saw her next, she would give me answers. All the answers. I would settle for nothing less. And if what Abram said was true, if she'd been peddling to kids, I was going to blow the lid off this deception. *I was going to—*

"Are you okay?"

Abruptly, I became aware that we were stopped in the middle of the sidewalk. Abram was still there, once again standing close enough for me to feel the heat of his body even though it must've been eighty-five degrees Fahrenheit in the shade. Interestingly and confoundedly, his hand was also rubbing circles on my back and I hadn't noticed.

But as soon as I became aware of his touch, I stepped away. Sucking in a raspy breath and holding it, I let my eyelids fall. I tried to swallow. My throat felt gravelly and raw.

No wonder my parents had freaked. If this got out to the papers, their pedestals might not survive.

"I guess it's not true?" His words were halting, like he was speaking his thoughts as they occurred to him.

What could I say? One of my anytime-situation phrases popped in my head (*And thus, I die*), but I quickly pushed it away. Opening my eyes, I glared at my reflection in his aviators and said nothing. I didn't know what she'd done to land behind bars. I had no idea!

"Where's this guitar shop?" I asked, glancing up and down the sidewalk, my voice extremely rough.

Abram hooked his thumbs in his jeans' pockets. "We're about a block away."

Clearing my throat, I motioned for him to proceed. Irritatingly, his initial footfalls were slow, which made it awkward for me to follow without walking next to him. I didn't want to walk next to him. I wanted to quietly fume and make plans for how I might uncover the truth as soon as possible.

But I couldn't do either because he was talking again. "So, the Tyler stuff is true, but the drugs stuff is not." He nodded at his own statement. "Good to know."

Staring forward, I erased my face of expression. *The drug stuff better not be true. . . OR ELSE!*

"But—" He scratched his cheek, seemed to hesitate before finishing his thought, "But you and Tyler are split? For good?"

"Yes."

"You've broken up before though, right?"

I nodded, only half paying attention. *If Lisa was selling cocaine to teenagers, I will go to a nerd-con and, posing as her, I would make out with a B-list celebrity and ensure we were photographed.* She would be horrified and might never recover. I felt certain of this in my bones.

"What's different this time with Tyler?"

Preoccupied by my perdition plans, I tried to remember my sister's response to this question when I'd asked two nights ago. "Never again. I'm done with that floating trash island of whale excrement."

Whale excrement? Where had that come from? Once again, I blamed *Moby Dick*.

Abram's chuckle was a burst of air, like my answer had caught him totally off guard.

"'Floating trash island of whale excrement, '" he quoted, sounding contemplative, drawing my eyes to his profile.

Since I was walking on his left, I caught the flash of his dimple and it—paired with his super handsome profile—was enough to distract me from my thoughts of revenge. "That's right."

"That's an interesting description." Abram's steps slowed, stopped, and he reached for the door of a shop, holding it open for me. "You have a way with words. You should write song lyrics."

I grunted, scanning the front of the building. The window facing the sidewalk showcased a two-by-ten array of guitars, all held aloft by a heavy-duty black wire cage display. Through the wire and guitars, the interior of the shop was scarcely visible. But, no matter. Clearly this was our destination.

"Why whale excrement?"

Abram's question drew my attention away from the guitars. He'd taken off his sunglasses and was folding them with one hand, holding the door open with the other. His gaze felt different. Oddly piercing.

"Because it's got to be the biggest piece of poop. Right? Whale poop should be massive."

He seemed to be fighting another smile and he opened his mouth as though to respond, but a voice called from the interior of the shop, "Are you coming inside? You're letting all the AC out the door!"

"Whoops!" I hurried past Abram and quickly found the owner of the voice. Giving him a little wave and conciliatory smile, I said, "Sorry about that."

"Yeah, yeah." The man didn't look up from where he stood in the far corner, one foot on an amp, the other on the floor, a

Martin D-45 Fire & Ice Dreadnought in his hands. Based on his level of preoccupation, he seemed to be tuning the acoustic guitar.

"It's expensive."

I turned to Abram, giving him a questioning look as the door shut at his back. "You mean the guitar he's tuning? The Martin D-45? Yes. It is. My mom has one and she never let us touch it."

His rich brown eyes seemed to glitter. "No. I mean"—he shook his head, now fully smiling—"Yes, the Martin D-45 Fire & Ice is expensive, but I was referring to whale excrement."

I wrinkled my nose at him. "What?"

"Have you heard of ambergris? It's found in the digestive tract of sperm whales."

"Pardon?"

"Yeah. They use it to make perfume—real perfume, not the fake stuff—it's expensive," he said conversationally, like this was true.

Crossing my arms, I waited for the punchline. Based on interactions with my brother, I was sure the joke's end had to do with both poop and sperm.

But when he continued to stare at me steadily with a small smile on his lips and those intense brown eyes while leaning a few centimeters closer, butterflies re-awoke in my stomach.

I was flustered again. *Stupid, distracting pretty man parts.*

Shaking my head, I lifted my chin and hid behind a frown. "That's the most ridiculous thing I've ever heard."

He leaned even closer, splitting his attention between my eyes and my mouth. "It makes scent, perfume, last longer. And some people believe it allows a person's pheromones to comingle with the perfume, increasing the intensity of both."

I said nothing. The butterflies swirled. He still smelled so atypically delicious, I fleetingly wondered if what I was actually smelling were Abram-specific pheromones mixed with fancy sperm whale poop instead of cologne.

"Look it up if you don't believe me." His statement sounded like a dare. His dimple and voice deepening, Abram's stare seemed to dance as it traveled lower, from my eyes to my nose, mouth, chin, and neck. And then, he smiled.

I turned abruptly—needing . . . *away*, from all *that*—walking aimlessly forward. "Aren't we here to get a guitar?"

"You really don't believe me?" He was trailing close behind and I didn't need to look to know he was shadowing my steps.

"I don't believe you."

"Why would I lie?" Abram's voice held his smile and was still deep and lovely. For some reason this caused a shiver to race down my spine.

"It was an acoustic, right?" Meanwhile, my voice was tight, held a hint of betraying nerves, and why was my neck hot?

Abram chuckled, like he was enjoying himself, and the sound— close to my ear—gave me new goose bumps. "No. It's a bass. You want to make a bet?"

NO BETS! Right then and there, I solemnly promised myself I would never make a bet with Abram as long as I lived, *with the universe as my witness.*

"I want to get your new bass guitar so we can get back to the house," I said stiffly, pretending to be interested in a used Rogue RA Dreadnought. How had a discussion about whale excrement turn into something that made my body temperature go wonky? And wasn't I supposed to be giving one-word answers?

Needing to hurriedly analyze the situation, I listed the facts: I'd just discovered my sister had—allegedly—been selling drugs to minors; I'd been roped into unwittingly covering for her; I was upset and flustered and off-balance and Abram had very pretty man parts I shouldn't be noticing, because they're irrelevant.

Conclusion: DEFLECT!

"How about if I'm right, then you—"

I spun, glaring at him towering over me. "Fine. Then Tyler is whale vomit. Happy?"

Abram sucked in a breath between his teeth while also—blatantly —still grinning. "Actually, whale vomit is also expensive."

"Now I know you're making this up."

"I'm not." He pressed a hand to his chest, laughing. "Partly indigestible beaks of squid cause sperm whales to have indigestion, and their vomit also contains ambergris."

Partly indigestible beaks of what? Scrunching my face, I shook my head, rejecting his nonsense.

He mimicked my headshake and face-scrunch while still smiling. "The indigestible beak causes irritation in the intestines, and this results in a build-up, like a rock, to form inside the whale. Ambergris is expelled."

"No."

He was laughing again. "It's like an extremely rare, smelly rock."

"Smelly rock. Riiiiiight."

Now he was laughing harder. "And they wash up on shore."

"You are full of *ambergris.*"

Now he was laughing so hard, he was forced to take a step back and was holding his stomach. *Goodness, that smile.* My heart thumped and stuttered; my chest ached; my mouth curved into an answering grin (against my will). *That smile is lethal. Wow.*

However, before basking in or allowing myself to comprehend the full effect of his smile, it was tempered by a sudden thought: was he laughing in good humor or laughing at my expense?

I'd never been gifted in the art of solving situations for this unknown variable. There'd been many incidences—especially during my freshman year of college—when I'd thought my classmates and professors were laughing in good humor. As it turned out, it had been the other . . .

"I will prove it to you." He reached for my arm.

I backed away before his hand could make contact, the butterflies ceasing abruptly, my stomach turning cold.

What did I know about Abram? He'd lucked out in the genetics lottery with his face and body and voice. He slept past noon. He'd dropped out of high school for reasons unknown. He wasn't a fan of consistently applying logic. Like my parents, he was a musician (ugh). He smelled like the Orion Nebula looked (beautiful). He didn't like Lisa. *He thinks I'm Lisa.*

He was probably laughing at me.

A lump formed in my throat.

So what if he was laughing at me? So what? Technically, he was laughing at Lisa. But that didn't make me feel better, either. I didn't want anyone laughing at my sister—*unless she's been selling cocaine to sixteen-year-olds. Then all bets are off!*

"Whatever," I said, glaring at him, trying to find fault with his maddeningly attractive face.

"I insist. I will prove it." He didn't see my glare, he was too busy pulling out his phone and swiping his thumb over the number keys to unlock it.

"Your source better not be Wikipedia. I don't trust crowd-sourced data. You could have created the page and edited it." These words came out more hostile than I'd intended. I told myself to relax.

"Fine." He peered at me, big fat grin on his face, eyebrow raised in a challenge, looking arrogant and tremendously attractive and standing too close. "What do you trust?"

"Peer-reviewed publications," I whisper-croaked, dropping my gaze to the glass case on my left and giving him just my profile.

Why couldn't he just pick up his guitar so we could leave? And why was my throat so tight?

His eyes were on me, I felt them. Mine were studiously focused on the glass case, but I wasn't looking within. A few seconds ticked by, during which I meditated on slowing my breathing and concentrated on pretending he wasn't there, pushing his presence and the echoes of his laughter aside.

Swallowing against the tightness, I ventured to my happiest place, picturing the concave dome of a planetarium above me, a blanket of deceptive white dots overhead, planets and galaxies and solar systems masquerading as stars. And between the white dots? Black matter. What we could not see, what we did not yet understand.

The universe—in all its infinite complexity and beauty—struck me as an apt reverse allegory for human interaction. We are deceived by the white dots. We label them stars. Often, they're so much more. Layered. Complex. Important. Surprising. Beautiful.

This was, I found, the opposite of people. In both cases, we label stars based on first impressions. The universe never disappoints or fails to inspire wonder, but people usually do.

Or maybe—maybe it wasn't a reverse allegory. Maybe it was exactly correct. After all, the brightest object in earth's night sky was usually our little moon. Whereas the majority of the dim, twinkling lights in the distance, the ones we barely noticed, were not only stars but something altogether more awe-inspiring once you took the time to investigate. To *know*.

"Hey."

The softly spoken word pulled me out of my reflections and I glanced at Abram. He was standing close, like before. His face was still unreasonably handsome, his scent still captivating, and his eyes appeared warm and interested. He was no longer (outwardly) laughing at me.

"Pardon? Did you say something?" I felt none of the earlier chaos or discomfort. Both had been replaced with cool dispassion. *Abram is a moon, most people are.*

His eyebrows pulled together as his attention flickered over me. "Are you okay?"

"Fine. You?"

He blinked, like I'd blown dust in his eyes, and he seemed to rock back on his heels. Abram's lips parted, perhaps intending to speak. But then he snapped his mouth shut, frowning like I'd done or said something to confuse him.

Giving him one more cursory glance, I twisted at the waist and called to the man in the corner, "This is Abram. He's here for a bass guitar. I believe you're holding it for him?"

* * *

As soon as we returned, I left Abram in the entranceway and reclaimed my seat in the mudroom by the back door. Picking up my book, I opened to the bookmark and stared at the words. I did not read them. My earlier cool dispassion hadn't lasted long. During the silent march home, I'd felt increasingly . . .

Hot. And aggravated. A vicious recursive loop of being aggravated at being hot and getting hotter by being aggravated.

Huffing, I set my book down once more and left the reading cubby, heading for the kitchen stairs and Lisa's room. I needed to cool down while also blowing off steam.

Conclusion: Swimming.

Opening and closing Lisa's drawers, I searched for a bathing suit. My choices were slim, literally. She owned nothing but string bikinis. Huffing again, I selected a plain white one with the tags still on. If I was going to put on a string bikini, I might as well use one my sister had never worn. Undressing, dressing, and then covering myself in her oversized terry cloth bathrobe, I made my way to the back-garden pool.

We didn't have a huge backyard, but the fact that we had one at all in this neighborhood was remarkable. My parents had bought a dilapidated brownstone on one side of theirs and torn it down, cleverly keeping the tall cast iron fence and the façade facing the street. From the sidewalk, one would never know a garden, a small shed, and a pool lay behind the wall instead of a house. The garden had been specifically designed to provide coverage and privacy from the neighbors while also allowing areas of sunshine for afternoon sunbathing.

Since it was just past three in the afternoon, the pool and its perimeter were dotted with sunlight peeking through the trees. That was fine. I'd never been a fan of spotlights.

Discarding the bathrobe, I walked to the water's edge and incidentally into a swath of sunlight, but then hesitated.

I still had on makeup. I needed goggles from the pool shed to see underwater. And what about my hair? If I went swimming, I'd have to do it again. Makeup was one thing, but I wasn't sure I could style my hair again on my own.

"Hmm." I dipped my toe in the water. It felt nice. And I missed swimming. And it was hot outside. And I was hot *inside*. . .

"Lisa, wait!" a voice shouted.

I stiffened, looking toward the house and spotting Gabby walking quickly toward me. At first I thought she was also wearing a bathing suit, but upon closer inspection her outfit turned out to be short-shorts and a tube top.

"What are you doing?" She dropped her voice to a harsh whisper as soon as she was close enough to be heard, her eyes wide and questioning. Not waiting for me to answer, she glanced over her shoulder hastily and stepped closer. "Please tell me you're not about to go swimming."

Movement at the bottom of the stairs leading up to the house caught my attention and I spotted Abram coming to a stop at the end of the railing. As our gazes connected, he stood straighter. But then his attention swept down my body and he took a step back. His eyes seemed to grow rounder, his dark eyebrows inching up his forehead, his lips parting.

Not thinking too much about the instinct, I shrunk backward toward the shade, away from the pool, placing Gabby in front of me so I wouldn't be as visible.

I wasn't shy about my body. I was wary. About everything. There's a difference.

For as long as I could recall, I lived with an ingrained undercurrent of discomfort in most social situations, including exposure of my façade. Did I wish I were more like Gabby and my sister? That I didn't dislike people looking at my body? Sometimes. It would be one less thing to be weird and anxious about.

But my ingrained undercurrent of discomfort in most social situations also carried over to my area of study. It made me a meticulous researcher. It meant I checked and double-checked and triple-checked. It meant I was always certain before I challenged others, which meant I was always right, which had led to my reputation of being credible, listened to, and taken seriously.

Funny how the very weaknesses that cripple us in some situations are often the foundation for our greatest achievements.

"I am about to go swimming, but first I need to get goggles," I whispered in answer to her objection. "By the way, how did you get in?"

"I have the gate code, and I ran past Abram when he opened the door." She waved this away like it was a minor thing. "You can't go swimming. You can't get your hair wet. I had to call in two favors to get you the blowout yesterday with George on such short notice. This hair has to last you for the next week."

"Would it really be a big deal if I wore my hair in a ponytail or a braid?" I split my attention between her and the bathrobe I'd placed on the chair.

"Yes. It would be a big deal. All the pictures in the house are of Mona with her hair back and Lisa with her hair down. What- what are you doing?" She followed my line of sight to where the bathrobe lay. "No, no. Do not put it on. Lisa would not cover herself. Do not put that bathrobe on."

Releasing a hissing breath between my teeth, I glared at my sister's friend, feeling increasingly antsy the closer Abram came. "Me putting a bathrobe on is not going to be a red flag for Abram."

"Yes. It will." An odd kind of urgency entered her voice. "The only time Abram and Lisa met, she was naked, okay? You covering up now would be weird."

What? Naked? What? I sputtered, my mouth opening and closing.

Giving me no time to recover, Gabby pasted a smile on her face, glanced over her shoulder again, laughed a fake laugh that sounded real, and turned back to me just as her expression switched to stern. "Act like a hot girl who is proud of her hotness, he's coming!"

[6]
ACCELERATION

"What do you mean she was naked?" I whisper-hissed.

"Shut up."

"Gabby—"

She didn't respond, instead looping her arm through mine and turning to face an approaching Abram. I flinched automatically and moved to withdraw. Gabby countered quickly, holding my arm in a tighter grip. My only excuse for not tempering my pulling-away instinct was that I remained stunned by her latest revelation. Indeed, my mind was still running through possible scenarios which might explain why Lisa would need to be naked in front of someone she didn't know.

Perhaps she'd stepped in an ant pile and they'd crawled under her clothes and she'd needed to rip them off? Or someone poured anthrax down the back of her shirt? Or . . . *what the heck?*

I was so entirely in my own head that it took me a few moments to realize that Abram and Gabby were speaking.

"I found her. You can go away Abram unless you're planning to join us by the pool." Gabby's tone was light and playful.

"You're not staying." His voice was like granite.

Distractedly, I glanced at Abram, found him examining me with wary eyes, like he half expected me to pounce on him. He was also a good ten feet away, pointedly keeping his distance. Even so, his gaze did move over me—legs, hips, stomach, and so forth—with the scarcest visible glimmer of appreciation, giving me the impression he was irritated with himself for noticing at all.

I had to wrestle with the impulse to step fully behind Gabby or otherwise use her to block myself from view.

"I can't stay long, I have to be somewhere," Gabby said, obviously pretending to misinterpret his meaning. "But if *you* put on a bathing suit, I'll cancel my other plans."

Abram crossed his arms, his wary gaze returning to mine. It seemed to soften. Or . . . maybe it didn't? Or maybe some plotting, rebellious part of me wanted irrelevantly attractive Abram to look at me differently than he looked at Gabby?

Yes. That's probably it. It's all in my imagination.

But then he asked "Lisa, are you going swimming?" and the tone he used was undeniably softer than the one he'd used with Gabby.

Oh.

So I croaked "Yes" and hated that the majority of my insides melted at the irrefutable evidence: Abram's expression and voice had gentled as he addressed me. Fact.

Gabby squeezed my arm.

I quickly put an end to the internal organ melting and came back to myself, adding firmly, "Preferably alone. Don't feel like you need to stay, Gabby."

She gave me the side-eye and a saccharine sweet smile. "You're funny. I do have to be someplace, but we have so much to talk about. I wouldn't think of leaving quite yet. Plus, I brought you dry shampoo. For your *hair.* You know you can't get your hair wet or else Abram will have to take you back to George."

"Who is George?" Abram took a step forward, glancing between us.

"George is Lisa's stylist in Chicago. Her stylist in New York is also George, but it's spelled G-O-R-G," Gabby answered, like it was the most natural thing in the world for a person to have a stylist with a name pronounced *George* in every city.

My upbringing meant I hadn't truly understood until undergrad how unusual it was for a person to have a stylist in every city, or even one in one city. My superstar mother was followed by a beauty and health entourage everywhere she went. When she and my father had taken Leo and I to movie premieres, or award shows, or wherever they'd be photographed with their two prized prodigy pedigrees, her life had been my initial baseline.

I'd spent the last four years readjusting my expectations of normal. Even so, since my Ivy League past and living with Dr. Steward were now my secondary baseline, I knew I was still hugely out of touch about many, many realities of the typical, normal, or average experience.

I didn't know what I didn't know, but I was working on it.

Abram lifted an eyebrow at Gabby's explanation. It looked judgmental. "You can't do your own hair?"

"Apparently, not in Chicago or New York," I said dryly, unable to help the note of sarcasm given my level of frustration. I just wanted to go swimming and cool down! Was that too much to ask?

Gabby shot me a dirty look, her elbow digging into my side.

But Abram's judgy single-eyebrow lift became a double rise of surprise, his gaze moving over me, his mouth curving into another of his reluctant grins.

"Given how much Abram loves your company, I'm sure he won't have any problem taking you to George to get your hair done." Gabby met my sarcasm and raised me a dose of mockery.

"Or maybe Abram could just change his name to George?" I appealed to Abram, pulling my arm from her grip.

"Sure. I can do that." He nodded, surprising me by playing along.

"There we go. I have my George. I can go swimming. Gabby, you can rest easy about my hair. And now you can both leave."

Gabby's mouth dropped open, and I could feel the squawking protest building inside her.

But Abram spoke before she had the chance. "Oh no, George can't leave. George has to go swimming."

Those statements earned him an intense eye-squint. "Why does George have to go swimming?"

"Don't you want a George nearby? Just in case there's a hair emergency?" He was grinning. Apparently he'd decided to stop hiding his smiles, just this once.

"No." I frowned, confused by the smile he was sending me. "Never mind. You're Ahab again."

Abram dropped his chin to his chest and covered his mouth with a hand, clearly trying to hide the fact that he was laughing. The maneuver didn't work because his shaking shoulders gave him away.

I sensed Gabby glance between the two of us, I also sensed her incredulity, but I didn't give her any of my direct attention. I was too busy battling warm feelings because Abram was laughing at my *Ahab* joke, which meant he was laughing *with* me. Which meant I was melting again.

It felt . . . good.

Eventually, he shrugged, his arms falling to his sides. When he lifted his head, his eyes were glowing, and he'd pressed his lips together as though to erase his grin. It didn't work, his dimples betrayed him.

"Too bad, *Liza*. George will be right back."

Scowling to hide this burgeoning warmth in my stomach and chest, I shouted at his back as he jogged away, "Where are you going?"

He turned and walked backward, looking very pleased. "To change into my swimsuit."

"Well take your time!" I crossed my arms, raging against some new, hotter emotion I didn't dare identify.

"I won't!" he yelled in return, giving us his back again as he climbed the stairs. "See you in a second."

I grunted, grinding my teeth, and not understanding why I wasn't more irritated. I should have been. My pool plans had been disrupted. Cooling down while blowing off steam would be impossible with Abram around.

The combination of Gabby's ill-timed text and his superfluously handsome man parts were responsible for making me hot!

Yeah, but now you'll see Abram shirtless. Worth it.

ARG!

Dammit, internal monologue. STFU.

"Well, well, well, *Lisa.*"

I moved my eyes to Gabby. Something about her tone made the hairs on the back of my neck rise. She sounded . . . pleased. *That can't be good.*

"Pardon?"

"You don't waste any time, do you?" Yes. She was pleased. Her gaze moved over me appraisingly and she nodded, as though agreeing with unspoken thoughts.

"What are you talking about?"

Gabby leaned close, her green eyes sparkling. "Abram."

"What about him?"

"What did you do?" She wagged her eyebrows.

"What are we talking about?"

"Look at you! He's vibing on you." Grabbing my wrist, she forced me to give her a high five before I could react. "Get it, girl!"

We were clearly having two different conversations. "I'm so lost. I know you're speaking, because your mouth is moving and sounds are coming out, but I don't understand a word you're saying."

She rubbed her hands together. "Oh, this is so good. I can't wait to tell your sister you got him in his swimsuit." Her eyes moved down and then up my body. "Or his birthday suit."

I flinched. "Gabby!"

"What? Did you see how he was looking at you?"

"Gabby."

"Maybe you will be sitting on his face after all."

"Gabby!" I covered my ears with my hands and shut my eyes. It was no good. Again, the sexy images, the spark, the flame, the fire. "Keep your power of suggestion to yourself."

She pulled my wrists away from my head. "I'm just saying, I've seen Abram work it before when he's surrounded by his harem, but a boy don't flirt like *that* unless he's thirsty for a girl's milkshake."

Harem? Flirt? Milkshake? *What?*

My eyes flew open and it took several seconds for me to decide which of her statements to contradict first. "He wasn't flirting with me."

She gave me a snort of disbelief and an eye roll. "You're kidding, right?"

"Why would he flirt with me? It would be completely inappropriate."

"Oh my god, Mary Sue, try to keep up. He wants your baa-day!"

"He shouldn't." I glanced at the back door to the house, dreading his return.

"Why the hell not? Have you seen him? Have you seen yourself in this bikini? I mean, yeah. You need a wax, but you two would be *hot*." She shrugged with her entire body. "I would kind of want to watch, to be honest."

"Oh my God!" A shock of two conflicting emotional states—one completely expected and logical, and one dark and secret and troubling —had me turning away from her and reaching for my bathrobe: repugnance and fascination, revulsion and curiosity, disgust and temptation.

She grabbed the terry cloth before I could and tossed it in the pool. "There. It's gone. Stop trying to cover up. Now give me one good reason why you two shouldn't take advantage of this fortress of solitude for the next few days."

My temper was lost along with the bathrobe and undammed feelings surged forth, coating my voice in viscous *emotion*. "Because he's in a position of authority over me. He could tell my parents lies about me—about Lisa not behaving, or seeing Tyler—if he wanted, and it would be my word against his. He could try to blackmail me into physical intimacy, if I don't do what he wants. So, no. He absolutely shouldn't be flirting with me!"

By the end of my tirade, Gabby was staring at me with wide-eyed confusion, but it quickly morphed into narrowed-eyed suspicion.

"Mona," she whispered.

"You mean Lisa."

"Mona," she whispered more insistently, her eyes moving between mine. "Did something happen to you? Did someone . . . did they do something?"

"No," I said, unable to hold her gaze. "I mean, no. Not really."

"What do you mean, 'Not really'?"

"I mean, nothing *happened*."

She bent and moved her face in front of mine, forcing me to look at her. "But someone tried to make something happen? While you were in college?"

I shrugged, waving my hands around. "No. It wasn't like that. I overreacted."

"About what?"

"Does it matter? If nothing actually happened?"

"I don't know, why don't you tell me what didn't happen?" She squinted until her eyes were nearly closed.

"It's not a big deal." Again, I glanced at the back door. *Shouldn't he be back by now?*

"Then it shouldn't be a big deal telling me what happened, or what didn't happen."

"I—" Now I felt silly. It wasn't a big deal. Every girl or woman I knew had gone through something similar, where she misinterpreted an innocuous situation, let her imagination get the better of her. If it happened to all women, then it wasn't a big deal, right? "It's stupid."

"I love stupid. Stupid is my favorite. Go on. And hurry, before the hottie gets back."

I vacillated, feeling inexplicably out of breath. I didn't want to tell her. "Fine. I'll tell you what happened if you tell me about Lisa being naked with Abram."

"Deal. Tell me."

Oh. Okay. Damn. I hadn't expected her to agree.

"You're going to be disappointed."

"Tell me."

I rolled my eyes at myself. "Fine. There was this postgrad TA. And he used to, you know, get touchy with undergrads. Give back massages or hug us from behind. I didn't like it, so I avoided him. Really, no big deal."

"That's it? How old were you?"

"That's not it. I was fifteen."

"Hmm. So what happened?"

"He . . ." *Why are you telling Gabby, of all people?* Why was I telling anyone? It was no big deal. No big deal.

"Mona."

"He cornered me—once—when I was alone in the chem lab. Made me feel uncomfortable." *Stop talking.*

"What did he do?"

"He—" my eyes lost focus as they drifted over her shoulder "—came up behind me and put his hand over my mouth. I didn't hear him come in, so I freaked out. I thought . . ." I shook my head at myself. "See? Stupid."

I didn't want to talk about this. My heart was galloping at the memory. Just like then, I couldn't seem to get my pulse under control. *So stupid.*

"And then?"

"I was kicking and elbowing him, because I didn't know it was a joke," I said, my voice growing quieter, more robotic. "But he was bigger than me, it didn't even faze him. When he let me go, he laughed. He said, 'You should see your face.' And then, when I finally calmed down, he acted like he wasn't going to let me leave again, and I got scared. Again."

Gabby, frowning, nodded slowly, apparently absorbing every detail. "What did he do next?"

This is Gabby. You don't trust her. STOP TALKING!

I hadn't even told Allyn about this, and I didn't stop. I met her stare and finished the story calmly. "He chased me, grabbed me again and pinned me against the wall. When I started to cry, he laughed again and let me go, said I didn't know how to take a joke, that I was easy to tease, like his little sister. And then he left, and it was over."

"Did you report him? Tell anyone?"

Her question cracked the shell of outward calm I'd erected. I looked at her like she was nuts. "Tell them what? That I got scared like a little kid?" I whispered harshly, because I was upset. I hated that this still upset me.

"Nooo." She drew the word out, but her eyes were tender, patient. "That he assaulted you. That he put his hands on you without your permission and frightened you. And when you told him to stop, he did it again."

"Come on, Gabby. It was a joke." Resurrecting cold reason to distance myself from the memory—*nothing happened, no big deal, nothing happened*—I took several deep breaths and my heart began to slow. The story was done, it was over, but for the life of me, I couldn't figure out why I'd said anything to begin with. Especially to Gabby.

"It was assault. You should have reported him."

"And then what?" I asked, once again employing my calmest, most rational voice. "I was fifteen, and he was the son of someone important. No one would have believed me. There was only one logical path forward, and that was to forget about it."

"Are you kidding? You were the perfect victim. Young girl genius, daughter of DJ Tang and Exotica, Mary Sue do-gooder, everyone would have believed you."

"First, there is no such thing as a 'perfect victim.' No one is ever perfect enough when there's no hard evidence of wrongdoing. Add to that, when the truth or identity of the alleged perpetrator—"

"'Alleged perpetrator?' Can you hear yourself?"

"—is inconvenient, no one wants to listen, no one wants to know the truth, let alone do anything about it. Second, I might have been terrified, but nothing actually happened. They would have told me it was no big deal, because it was *no big deal*. I wasn't hurt, I was just scared." Inexplicably, despite my determined sensibleness, my eyes stung.

Gabby glared at me for several seconds. Whatever this expression was on her face, I'd never seen it before.

I was just about to speak, to reiterate how minor of an event it had been, when she said, "No. Not hurt, just scarred."

I blinked against the hot sensation behind my eyes and labored to form a complete thought for a few moments before finally managing, "Pardon?"

She gently—but suddenly—encircled my wrist with her fingers and I winced, instinctively yanking it back without thought.

"See? Scarred." Her smile was small and sad.

My face flushed anew, my tongue tasting like ash. "Just because I don't like—"

"You didn't think I noticed? You don't think Lisa noticed? You've changed. Not answering Lisa's letters from boarding school is one thing, but cutting her out completely?"

OH MY GOD! The letters. The damn letters!

"I had no control over the fact that her school didn't allow emails or internet. And I answered her handwritten letters. I answered every single one of them, and yet she continues to point to them as a reason to be mean-spirited."

I'd answered them as soon as I'd received them, which was months late. As an eleven-year-old, I'd begged my tutor to stop holding them, parsing them out as prizes for accomplishments. When that didn't work, I'd asked my parents to intervene, but they agreed with my tutor (which really meant they didn't want to rock the boat). I'd even asked Leo for help and discovered his teacher was doing the same thing to him!

When would Lisa and Gabby get it through their brains that there'd been nothing I could have done?

"You responded months after she sent them. Months and months, Mona. She was sent away—because of you—and you were too busy to respond. And she's never been mean to you, not as far as I know."

"That's so untrue! You know she can't stand me."

"False."

"Oh yeah? What about that prank? With the university newspaper? Plus, as I've explained a hundred times, I didn't get the letters—"

"Whatever, that prank was a joke. You're just too busy thinking the worst of her to realize it." She flicked away this fact with a wave of her hand. "The point is now. You don't even like it when your twin sister hugs you. What happened changed you."

"That's preposterous." I was sputtering again, "I-it-what happened didn't change me. I've never liked. . . I just don't like not knowing when- when- nothing—"

I didn't get a chance to complete my thought or reiterate my objection because Abram chose that moment to exit the house, the sound of the door drawing my attention. I watched him, some forty feet away, as he descended the stairs dressed only in board shorts.

I flinched.

"Good. Lord. That man is gorgeous." Gabby's breathless exclamation felt like sand in my bathing suit. My eyes still stinging, I frowned at the back of her head for a beat before glancing again at Abram.

Perhaps it was the recounting of my no-big-deal story just moments ago and the strange emotional toll that had taken, but as my attention moved over Abram, all I experienced was an aloof observing of a fact.

Objectively, I could admit that Abram was, his body was, breathtaking. Big, wide shoulders—linebacker shoulders, but still lean—on a tall frame, defined stomach, narrow hips. He wasn't just strong, he was exceptionally formed. He was perfect proportions and elegant lines and exquisite angles.

He was gorgeous. However, my accompanying thought was, *so what?* Abram was gorgeous, so what? The sky was blue, so what? I have no idea why my damn eyes are still stinging, so what?

And then he looked up. Met my gaze. A whisper of a smile curved his lips and I experienced an odd sort of tunnel vision as he approached. His warm brown eyes didn't stray from mine though his smile waned, and the focus, the concentrated intensity of interest obvious in his stare seemed to increase the closer he came.

Suddenly, he was there. Standing in front of me.

"Hey," he said softly, those warm eyes of his moving over my face, a concerned-looking wrinkle appearing between his eyebrows. "Are you okay?"

Am I okay?

"Of course," I said automatically, feeling oddly flustered by the question.

The wrinkle between his eyebrows deepened and he shifted closer, confusion and urgency behind his gaze. "Are you- have you been crying?"

[7]
MOTION EQUATIONS FOR CONSTANT ACCELERATION

I t was 2:47 AM. I couldn't sleep. *Maybe I didn't get enough exercise . . .*

I hadn't gone swimming, and I had only myself to blame. More specifically, my wonky emotions were to blame. Or maybe it was Gabby's fault and her potent power of suggestion. Whatever it was, I was paying the price now.

Instead of getting control of myself like a sane person, Abram's intensely gentle concern for my well-being freaked me out and drove me away from the pool. I'd made some lame, hurried excuse about needing to wash the bathrobe, fished it out of the water, and sprint-walked to the house. Then, feeling like a fool, I brought the robe upstairs to the bathroom, tossed it in the tub—planning to wring it out and dry it later—and ran into Lisa's room.

Any plans I'd had of going swimming or cooling off were forgotten, which was fine. After recounting my stupid, ridiculous story to Gabby, I'd no longer felt hot anyway. I'd felt nothing.

I'd wanted to go to my own room but didn't. That wouldn't have been prudent. Changing back into day clothes, I searched my sister's room for something to do, something—anything—that might occupy my mind and time. After a short hunt, I discovered one of our old violins in the back of her closet along with a pile of early workbooks and advanced sheet music.

I took it all out, attempted to tune the instrument, reacquainted myself with how to hold the bow, where to place my fingers on the bridge, and began playing. I started with "Twinkle, Twinkle, Little Star." I played it ten times and then flipped the page of the Suzuki Method, Book One to the second piece, "Old MacDonald."

I'd just made it to page eighteen when I thought I detected someone approaching, reverberating footsteps on the stairs, on the landing, coming closer. Closing my eyes, I replayed the song from the previous page—which I had memorized at this point—and silently chanted in time to the music, *Please go away, please go away, please go away.*

Whether it was Abram or Gabby, I would never know. Whoever it was, they left after two stanzas, continuing upward to the third floor. *So, probably Abram.*

I played and I played until my neck ached, and my wrist cramped, and my fingertips stung, and I suspected the violin had given me hickeys on my neck. And then I played some more. When my arm started to spasm, I put the violin back in its case, but didn't place it back in the closet. I left it out for tomorrow.

That had been hours ago and I'd only left Lisa's room to sneak into the bathroom twice. I spent the rest of my evening going through her record, cassette tape, and CD collections. Despite living in the digital age, my sister still collected hardcopy forms of music.

Where my shelves were stuffed with books, hers were stuffed with music, vintage devices used to play the music, and fashion magazines. She owned an old boombox with a double cassette player, an AM/FM radio, and a CD player; a Sony Walkman; a record player; and several sets of quality Bose headphones. I'd listened to various and sundry music until late, lying on the carpet, my feet in the air or against the wall.

Then, at 1:00 AM, I'd gone to the bathroom to wash my face. There, on the counter, I found a note from Gabby folded under a brown plastic bottle with a pink label.

Hey you,

I'm leaving dry shampoo here, use it. I'll check on you tomorrow.

Love, Gabs

PS Sorry if I upset you

She'd also wrung out and hung up the bathrobe.

Numbly setting her note to the side and promptly pushing it from my mind, I washed my face, braided my hair, and changed into a pair of pink tank top and boy-short PJs. I then tried to go to sleep.

Maybe I can't sleep because I'm hungry? This was a distinct possibility, given the fact that I'd eaten only a granola bar yesterday.

My stomach rumbled, long and loud, and I pressed my hand against it. Grunting into the darkness, I tossed off the covers and stood from Lisa's bed. Food on my mind, I slipped out of the room and down the stairs. The kitchen was dark, but instead of flipping on a light—which might've alerted Abram as to my whereabouts . . . which he probably didn't care about so long as "Lisa wasn't doing anything crazy"—I crept on quiet feet to the fridge and opened it.

Momentarily dazzled by the bright light within, it took several seconds of squinting and blinking before the scant contents became visible. I frowned. In addition to the pizza box, two suspicious-looking containers of Chinese takeout, and various condiments, I found: shredded cheddar/jack cheese blend, a zucchini, a half a pint of mushrooms, and hot salsa. Opening the hot salsa, I smelled it, and then I dipped my pinkie inside and tasted it while examining the lid. It looked, smelled, and tasted fine.

Placing my finds on the island counter, I shut the fridge. The sudden extinguishing of the bright light meant that the kitchen was now pitch black. Shrugging off my lack of sight, I extended my arms and blindly felt my way over to the pantry until my hands connected with the torso of a person.

A person.

A PERSON!

I jumped back on instinct, my leg hitting one of the stools at the island counter and sending it crashing to the ground. My heart in my throat, I screamed, turned, and darted forward, but my feet tangled with the felled stool and I pitched, bracing myself for a gravitational collision with unseen wooden bars and a granite stool top.

But then strong arms caught me, deftly spinning and lifting me into the air. Cold dread rushed through my body, tensing every muscle. I couldn't think. I didn't think. Instinctively, my legs and fists pumped, fighting against my captor. Rocks in my throat as I readied another scream, a hand covered my mouth just as I belted it out.

"Whoa! Calm down. It's me." Abram's voice at my ear soothed, his bulky arm a tight band around my torso, my back to his front, my feet not touching the ground. "Calm down. Shhh. Calm down."

Hot breath teased my hair and neck, and I stilled, relief at discovering it was Abram didn't quite chase away the viral panic still attached to my hemoglobin, coursing through my veins. I shook. I was shaking. And I was gasping through my nose, greedy for air.

Perhaps he heard or felt my strained breathing because his arm loosened, lowering my feet to the ground, and his hand covering my mouth slid away. "Are you okay? Are you hurt?"

"I'm fine," I said, not sounding convincing. Truth was, I felt like throwing up. "Can you, uh, let me go?"

His arms immediately fell away and I stupidly rushed forward, once more crashing into the stool.

I heard Abram mutter a curse under his breath just as he caught me again, lifting me off the ground again, and saving me—again—from another gravitational collision. This time he turned us away from the stool and carried me across the room.

I didn't fight him this time. In fact, I relaxed into him. Wired and exhausted, but mostly embarrassed, I allowed myself to be transported without protest. We left the kitchen and I was finally able to see dim outlines of furniture and walls, courtesy of the streetlamp illumination spilling through the windows of the living room.

Abram carried me to my mother's favorite piece of furniture in our house, a gold velvet chaise lounge said to have once belonged to Napoleon's sister, Pauline Bonaparte. Depositing me on the soft surface, Abram crossed to one of the Tiffany lamps and pulled the chain, bathing the room in soft blue and yellow, colored light filtering through the stained glass.

He then returned, knelt in front of me, one hand on my leg, the other cupping my cheek. "Are you okay?"

"Yes," I said, cleared my throat, unable to lift my eyes higher than his black T-shirt, and said again, "Yes."

He blew out a breath, pushing his fingers through my hair. By doing so, he forced my chin up and caught my gaze. That wrinkle of worry appeared between his eyebrows, and his very pretty eyes— which glowed and sparkled like polished amber cabochons—moved between mine.

"You really freaked out."

I stiffened, gritting my teeth and yanking my head back, out of his reach. "I didn't know you were there."

Watching me with watchful watchfulness, he let his hand drop slowly until it rested on my left leg, next to his other hand which covered my right knee. "I said your name—twice—when I walked in."

"I didn't hear you." I glanced from his eyes to where his palms were hot on my skin. "And I couldn't see. I'd just shut the fridge, my eyes hadn't adjusted."

"Did you think I was a robber?" His left eyebrow lifted as did the side of his mouth, just a hint.

Clearly, he was trying to lighten the mood. Unfortunately, I still felt shaky. And embarrassed.

"I- I didn't think," I admitted, releasing an unsteady breath. "I wasn't thinking. Sorry I fell."

"No need to apologize. It wasn't like you could help it."

"Yeah. Gravity can be such a downer."

He made a light, laughing sound. "What?"

"Uh, nothing. Whatever." *No physics jokes!*

His frown returned, his fingers flexing slightly on my legs. "Are you sure you're okay?"

Reaching for his hands, I removed them from my knees, setting them away. "I'm really fine. I just don't like—"

He glanced at my knees. "Being touched?"

"When it's unexpected." I crossed my arms.

"That makes sense. But your reaction, even after you knew it was me—" He paused and sat back on his heels, as though debating how to continue and finally settling on, "It was a big reaction." Abram continued to study me with his big, pretty, knowing brown eyes. "Hey, I would never hurt you."

I winced, just a little, my gaze falling to my knees where his hands had been. I wanted to huff a laugh and roll my eyes, maybe say something like, *I know, don't be ridiculous.*

But the word "Okay," small and fragile sounding, slipped out instead. I immediately wished it back, because I didn't understand it. I didn't know why I'd said it, and I hated not knowing.

Get ahold of yourself, Mona. Pull it together. You are fine. Nothing happened.

Meanwhile, he continued his examination of me, I felt his stare, assessing my downturned face. "Out of curiosity, and no big deal if you don't want to say, but did something happen to you this last year?"

My back straightened and I sucked in a slow, deep breath before asking calmly, "Like what?"

"You're very . . . different than you were before."

"Because I don't want you touching me?" I tried to infuse my words with challenge, strength—wanting to shake off any earlier impression of weakness—and mostly succeeded. Peeking at him, I gauged his reaction from behind a hastily built wall of dispassion.

But then Abram dropped his chin to his chest, a massive grin lighting his features, and the fragrance of him hit me. My lashes fluttered as though he'd blown dust in my eyes, penetrating my wobbly wall of dispassion and sending it crumbling to the ground.

God, he smelled so good, and—unlike visual stimuli—I couldn't stop whatever cascade of relaxing, soothing, melting awareness smelling his scent set off. Unthinkingly, I leaned forward an inch, chasing and inhaling the smell of him while he cleared his throat, like he was trying not to laugh.

Why he was fighting a laugh, I didn't know, but the apparent genuineness of Abram's struggle to subdue his grin only served to increase his attractiveness.

A moment later, he lifted his eyes and they connected with mine. He'd conceded to a shy smile. It was *quite* a smile.

"Yes," he said.

"Yes?" I parroted dumbly. *What were we talking about? And would it be weird if I buried my nose in his neck?*

"Yes. You not wanting me to touch you means that you are very different now than you were before," he explained.

I appreciated the completeness and thoroughness of his sentence.

My cheeks were hot. I pressed my hands against them while I examined him with suspicion. What was he doing to me?

"How so?" I asked, hoping to keep him talking so I could hunt down the splintered pieces of my concentration.

His eyebrows pulled together as his shy smile became a smirk. "You're telling me you don't remember?"

"Tell me your version of events," I demanded, side-stepping a lie and still holding my cheeks.

"Uhh . . ." He scratched the back of his neck, peering at me like I both confused and amused him.

I was used to confusing people, but not amusing them. My cheeks burned hotter.

"Do *you* even remember?" I pushed, knowing my tone was belligerent.

He made a sound like he was choking on a laugh. "Yes. It's hard to forget waking up to a naked girl in my bed."

Jaw dropping, my eyes grew to their maximum diameter.

Naked. Girl. In . . . bed?

"Are you serious?" I whispered, my mind darting in all directions, attempting to form a reasonable hypothesis for Lisa's behavior and coming up completely empty. Suddenly, I couldn't catch my breath.

He shook his head, giving me an astonished once-over. "You honestly don't remember?"

My mouth opened and closed as I struggled to speak, but it was no use. I was too . . . I was too many things. Shocked. Confused. Incredulous. ANGRY.

LISA!

What had she been thinking? She'd been eighteen! How would she have liked waking up to find a strange, naked, eighteen-year-old boy in *her* bed?

I was beyond shocked. I was horrified. I was electrocuted by the reality of my sister's brazen-slash-creepy quotient, because I couldn't imagine doing anything in the same sphere of possibility. I was beginning to believe that if my twin and I were represented by a Venn diagram, our only areas of overlap would be physical. A minor sliver of shared corporal characteristics, and that was absolutely it.

"Lisa?"

Blinking at Abram, and promptly becoming tangled in his searching gaze, I realized he was still there. And I was still here. And my hands were still pressed against my cheeks as I warred with what I now identified as hot mortification.

What else could I do? I shot to my feet and marched out of the living room, dropping my hands and running up the main staircase.

She owed him an apology and . . . and . . . a voluntarily executed restraining order, a promise to stay one hundred meters away at all times. I clutched my forehead as I made it to the second floor, pausing only for a second when I registered the sound of his footsteps rushing up the stairs behind me. Sucking in a large breath, I jogged to my room —*dammit!*—and pivoted as soon as I realized the error, turning to Lisa's room just as Abram crested the top stair.

"Hey, wait. Wait." Abram stepped in front of Lisa's door and held his hands out as though to catch me by the shoulders, but I rocked back before he could make contact. He looked bemused and amused.

"You think this is funny?" I asked, though it was really an accusation.

"I guess I do." His gaze traveled over my face, and—like before— he was looking at me like I'd surprised him, delighted him, like I was something new.

I was too angry at Lisa to worry about what this look might mean.

Did he suspect I was Mona? I didn't think so, but I couldn't be sure because I couldn't concentrate. My attention was split between my disgust with my sister's actions and trying to shake off all the damn noticing I was doing of Abram's every damn mannerism.

Plus, his current obvious amusement did not help.

Gritting my teeth, I was having trouble holding his gaze but forced myself to do so anyway. "How can you think this is funny? I think it's horrifying."

Abram lifted an eyebrow. "You think it's horrifying?"

It was a wonder he'd been so nice to me—to Lisa—up to now. No wonder he'd been so standoffish when we arrived. No wonder he'd looked at me with such hostility. If I'd been him, I would have refused Leo's request. *Abram is a saint!* A SAINT!

And Gabby knew about it this whole time . . .

"You're owed an apology." Crossing my arms and lifting my chin a notch, I nodded my head. "On behalf of—on behalf of that Lisa, who did that to you, who behaved in an unforgivable way, I apologize."

His eyes softened, the focus of their warmth shifting from inward amusement to outward . . . something else.

"You're forgiven," he said in a way that was a little breathless, dazed. His stare had turned hazy, velvet and hot. I felt the words and the weight of this new look straight to my heart, and now I was also breathless.

What is happening?

We passed a moment, staring at each other, where all I felt was confusion and chaos and a frenzied sort of all-directional momentum. Though I know it is theoretically impossible, which really just means improbable, time slowed until it merged with the physical plane, and I lived every infinite possibility that touched this second: leaving, staying, staring, kissing, shaking hands, touching, grabbing, high-fiving, walking backward to a bed—

But then Abram leaned closer, his attention dropping to my mouth. He blinked dazedly, and whispered, "Lisa."

Lisa.

. . . LISA!

Her name was a vomit pie to the face and merged all the infinite possibilities into just one inescapable path forward.

The bizarre moment broken, I huffed a shaky laugh. Unable to maintain eye contact, I backed away. I didn't believe in predestination, but Abram and I were predestined to be less than friends, hopefully not even acquaintances. For order to exist and be maintained in my universe, we must be absolutely nothing to each other.

"Don't forgive me," I said, my voice gravelly, surveying the space between Abram and my sister's open door behind him, looking for a way into the room that wouldn't bring our bodies into contact. Finding none, I turned for the stairs, calling over my shoulder, "In fact, do us both a favor: hold a grudge."

*　*　*

I slept in my parents' room, but not in their bed. Their bed was huge and huge beds had never held any allure for me. Since going to college, I'd been a nervous sleeper, waking up several times a night, tangling myself in my sheets. I never make my bed because it would be an inefficient use of time, and big beds with big sheets give me drowning dreams.

The cushioned window seat was my bed for the night and I used one of the many plush blankets piled high in the linen closet. They smelled of geranium and rose. The housekeeper had layered the blankets with linen squares scented with essential oils, as per my mother's instructions. She had a sensitive nose and had always been very particular about how things smelled.

Other than my looks, I'd never considered that I might share any traits with my mother. She was very glamorous, vivacious, and charismatic.

I was . . . not.

But as I tossed and turned on the cushioned seat, and despite the aroma of geranium and rose, I couldn't stop thinking about Abram and how delicious he smelled and how the fragrance of him fogged my brain.

I'd always enjoyed good smells—fresh baked bread, warm cookies straight out of the oven, cinnamon, donuts, apple cider, orange blossoms, lavender and lemon—but I'd never thought of myself as being sensitive to them. Until now.

Thoughts of Abram's heady scent on my mind, I forced my eyes closed by laying a forearm over my eyelids. I must have eventually fallen asleep because I dreamt of him. I dreamt of that moment in the hall and all those infinite possibilities.

I looked into his eyes, hazy and velvet and trusting. Instead of saying my sister's name, he'd said, "Mona . . ."

And knew what I wanted with a clarity that, even though I was merely dreaming, it was jarring.

In general—in my experience—good decisions were always made by default. Living your best life wasn't about active choice, it was about the risk/benefit ratio, an equation that balanced the greatest good against the least harm. The logical path forward was the only path forward.

But I wanted him.

So, I made an active choice to be reckless.

I placed my hand against his cheek without an invitation. I dropped my eyes to his lips and thought of nothing but my own selfishness and how much I wanted to taste them. I stepped closer, into his warmth, absorbing his heat, pressing my body to his without asking for permission, and finally—*finally*—took his beautiful lips with mine.

And then inexplicably, just as an explosion of heat and taste invaded my mouth, he said, "Rise and shine, sleeping beauty."

The soft slide of fingers brushing loose strands off my forehead paired with his soft, grumbly whisper made no sense. We were kissing. How could he be speaking when we were kissing?

But we aren't kissing, not really.

Rousing reluctantly, I turned my face toward his voice, stretching languidly, feeling relaxed and calm and inhaling a chest-expanding breath.

"What time is it?" I asked, brushing the back of my knuckles against my lips.

"Ten," he said.

He said. . .

Who said?

Abram.

And just like that, I was awake. But I didn't open my eyes. Nor did I tense, or shrink away. Instead, for reasons unknown, I held perfectly still.

His hand made another pass over my forehead. His fingertips, rough and callused, pushed into my hair gently, curving back around so that his knuckles skimmed over my upper cheek, down my jaw, the pad of his thumb caressing a little circle around my chin. It felt like he was tracing me, drawing me into wakefulness, and—once I stopped attempting to calculate the risk/benefit of this moment—it felt really, really nice.

"Sorry I have to wake you," he said, sounding sorry, and sleepy, and extremely close. "But we have to go."

"Where are we going?" I asked, still not opening my eyes, hoping he'd trace my face again.

He did, his fingers followed the same lazy path. "To Michigan."

"What's in Michigan?"

Finished with his third tracing, his hand paused on my shoulder, and then slid slowly down my arm. That felt good too. The rough spots a surprising texture, his touch a three-dimensional, complex experience. He had nice hands.

"My parents' house."

My eyes flew open, reacquainted themselves with his big, pretty ones—which were currently smiling down at me tiredly—and blinked. "Your parents' house?"

His warm hand made a return trip up my arm and came to a rest on my shoulder. "Yes. It's my mom's birthday. We have to be there by two thirty, so we have to leave soon."

"We?"

"I let you sleep as long as I could, and I didn't sleep." He stopped here to yawn, taking his hand away to cover his mouth. "Sorry," he said around his display of exhaustion. "But we have to go."

I shook my head and squinted at him, at the circles under his eyes, at the ashen quality to his skin. "You didn't sleep? Why didn't you sleep?"

"I couldn't." He smiled, plainly happy, standing and shrugging.

"You couldn't?" I sat up and held the blanket to my chest, tracking him as he backed away.

Abram pointed at me with both index fingers. "Too many ideas, my muse!"

"Ideas?"

"Be ready in a half hour." He yawned. "You're driving. I'll sleep in the car on the way. I'll be fine."

I'm driving?

How could I drive? I had my (Mona's) driver's license, but I didn't have Lisa's. Obviously, I couldn't take mine. Wasn't it illegal to drive without a license? And what if I were pulled over? Who would I say that I was?

"Abram." I stood, shaking my head at the tangled strands of information he'd just dropped in my lap. "Wait. Stop. Let me get this straight. You want me to go to your mother's birthday? What if I promised to stay put?"

"Where I go, you go."

"I won't leave the house."

"I don't have a choice, and neither do you. I promised your brother."

I couldn't argue with that. "So, we're going to your parents' because it's your mother's birthday? And you have to be there by two thirty, but you haven't slept, so you need me to drive, and you're expecting to sleep on the way?"

"Correct." He was almost to the door, his steps shuffling, like he was too tired to pick up his feet.

Hastily discarding the blanket, I followed him. "Do you have a present?"

"I'll pick something up on the way." He yawned again. "Maybe a card. She likes flowers."

Frowning at his blasé comment, I persisted. "No, no. Don't get her flowers on the way. We have—I mean, my mom has—a stash of stuff. Designer bags, perfume, silk scarves for last minute gifts. Let me put something together."

Abram stopped walking backward, but he also made a face. "Silk scarves?" he slurred, his eyes blinking like he was having trouble keeping them open.

"Trust me. Just, go get ready. I'll get the gift and meet you downstairs in a half hour." I walked around him, pressing the call button for the lift. "And take the elevator. You're exhausted."

"I'm fine. It's just one floor down." He waved away my comment, but promptly had to cover his mouth again for another yawn.

Thankfully, the doors opened immediately, and he didn't protest as I pushed him onto the elevator. In fact, my pushing seemed to amuse him.

"Okay, see you soon." I ignored the way my skin heated at his warm expression, focusing instead on what needed to be done. "And if you use the stairs, promise me you'll hold onto the rail. I don't want you falling down."

"Yeah, gravity can be such a downer," Abram mumbled, repeating my words from the prior evening, and that gave me pause.

I watched him closely as he leaned backward against the wall of the car, as though standing upright took too much energy. His sleepy, half-lidded gaze moved over me. His smile grew.

"You look . . . nice," he said, his voice dropping an octave.

Frowning in confusion, I glanced down at myself, at my braless chest in the skimpy pink tank top and boy-short PJs. Awareness caused a shock of pinpricks beneath my skin and I lifted startled eyes, catching the tail end of his transparently hot and appreciative look just as the doors slid shut.

[8]
FALLING OBJECTS

I assembled a birthday package for Abram's mom, pulled on one of my—Mona's—dresses as it felt more appropriate for the situation; unbraided and brushed my hair, ignoring the bottle of dry shampoo; applied the eye makeup; and grabbed two granola bars. The bars I washed down with a glass of milk just as Abram called Lisa's name from the foyer.

"That's a nice dress," he said, leaning against the front door and watching me as I entered.

Glancing down at my somewhat fitted skirt, I shrugged. His gaze persisted, but I ignored it, instead turning to the mirror and pretending to fuss with my appearance.

"Very librarian chic." His voice was deeper than usual, probably because he hadn't slept at all. "All you need now is glasses, a ruler, and a very disapproving scowl."

I fought against the sudden urge to scowl disapprovingly—just to see what he'd do—and said, "It's Mona's."

Telling the truth here made the most sense. I'd never worn it before, so I didn't have to worry about any pictures of me (Mona) in this dress somewhere in the house. Yet, it definitely wasn't Lisa's style: "boring" navy blue cotton, capped sleeves, a conservative neckline with a little collar, and an equally conservative hemline that fell just past my knees. However, it was form-fitting, which was why I'd never worn it, but was why I thought maybe it was a good compromise for today.

Abram pushed away from the door and strolled to my shoulder. "You'll need this."

Avoiding eye contact (and speaking and smelling), I turned to him and accepted the phone he held. Google Maps was already pulled up, and an address in Michigan was already mapped out.

Wordlessly, he guided me out the door, ten meters to the right beyond our gate, and to his car, a 1999 Honda Civic. Good thing I knew how to drive a stick shift. But, unfortunately, the stick shift also meant I had to hike my fitted skirt up a bit to use the clutch. Feeling acutely self-conscious—especially after the look he'd given me this morning before the elevator doors closed—I had difficulty swallowing until I glanced at my companion.

Abram had already fallen asleep, zonking out as soon as I'd pulled away from the curb. Seeing this, I laughed at my silly self-consciousness, hiked my skirt up a little more for ease of clutch-usage, and released a giant sigh.

I must be in an alternate dimension. My brain has officially gone off the rails.

I felt . . . lost. Not geographically lost, thanks to Abram's GPS, but mentally and emotionally and physically muddled. Since talking everything over with Allyn was out of the question, I used the long, quiet drive to sort through the tangle of thoughts in my brain and the bundle of nerves in my stomach without her help.

First and foremost, I was nervous because I'd never operated a motor vehicle without my driver's license before. If sleeping in my day clothes felt disobedient, this felt exponentially disobedient. I couldn't relax. I felt the illegal nature of my actions like an elusive hair in my mouth, but instead *IN MY BRAIN.* Which was why I drove ten to twenty miles under the speed limit the entire way, with both hands on the steering wheel. At all times.

Second, there was that dream from last night and *that look* from this morning. I tried to talk myself into believing *that look* had been imagined. But then I'd recall the image of his hot eyes in his super handsome face, staring at me daringly, brazenly.

No matter how much I tried, I couldn't talk myself into believing something false. Abram had been ogling me. Fact.

No. Not me. Lisa.

Except, in that moment, I wasn't Lisa. But, I also was her. *Confusing.*

Which brings me to the third item: everything else. The tense moment between Abram and I last night in front of Lisa's door and whatever that meant; the revelation that Lisa had appeared naked and uninvited in his bed last year; the fact that I'd told Gabby about that stupid story with that stupid TA my freshman year (W*hy oh why had I done that?*); the possibility that Lisa had been dealing drugs to teenagers; the unknowns surrounding her arrest; and the fact that I was a lying liar, pretending to be her, right now. What a mess.

I didn't like all the unknowns.

My life had been supremely tidy up to now, by design. And Abram was the definition of messy—from the way he dressed to how infrequently he shaved to eating cold pizza, sleeping at random hours, approaching his responsibilities with a laissez-faire nonchalance, waiting until the last minute to get his mother a birthday gift, and *did the man even have a job?*—and liking him had the potential to be incredibly messy.

And yet, I did.

I liked him.

Talking to him was confoundedly easy. One might even say *seductively* easy. Seductive because, when we spoke, I was constantly forgetting to lie, or speak in one-word sentences, or try to be Lisa-like. I couldn't help but default to being myself.

I liked, now that I understood the situation better, that he'd shunned Lisa (I know, I know, I'm strange) and firmly rejected her BS, setting down rules and laying out expectations with both her and Gabby upon our arrival. Lisa had behaved horribly to him in the past. Still, he'd agreed to help my brother and had forgiven her—me—as soon as I'd apologized.

Also, I was now mostly convinced he hadn't been making fun of me during the sperm-whale-poop conversation at the guitar shop. He'd been teasing me and, upon recalling the conversation, I liked how his teasing had been clever and informed. He'd caught me by surprise with something I hadn't known. I liked that his sarcasm was funny and quick-witted rather than biting and mean-spirited. Clearly, he was intelligent, though it was a species of applied, pragmatic intelligence mostly foreign to me.

But! He's a slacker. And you've only known him for two days, Mona.

True. Very true.

In my world of faculty and fellows, data and research, practical smarts weren't a requisite. In fact, I'd been told they were an impediment to expansive thinking. Theoretical intelligence was all that was needed, application of theory was for capitalists and corporations.

And yet, I couldn't help but enjoy Abram's pragmatism, like when he'd told me to take a bath instead of engineering a shower helmet (he'd been right!)

And finally, I liked how gentle he'd been last night when I'd freaked out. He'd been comforting and concerned. Of course, there was this morning, and how he'd woken me up with more gentleness. Even though there'd been unexpected touching, I'd liked everything about it.

But, again, you've only known him for two days!! And Lisa will be home very, very soon . . .

Also true. Very true.

When Lisa arrived home, ideally, she'd continue the lie. Abram would have to believe we were the same person. Which meant any friendly overtures, or clever teasing, or any looks of appreciation he sent my way would all eventually be shifted to her.

Twisting my lips to the side, I removed one of my hands from the wheel just long enough to rub my sternum. My chest ached, a strange expanding tightness against my lower ribs, and the thought of Abram teasing Lisa made me want to pull over and punch that stupid guy in his stupid hat on that stupid billboard I kept seeing all along I-94.

Once or twice, when the highway was free of other cars, I gave into the temptation to glance over at Abram's silently sleeping form. Entirely quiet and motionless, his stillness verged on eerie. At one point I debated whether or not to pull over and check his pulse. That would've necessitated touching him, which I had mixed feelings about —he couldn't give consent, but then again, he might be dead—which was ultimately why I didn't do it. However, if I'd had a mirror on me, I probably would've pulled over to hold it under his nose.

Who sleeps like that?

Not me.

But back to Abram. I snuck another look and my stomach flip-flopped. He'd called me sleeping beauty, but the label firmly belonged to him and his dark lashes, his gently parted, gorgeous lips, the angle of his strong jaw, and the perfect curve of his bicep supporting his head. This was all transposed against tousled hair and rumpled clothes.

He was a messy Adonis and, despite myself, I just . . . really liked him.

But why?

To what purpose?

What are you doing, Mona? Stay on the path. Liking him is irrelevant.

My chest flared with another ache. Indigestion? I probably should have eaten something more substantial than granola.

Conclusion: I needed a healthy meal, and I needed to get control of this situation.

More precisely, after today, I needed to redouble my efforts to avoid Abram, and I needed to take care of my physical urges. Because that's all this was really.

Embrace the null hypothesis, Mona!

Liking Abram was madness. It would never lead anywhere. Therefore, there was no decision to make. My choice was made by default. I didn't actually like Abram. I had physical needs. Thanks to Gabby's insidious text yesterday, I was having trouble concentrating.

I thought I'd be able to wait until I made it back to California, but that wasn't going to work. I'd have to take care of the physical urges now.

I glanced down at my form-fitting skirt hiked up to my mid-thigh. Well, not *now now*. More precisely, this evening *now*.

Maybe once that box was checked I'd stop noticing the prettiness and amber color of Abram's eyes, and how great he smelled, and how the man chewed, and how achingly gentle and sincere he was with me when voicing his concern for my well-being, and I would be able to properly avoid him. Yes. This was a good plan. The moment we returned to the house? I was definitely going to avoid him and . . . do something.

But first, I needed to get through this expanse of highway, operating this vehicle without my license, his mother's birthday, and the drive back to the house. After that, it would be all avoidance, all the time.

Four hours into our journey, just when a rest stop sign appeared and I was seriously close to pulling off and placing two fingers against his neck—not because I was itching to touch him, but because who wants to drive not only without a license but also with a corpse?—Abram finally stirred.

Without meaning to do so, I exhaled a large sigh, mumbling one of my anytime-phrases, "As the prophesy foretold," and felt my shoulders relax.

In my peripheral vision, I saw Abram lift his head, rub his eyes, and peer out the windshield. "Hey. What time is it? Where are we?" His voice—deep and sleep-sandpapery—slid over me, making me sit up straighter. His voice was pleasing all the time, but newly awake Abram-voice was real nice.

But irrelevant.

"On I-94." I cleared my throat, glancing at the car's clock before remembering it was broken.

"What time is it?" he asked, peering at his phone where it was held suspended on the dash. "It's after three? Did we- did you miss the turn off?"

"No. It's still a few miles away." I gestured to the looming green sign. "We passed Kalamazoo twenty minutes ago."

I sensed rather than saw his stare. "Did you pull off for a while? Take a break from driving?"

"No."

"No?"

"No."

He waited a beat, and then asked, "Is there something wrong with the car?"

"No."

"No?"

"No."

Again, he waited a beat before questioning me further, but this time I felt a mood shift. "Then what happened? We should have been there an hour ago." He grabbed his phone from the dash, moving his thumb along the screen. "My mom has texted me five times."

"Your mom texted you five times?"

"Yes. Haven't you noticed the messages?"

"Yes, but I didn't read them or know they were from her. I hid them when they came in."

"You didn't read them?"

"They're not my messages, it would have been an invasion of privacy." I gave a weak shrug. "Why? Why did she text?"

"Lisa, we're very late and she's worried." He said this like it was obvious, as though all parents worried and texted their kids when they were late. "We've gone a hundred and fifty miles in four hours, why are you driving so slow?"

"I don't have my driver's license."

He waited, like he expected me to continue. When I didn't, he asked, "So?"

"So, I didn't want to get pulled over." I glanced at him, found him staring at me. "Hey. Don't give me that look. You're not the one operating a motor vehicle illegally."

"It's not illegal to drive without a license. It's illegal to drive if you have no license."

Sending him a quick glare, I readjusted my hand placement on the steering wheel. "Is that some kind of riddle? If I say your name backward three times, will you drive?"

Abram barked a laugh, drawing my attention. I found him looking at me with glassy eyes, his hand over his mouth, hiding his smile while shaking his head. His shoulders shook with quiet laughter.

"You are . . ." he started, stopped, sighed, then chuckled. "I should be mad at you."

"You're mad at me?" I felt equal parts indignant and contrite, which was a weird, new combination for me.

"But I'm not. You are so much different than I thought you would be."

Unsurprisingly, that had me gripping the steering wheel tighter and flailing for something to say that might sound Lisa-like.

But then I stopped flailing.

If my actions and our conversations over the last few days hadn't made him suspicious, then he wasn't going to be suspicious. At all. In fact, now I had a suspicion Abram wasn't ever going to be suspicious of me.

Conclusion: No need for me to worry about acting Lisa-like, because—to him—I was her.

Which, I conceded with a good measure of uneasiness, when she arrived, she'd have to act like me.

* * *

I'd never been to a suburb before.

Driving through Abram's parents' neighborhood was like visiting a movie set. The houses all looked remarkably similar, the front lawns were perfectly maintained, US flags flew from flagpoles, wreaths hung on doors. I even spotted a few picket fences.

Honestly? I loved it.

"You grew up here?"

"Yes."

"What do your parents do?" I asked, making a left onto another street that looked just like the last street. Everything was so delightfully tidy.

He didn't answer immediately, so I glanced at him. He looked uncomfortable.

"What?" I split my attention between him and the street. "Do they run a grow house?"

Abram coughed a laugh, now staring at me. "No! My parents don't run a grow house!"

"This neighborhood reminds me of that show, *Breaking Bad*. Of course, we're in Michigan, not New Mexico, and the house styles are different, but the neighborhood has a similar feel. Have you ever watched it?"

"No." His tone held amusement, but also maybe defensiveness. Or something like defensiveness.

"It's a good show. The chemistry stuff is spot on," I said distractedly. A house with a picket fence, a rooster weather vane, *and* a towering flagpole with a US flag snagged my attention. The outside was painted white, the shutters were trimmed forest green, the door was red. A summery-looking wreath with yellow flowers was affixed to the door. It probably had a welcome mat.

I want to live there.

"How would you know about the chemistry stuff?" he asked, also sounding distracted.

Instead of being flustered or worried that I'd made a mistake by mentioning chemistry, I saw his question for exactly what it was: a way to avoid answering my earlier query about his parents.

So I said, "Mona knows chemistry stuff," which wasn't a lie, but rather a true statement meant to deflect, and then asked again, "So, what do your parents do?"

Abram released an audible breath, shifted in his seat, and then finally said, "They're retired."

"Retired?"

He nodded.

"What did they do before they retired?" I lifted my eyebrows expectantly. When he didn't answer, I suggested, "Run a grow house?"

"No."

I peeked at him, found him grinning and trying to hide his grin by covering the bottom half of his mouth with his hand, his elbow propped on the window sill. He was giving me an amused side-eye.

Finally, he answered, "My dad was a general contractor and my mom ran the business part. They had my sister late, and me even later."

"Oh." I made a right. "How late?"

"Mom was forty when she had me and dad was forty-seven."

"Oh." I made another right, scanning the scrolling numbers on the side of the mailboxes. We were four houses away. "How old are you?"

"Twenty-three."

That's right. Gabby had said something about him being three or four years older than us.

"So she's sixty-four today?"

"Yes."

"Oh." I slowed as we approached the address, studying the two-story yellow house.

I found myself swallowing against a pang of longing as my gaze greedily noted the details of Abram's childhood home. Navy shutters, white drapes, maroon door, and a wreath of pink and white flowers. No picket fence, but it did have a stone path leading to the front door which was lined with abundant rose bushes, all fully in bloom.

Forget that other house. I want to live here.

"Is this why fate brought us together?" I mumbled another of my anytime-phrases, the one I typically reserved for inanimate objects I desired.

"What?" Abram's question brought my attention back to him.

"It's so pretty."

His eyes narrowed. "What?"

"Your parents' house. It's so pretty."

His eyes narrowed further, moving over me in a way that felt apprehensive, like he didn't believe me, or he thought I was making fun of his family, or he was waiting for me to add a *but*, or a *for a plebeian's house,* or something equally judgmental and pretentious.

Shifting my gaze back to the house, I allowed the envy in my features tell the truth of my words; tall yellow rose bushes flanked the porch; adjacent were several shorter bushes with lavender-colored blooms.

"Are those Blue Moons?" I lifted my chin toward the purple flowers. I didn't know all the different varieties of roses, just a few of my favorites: Princess Anne, Boscobel, Blue Moon, but Eden was my absolute favorite. They smelled like how heaven must feel.

"I honestly don't know. But my mom will." Abram seemed to hesitate, and then mildly surprised me by placing his hand on my bared leg, drawing my gaze back to his and causing an immediate swirling heat low in my stomach.

But not alarm. *Interesting.*

When I looked at him, I found his eyes were uncharacteristically—insomuch as I knew his character—somber. "Hey, one more thing. And promise me you won't freak out."

I lifted my eyebrows at the irony of the situation: here I was, trying to ignore how very, very nice the heat of his hand felt on my thigh and he was asking me to not freak out. Meanwhile, I'd usually be freaking out about an uninvited hand on my leg.

But I wasn't. I *liked* it. And I was just barely holding the door closed on all sorts of odd, inappropriate hopes. Like maybe he'd pull the hem of my skirt just a little higher, or reach underneath . . .

Pushing those thoughts back behind the closed door, on a rush I said, "I can't promise you I won't freak out until you tell me what I'm not supposed to freak out about."

His lips quirked to the side. The left side. My gaze dropped to the dimple I felt certain would make an appearance. I wasn't disappointed, even though it was promptly hidden again.

"Okay, makes sense." He breathed in, he breathed out, his fingers flexed on my leg and I swallowed thickly. "Here goes: my sister, who is probably already here, is a journalist."

My eyes cut to his. All inappropriate heat and hopes extinguished. *A journalist?*

"Pardon?" My single word was sharp.

"My sister, Marie. She's an investigative journalist." He seemed to be watching my reaction closely. "Leo said you guys—your family doesn't like journalists."

An investigative journalist? Of the exposé variety?

I didn't freak out, outwardly. I freaked out inwardly. "What does she investigate?"

"Whatever she finds interesting or whatever she's assigned." He shrugged. "She's freelance, part of the AP, so she does all kinds of things."

A member of the Associated Press? She was the real deal. So many questions, none of which I could voice, and most involving worst-case scenarios.

What if this is a setup? Unlikely. His mother's birth date wasn't something Abram's sister had any control over.

But, what if his sister knows who I am? Or, I've met her before now? What if she's interviewed me? What if this benign birthday party leads to exposing Lisa's arrest? Like most professions, the world of professional journalism was a lot smaller than people realized.

"What's her name?" I asked.

"Marie Harris. She's awesome, and I told her she wasn't allowed to ask you anything on the record."

"Hmm . . ." The name didn't sound familiar, but that didn't mean anything.

"Also, she just broke up with her boyfriend recently, a few months ago. He was a chef in Chicago, kind of a dweeb, actually. She deserves *a lot* better. Don't bring up anything related to that. I think she's still sensitive about it."

I was only half-listening to him. Leo had been right. My family had a love/hate relationship with the media. According to my parents, none of them could be trusted. Ever. But they served a purpose.

For my part, I hypothesized that there were three types of journalists: those who wanted to do another fluff piece on music's most beloved power couple's "odd-ball, genius daughter" (say that ten times real fast), or those who wanted dirt, or those who wanted both.

Having been interviewed countless times, the interviewers always seemed content to follow the same, predictable path, painting me using the same brush, prosaic questions the brush strokes: What's it like to be so smart? What's it like to have DJ Tang and Exotica as parents? Are you dating anyone? Blah blah blah.

However, having been interviewed countless times *and* having never been surprised meant I rarely remembered the interviewers' names. In summary, I'd never met a journalist who pleasantly surprised or impressed me.

"Any stories on, uh, the children of celebrities?"

Abram shook his head. "No. Politicians are more her speed." His gaze lost some of its focus as it moved over my shoulder. "She also writes some weird stories too. Stuff that gets her in trouble."

"Trouble?"

"Yes." His gaze came back to mine and he smirked. "Ask her about bodybuilders."

"Bodybuilders." I relaxed. A tad. My gaze flickered over him. "Okay. So . . . what are we going to tell her? What's the story?"

"The story?" He turned a little in his seat. His hand slipped from my leg and he pushed his fingers into his hair, moving the dark mahogany strands off his forehead.

"What's the story about why I'm here? With you? What are we telling your sister and parents?"

"Uh . . . the truth?"

I sat up straighter while having a minor heart attack. "The—the- "

"That you're Leo's sister and you came home while I was house-sitting your parents' place in Chicago. We've shacked up together for the summer, you're my muse, and I've fallen madly in love with you over the last—" he grabbed his phone from the dash, glancing at the clock "—forty-eight hours."

With that tornado of an esoteric suggestion, Abram opened the passenger door and exited the car. Unhurriedly unfolding his long form from the Civic, he stretched. I stared at the band of back, side, and stomach skin (and muscles) left exposed as he lifted his arms over his head and twisted at the waist—first left, and then right.

In love? Muse? Is he . . . ?

He's . . .

I shook my head in an effort to rouse my brain. Tearing my stare from his body, I chuckled and rolled my eyes.

He was joking, of course. *Oh, Ahab.*

I decided right then, that whenever Abram said or did anything nutso, I would think of and refer to him as Ahab.

"Ha ha ha," I said to myself, adding for good measure, "And then the wolves came."

I guess we were winging it. I didn't like the idea of winging it, but I trusted Abram . . . insomuch as I was capable of trusting anyone I'd just met two days ago.

Finished stretching, Abram sauntered around to my side while I turned my attention back to the likelihood of having met Marie Harris in the past, talking myself into, and then out of, a freak-out.

Worst-case scenario: She'd interviewed both Lisa and me at some point, but so what? If she had, it had been only once. How much could a person remember from a ten-minute interview? And what could she do? Call me Mona and sew a scarlet M to my chest? Nah.

As Abram opened my door and extended his hand, which I accepted distractedly, and then allowed him to pull me from my seat, I reasoned that—even if his sister was a journalist of the dirt-digging variety—she couldn't expose me as Mona in the span of an afternoon. I would just . . . not talk much. Speak only when spoken to.

Keep my answers polite, but vague.

Yes. Good plan. *I can do this.*

INTRODUCTION TO TWO-DIMENSIONAL KINEMATICS

"Ah!" Glancing between the bundle Marie had placed in my hands and the woman herself, I added the apt anytime-phrase "Is this why fate brought us together?" because it was perfect for the situation and needed to be said.

Marie tossed her head back and laughed. And then Abram's mom was also laughing. And then I was laughing, because the Harris women's laughter was contagious. For reals, it was an airborne illness of awesome.

Marie reminded me of my friend Allyn in some ways—how open she was, how friendly and engaging—but without the naïve awkwardness I found so charming in my friend. Marie was . . . well, she was a woman. Or, how I thought a woman should aspire to be: Knowledgeable. Confident. Kind. Reasonable. Empathetic. Inclusive. An adult. There was so much I could learn from her. Basically, Marie was who I wanted to be when I grew up.

But Pamela reminded me of no one. I'd never met anyone like her, and therefore I felt like I could learn a lot from her as well.

Perhaps I should have been disappointed in myself for not sticking to the plan. But try as I might, I could not stop talking. I was having too good of a time to care about the logical path forward. It was official: I loved both Abram's mom and his sister and I wanted them both to adopt me.

Here's how it happened: Abram and I had walked in, and I'd been determined to be on my best rigid behavior. But then Pamela—Abram's mom—pulled me into a hug, kissed my cheek like I was something precious, and slipped me a cookie under the premise of wiping lipstick from my face. She also winked. Stunned, I ate the cookie. It was shortbread and it was so good I wanted to cry.

I handed off the present I'd brought to Abram and, with her arm around my waist, Pamela walked me into the kitchen where Marie—who was Abram's opposite in coloring and willingness to show her smile—also gave me a hug and gave me a cookie. Another shortbread.

Is this all it takes to earn my trust? Cookies and smiles?! Can I be bought for so little?

Apparently, yes. Which I felt was the right answer. Besides, who is to say cookies are cheap? Cookies are priceless! (Don't @ me.)

Anyway, Marie promptly confided that both she and Pamela were Hufflepuffs, but that Abram was a Gryffindor with Slytherin tendencies, and then asked me which house I was in.

It all happened so quickly. One moment I was discussing how I preferred the blue and bronze scheme from the book to the blue and silver combo in the films (for the Ravenclaw house colors), and commiserating on the absence of Peeves in the movies, and in the next moment—really, six hours later of near constant enthralling conversation—Marie was showing me her hand-knit collection of fingerless gloves and asking me if I wanted a pair.

Which brings us to now.

"You are hilarious. 'Is this why fate brought us together?'" Abram's sister quoted me, wiping at her eyes. "They're just fingerless gloves. Take them."

"I will. I will take them." With no shame, I clutched the gloves to my chest. "Thank you." Not only were they warm, they were blue and bronze, *my real house colors.*

Since I worked and spent most of my day in cold offices sitting in front of a keyboard, my fingers were often cold. I'd tried full-fingered gloves to various degrees of failure. Explaining my cold finger lament to the ladies over peppermint tea—leaving out any particulars that might reveal me as Mona—Marie had immediately offered me a pair, volunteering that she was a knitter and had several spare sets in her old room, along with scarves, blankets, hats, and so forth.

"My apartment in Chicago is too small to hold everything I make, so I store a lot of stuff here. And you're welcome," Marie replied warmly, her face and her smile sunshine. "Thanks for giving my mom such generous gifts for her birthday, they were very thoughtful." Her gaze flickered over to her mother.

"Yes, thank you so much." Pamela placed her fingertips on her chest, immediately flustered all over again, just like she'd been when she'd first opened the presents.

I wanted to tell her it was no big deal. My mother received free luxury goods from all the major names, so a Burberry bag, scarf, and bottle of perfume had been—quite honestly—nothing from my perspective. But after seeing how Pamela had been almost afraid to touch the bag, scarf, and perfume upon opening them, and how agitated and grateful she'd been, I decided to keep this information to myself.

"I hope you enjoy them" was all I'd said then—which had earned me a soft smile from Abram at the time—and it was all I said now.

"Well, I absolutely will." Pamela sent me another affectionate gaze of gratitude, which only made me want to change the subject.

I wasn't comfortable with her appreciation. It wasn't deserved. Plus, I'd intruded on her birthday celebration. I was the one who needed to express gratitude.

"Thank you so much for having me today. Thank you for letting me crash your party."

"Oh pshaw. You didn't crash anything. You're welcome anytime. Did you get enough to eat?" Pamela motioned to Marie's bedroom door. "Do you want another piece of cake?"

I laughed. "No, thank you. I think two is enough."

"And you're assuming, Mom, that Abram hasn't already finished it off." Marie crossed to her bed and sat on the end of it, motioning that I should do the same. "I don't think we've ever had a birthday cake last twenty-four hours in this house."

"He's always been a good eater," Pamela said proudly, lowering herself into the chair in front of Marie's desk.

Marie glanced at me, giving me a closed-lipped smile. "Does he finish your food when you go out to restaurants? I swear, he only visits me in the city when he's hungry."

I straightened my spine, the question catching me unprepared, and opened my mouth to respond, but said nothing. This was the first time since I'd arrived that either Marie or her mother had asked me about Abram or made any reference to the possibility that he and I existed as a unit.

I'd been partnered with Marie and Pamela all day while Abram had gone off with his dad. We'd reconvened for a leisurely dinner, during which Abram sat across from me. The seating arrangements hadn't done much to settle the knots in my stomach, but they had strengthened my resolve to avoid him upon returning to the city.

First of all, I caught him staring at me. More than once. And worse, he'd caught me staring at him, *a lot* more than once. Each time it happened was like cymbals crashing between my ears as our eyes collided, snagged, and were hastily ripped away. After the crashing came the hot flare of mortification in my chest and up my neck.

And yet, I did it over and over, almost compulsively, like my free will had been hijacked. It was the most maddening thing, but my eyeballs drifted to him, seeking out his face, wanting to watch his features as he conversed quietly with his dad, or sparred good-naturedly with his sister, or told his mom how pretty she looked on her birthday.

I was mesmerized during these little interactions; how he demonstrated affection for these people he loved; how they in turn showed their affection for him. This family seemed to know each other intimately, and—for some inexplicable reason—Abram's attractiveness increased exponentially as I watched him love through quiet, small gestures. It made . . . *it makes me* . . .

It gave me heartburn.

Wonderful, dizzying, problematic heartburn.

And, yes, I also found myself once more mesmerized by the action of his jaw and throat and lips as he chewed. *Why am I such a weirdo?*

Dessert and presents followed, but then we split again. While the men did the dishes, the women sipped tea and talked.

Over the course of the afternoon and early evening, we'd discussed books, movies, historical events, current events, recipes, and even scientific advances, but neither of them had asked me a single thing about Abram. Or why he'd brought me. Or who I was.

Presently, Marie's eyes moved over me as I struggled to answer her question, her gaze feeling remarkably patient. "I'm sorry. I didn't mean to make you uncomfortable."

"You didn't," I said automatically, wanting to reassure her. "It's, uh, just that he's never finished my dinner at a restaurant because I've never gone to a restaurant with Abram."

Pamela made a clicking sound with her tongue and teeth. "What is he thinking? I swear, I raised him better. I know I did."

For some reason, her irritation made me chuckle even as I sought to clarify that Abram and I weren't a unit. "Oh, no. No, no- Abram and I aren't—"

"It's just, this is the first time my brother has brought anyone home." Marie leaned closer to me, her voice lowering, like she was confiding something important. "It's been great to see him smile so much."

"Smile?" I looked between the women. "He doesn't smile?"

Pamela nodded. "He was my stoic little deep thinker growing up and wasn't what you would call a happy baby. Or child." She sighed.

"Or teenager, or adult," Marie added, laughing.

"But that's okay. If I wanted sunshine, I'd spend time with my Marie." Pamela sent her daughter an affectionate smile. "That's not to say Marie isn't a deep thinker—she is—but she doesn't rain all over your parade with her deep thoughts."

Marie laughed harder and shook her head at Pamela's obvious frustration with Abram. "I think what my mom means is that Abram has always been one to push back, question authority, and has a deep sense of right and wrong. He often expresses his opinions as sarcasm and his sarcasm can be difficult at times."

"You mean his sass-back." Pamela's eyes narrowed, her lips compressing as though she weren't impressed.

"I mean his *sarcasm*," Marie said diplomatically.

It was at this point I should've clarified that Abram and I were not a unit, we were not dating. I shouldn't have allowed these fine women to believe otherwise. Continuing to sit quietly and listen without correcting their misconception was dishonest. I knew that.

And yet, I sat quietly, my eyes ping-ponging between the two women, my pulse quickening, my mind arguing with itself.

Speak up! You are lying by omission.

A voice that sounded suspiciously like Gabby's shushed my altruistic instinct, *Don't you say a word. Just go with it, Mary Sue.*

"Well, you know what that's all about, don't you? The sarcasm?" Pamela asked, sounding exasperated, but I couldn't tell which of us she was addressing or if she was merely speaking to herself. "It's what he does to hide that big, sensitive heart of his. That's all that is. Abram has always been extremely sensitive. He wasn't a cheerful child, but he was a cuddly one, always needing hugs. And the world isn't nice to sensitive little people, so they learn to hide it, unfortunately."

"Mom—"

"They withdraw behind sass-uh-sarcasm, and pretend not to care, act like nothing matters. But when they do care—" Pamela puffed out a breath and lifted her eyebrows meaningfully, glancing between Marie and me with rounded eyes "—watch out, 'cause when Abram commits that heart to something—like he did with his music when he dropped out of high school, leaping without looking—he doesn't know how to hold any part of himself back. Good or bad, even if he crashes and burns."

I won't ask questions about Abram because I am not at all curious, because knowing more about him is pointless.

Okay, okay. You got me. I *was* curious.

Apparently, I was exceptionally curious, because I was now sitting on the edge of the bed, gluttonously gorging myself on this incredibly fascinating glimpse into Abram's history and personality courtesy of his mother, greedily coveting and storing and consuming every single word, detail, and insight.

I wasn't, however, ready to admit how ravenous I'd been for information about Abram. Nor was I willing to cross the snooping line. Passive listening was one thing, allowing them to misunderstand the nature of my relationship with Abram through a lie of omission was also one thing, but actively drilling them for information on this man I liked—but shouldn't like—was a gamma ray of a different wavelength.

So, I refused to ask any questions, accomplishing this Herculean task by gripping my new fingerless gloves very, very tightly on my lap, holding my breath, and rolling my tongue to one side within my mouth.

"But mostly good, right Mom? Abram's choices are mostly good?" Marie cut in and her tone held an undercurrent of hardness, one my sister and my mom used on me and my brother when they didn't want us embarrassing them in public.

Clearly, Marie was trying to be a good sister. I adored her for it, but I also wanted her to mind her own damn business and let her mother spill all the Abram beans.

"And he's like a big thundercloud when he's upset—" Pamela sighed again and set her chin in her palm, obviously not taking Marie's hint, but she also wore a soft smile "—won't listen. Stubborn."

"Mom—"

"Remember when he found out about Santa Claus?" Pamela pointed at her daughter but didn't wait for her to respond. "Took him a year to forgive his dad and me. A year! Even longer to forgive Marie, since she knew before he did. Said the trust had been broken and we'd all lied to him. He was seven. Thank God we never did the Tooth Fairy or Easter Bunny with him, he might've sought emancipation! Always been that way." She made that clicking sound again with her tongue and teeth. "And so broody. Quiet. Keeps everything bottled up, like his dad. Won't talk. And once he sets his mind to something, doesn't matter how nonsensical and foolhardy, there's no changing it."

"*Anyway*, I think today is the most I've seen him smile. Ever."

Marie tried again to shift the conversation back on track, adding softly, "He's clearly smitten with you."

Again, she'd caught me off guard. Again, I opened my mouth to respond, to explain that Abram and I were not a unit, or together, or dating, or anything of the sort. But this time guilt kept me from speaking. I'd let them talk and talk and talk about Abram, revealing things they may not have revealed if they'd known the truth about us.

There was no *us*.

And admitting that we weren't a unit now would certainly crush me under the weight of confession-awkwardness. So, I closed my mouth, and I returned her smile.

And I said nothing.

[10]
VECTOR ADDITION AND SUBTRACTION

Abram was the one who drove us back to Chicago through some unspoken, implicit agreement.

But then, once we were on the highway, he said, "You don't mind if I drive, do you? I'd like to get back before my next birthday."

Glaring at him from the passenger seat, I asked, "When is your birthday?"

"In a few months."

I rolled my eyes, pressing my lips together, pretending to be irritated. This made him laugh, a good, deep sound. I liked the sound, and I liked the way a smile looked on his face, which was why I'd pretended to be irritated. He seemed to enjoy teasing me. And, you know what? I liked it too.

Lisa's teasing hadn't been actual teasing—but rather passive aggressive barbs—in a very long time. Leo used to tease me, but we'd been speaking so infrequently these days and our calls had grown shorter and shorter.

Other than Allyn, no one teased me. I'd been in very real danger of taking myself too seriously, a personality trait of my parents' I'd never wanted to share. I firmly believed that good-natured teasing was good for keeping the ego in check, and therefore, it was good for the soul.

We drove in silence for a while and I thought about the day's events, feeling a small smile on my lips wax and wane at intervals. My brain kept snagging on and returning to one short conversation during dessert where Abram's dad, a man of few words, had questioned Abram about his music.

"How's the song writing going?" He sounded genuinely interested and I found this enthralling.

As far as I could piece together, Abram had dropped out of high school to pursue music. Where most parents would still be holding a grudge about potentially being embarrassed by their child's rash choices (in front of their friends and colleagues), Abram's parents seemed more interested in having a relationship with their son.

Fascinating.

The attention evident in Mr. Harris's voice was one of the main reasons I'd kept smiling at the memory. How would that be? To have a parent interested in what brought you joy? To have a parent who valued the actual relationship over the value of having the relationship?

The other reason I kept smiling had to do with Abram's response.

"Great," Abram answered immediately. But then, as though needing to clarify, he added, "*Now* it's great."

"Now?"

Abram lifted his chin in my direction, his gaze sliding over me in a way that had my breath catching before his eyes dropped to his cup and he cleared his throat. "Since Lisa, it's been going great."

"Really?" I sat up straighter, equally confused and surprised by this news.

"Yes." He rolled his lips between his teeth, not raising his eyes from the surface of his coffee. "Really."

I'd felt myself smile in wonder, still confused, but also flattered. An enjoyable, spreading warmth had expanded in my chest, a feeling I couldn't seem to stop chasing on the quiet drive home.

I appreciated the quiet. Finding other people who also liked quiet, with whom it wasn't strained or awkward, seemed to be a rare occurrence.

I thought I'd be spending the time grappling with residual guilt instead of trying to relive the best parts of the day, but I didn't. In retrospect, passively plying Abram's mom and sister for information about him didn't feel like such a terrible thing.

Sure, in the moment, I'd worried that all my morals and ethics were crumbling around me, that failing to correct someone else's misunderstanding today would undoubtedly lead to running for a US senate seat and golfing with big tobacco tomorrow.

The slope wasn't nearly as steep or as slippery as I'd assumed.

But then randomly, an image of Lisa stripping off her clothes and climbing into bed with a clueless and sleeping Abram flashed in my mind's eye. I frowned, shifted in my seat, and glared at the unpleasant image.

Or . . .

Or is the gradual steepness of the slope exactly the problem? Was this how Lisa's lies had started? By her own admission, she was now a serial liar. One trivial omission had become a white lie, which had become a gray lie, which had become a Tyler-trash-island whopper?

"What's going on over there?"

Abram's question didn't quite pull me from my musings and I said distractedly, "Incremental temperature increases."

"What?"

"If you boil a frog slowly, it doesn't notice."

I felt his eyes move over my profile, which finally stirred me from the morbid reflections. "Sorry. Just thinking."

"About boiling frogs?" His voice did a cute little catch thing at the end of his sentence, like he was worried that boiling frogs might lead to boiling bunnies.

I slid my eyes to the side, clandestinely peering at him and wondering what he thought—what he *really* thought—of Lisa's behavior last year. He'd been pissed at me (her) a few days ago, but when we'd discussed it last night, he'd forgiven me (her) easily.

"Do you mind telling me about the night I, uh, the night we met?"

Abram's eyebrows climbed a half inch on his forehead. "You really don't remember anything?"

"Humor me."

He glanced at me once, twice, three times before saying, "I guess- I mean, you *were* pretty drunk. Do you remember the party?"

"The party," I said vaguely, using a tone I typically employed when my professors or classmates would suggest something foolish and I didn't want to sound judgmental, but rather wanted to give them the time and space to correct or withdraw their faulty suggestion.

"Yes. You and Gabby showed up at Leo's party?"

"Ah. Okay. Yes. Then what happened? I mean, from your perspective. What happened from your perspective?"

He shifted in his seat, placing his elbow on the window sill, his index and middle finger lightly brushing against his lips as he stared out the windshield. "Let's see . . . You came in and your brother pointed you and Gabby out. It was dark, there were a lot of people, so I didn't get a chance to officially meet you. Plus, I was preoccupied with the upcoming set."

"Ah, yes. The set." I assumed he meant a music set, i.e. he must've played a set of music for the party.

Abram cleared his throat. "I thought it went well, given I'd never played for that many people before." A hint of uncertainty edged into his voice, which had me smiling at him automatically.

"The set was great," I said unthinkingly, the falsehood slipping out of my mouth and sounding sincere. I didn't know whether to be disgusted or impressed with myself, nor did I know why I'd said it.

But then he looked at me again and smiled, another hitting-me-right-in-the-center-of-my-stomach grin, melting my brain with fuzzy feels. And I understood at once why my subconscious had decided to lie so convincingly.

Conclusion: My subconscious wants to see him smile.

Abram's gaze flickered over my face, his eyes warm and appraising as he said quietly, "You have a really nice smile."

I blinked at him, and then turned my attention back to the road, surprised to discover that I'd been smiling as well. Surprise was accompanied by a rush of flustered heat to my cheeks at his unexpected compliment. It's one thing to admire a person in the comfortable privacy of one's own thoughts, but for those thoughts to be reciprocated *out loud* was highly disorienting.

Struggling in the ensuing silence for a response, I finally settled on, "Thank you. Also, your smile is also nice. Also." Instead of wincing at the stilted quality of my response, I cleared my throat and expression. "So, after your excellent set. What happened next?"

I anticipated the next words out of his mouth with both dread and anticipation, but he didn't leave me in suspense for long. "Leo introduced me to this guy named Broderick—a producer out of New York —and the three of us talked 'til late, calling it a night around four. I went to bed, fell asleep, and then . . ."

"And then?"

He sighed. "And then I woke up and you were there."

"Naked."

"Yeah."

"Yikes."

We were both quiet for a short moment, and again the image of Lisa crawling into bed—okay, maybe she didn't crawl, but crawling is skeevy and therefore in my imagination, she crawled—flashed within my brain. I was so irritated with her. Irritated and disappointed and . . . *wait? Is that jealousy? WHAT?*

"You were pretty drunk."

"Don't make excuses for- for me." I swallowed around a lump of unpleasant feelings constricting my throat. We'd just exited the highway and Abram had to stop at a red light.

He opened his mouth, as though to argue, but I cut him off, "How did you even recognize me? It was crowded at the party, we weren't even properly introduced."

Abram's eyelids lowered and he gave me a *cut the crap* look that reminded me of Leo.

I shook my head. "What?"

"Come on, Lisa."

"What?" I glanced left, I glanced right. What was I missing?

"You know you're crazy beautiful," he said, not sounding happy about having to say it.

Startled by this explanation, and confused about how irritated it made me feel, I straightened my spine and glared at him. *He thinks Lisa is beautiful.* Which, I reminded myself calmly, meant he thought I was beautiful. Because we were identical.

. . . I hate that he thinks she's beautiful.

Shaking my head again, I mentally swatted away the irrational thought just as the light changed and he turned his attention back to the road. "Right, well—"

"It's impossible not to notice you," he interrupted gently. "Even in a crowded room."

Suspended on those words, I felt my glare dissolve, again not knowing what to feel. Or, perhaps more importantly, why I was feeling anything at all. Settling back in my seat, I refocused on the questions I wanted to ask and the information I was lacking.

"Right, so," I started again, concentrating on balling my hands into fists. "You knew it was me. What did you do next?"

"I tried to wake you up. When you didn't wake up right away, I checked your pulse and breathing. You seemed fine." His tone was flat as he told the story, giving me the impression this memory was not one that he enjoyed. "So I got dressed, put a T-shirt on you—I didn't look!" He added this last bit sharply, sending me a hard glance. "And then I called your brother."

"You called Leo? Did you wake him up?"

"No. He was with Gabby. They were both frantic, looking for you."

"Gabby was looking for . . . me." I thought about that. I turned it over in my head. I examined it from many different angles.

"I guess you disappeared on her and she freaked out, because she knew you were drunk. Haven't you talked to her about this?"

"Of course." Crap. I was going to need to be more careful with my questions. "From your perspective, though, what happened next?"

He sent me a questioning glare as he readjusted his hands on the wheel. "Gabby and Leo showed up, you were mostly awake by then, climbing all over me. I was trying to keep you from hurting yourself, but also . . . " He paused and shook his head, making a face of intense irritation.

"Oh no." I covered my face and peeked at him from between my fingers, frustration and anger nearly choking me. "I groped you, didn't I?"

He shrugged, not looking at me, but there was a palpable mood shift. He suddenly felt very distant, faraway. "Anyway, I wasn't too happy. Gabby and I got into it. Leo carried you to your room. Gabby left. The end."

With more force than necessary, Abram flipped the turn blinker and made a right onto our street while I sat perfectly still. I felt so . . . so . . .

ANGRY.

How could he forgive her? What was wrong with him? He should have- should have- *I don't know. But he should have done something.*

Wordlessly, he parked in front of the house, turned off the headlights, and cut the engine, all the while staring forward. I let my hands drop from my face to my lap and also stared forward, now nauseous.

But then, just as the stillness and silence settled around us, he faced me, drawing my eyes to his, Abram's features now mostly in shadow. "Can we just forget about that? Can we just pretend it didn't happen? I mean, what did happen? Nothing happened."

Nothing happened.

A bubble of laughter erupted from between my lips and I shook my head, closing my eyes. I sighed.

"Lisa." He placed his hand over mine.

I didn't yank it, but I did slide it away and turned to open the door. "Come on. Let's go inside."

Exiting the car, I took a moment to fix my skirt before walking to the keypad and punching in the code. I heard Abram's door close behind me and he opened the gate just as it unlocked and buzzed. I walked through it and we climbed the stairs side by side, his hands in his pockets, my arms crossed over my chest.

When we reached the top stair, he side-stepped, cutting me off, stopping directly in front of me, and forcing my eyes to his.

"Listen, I was pissed at the time. But I'm not upset anymore."

"If the roles had been reversed, if I'd found you, an unknown person, naked in my bed. And then you groped me? Should I forgive you so easily? Should I not be upset?"

He frowned, looking frustrated. "I'm not saying what you did was okay, and I'm really glad—I mean, really fucking glad—you feel remorse about it. You apologized. I forgive you."

I scoffed, shaking my head.

His tone turned stern. "No. I get to decide what and who I forgive, and I forgive you. But, fine, forget about that for a minute. There's one fundamental difference between what happened that night and the hypothetical, role reversal situation you're proposing."

"Oh yeah? What's that?" I lifted my chin a notch.

"At no point was I afraid of you." His gaze seemed to narrow, as though watching my reaction very carefully, and he added slowly, "But I'm guessing, whatever happened to you, was scary as hell."

I didn't flinch. But holding his eyes, I felt mine sting. A searing numbness settled in my stomach and I found I had to swallow before I could speak.

"Nothing happened." I parroted his own words, my voice gravelly, and then stepped around him, walking calmly to the front door.

I remembered I didn't have any keys just as I spotted two slips of paper tucked into the door jam. Retrieving them, I read the first,

Hey you,

I stopped by. Wanted to see how you were doing. I found this postal service slip just inside the gate on the cement so I brought it up to the door.

I'll be by tomorrow. Maybe we can have breakfast and catch up.

Love ya, Gabby

I handed her note to Abram when I finished and glanced at the second slip. Sure enough, it was one of those orange United States Postal Service slips.

Sorry we missed you! We tried to deliver your package. It is now being held for you at Wicker Park Commons on N Ashland Ave. Please stop by with a photo ID to collect your package.

"Must be your cell phone and stuff," he said.

I turned my head and found him at my shoulder, reading the postal service slip.

"Yeah. Must be." I handed it to him as well and stepped to the side so he could unlock the door.

Abram shoved the notes in his back pocket and retrieved the keys, his eyes on me the whole time, his features mostly clear of expression. But he didn't unlock the door.

"Hey," he said.

"Yes?" I said.

"So, can we forget it happened?" He took a shuffling step toward me, dipping his chin.

"Are you going to unlock the door?"

"Can we forget about it? Start over?"

I didn't have to think much about his request, because the only logical path forward was obvious. "No. We're not going to forget about it. You're going to hold that grudge."

He exhaled a frustrated-sounding breath even as his lips tugged to the side. "Oh yeah? Why would I do that?"

I told him the truth, "Because you never know when *that* Lisa might come back."

[11]
NEWTON'S FIRST LAW OF MOTION: INERTIA

I needed coffee.

I didn't usually drink coffee, but I awoke the next day with an insatiable desire for coffee. And donuts. Okay, actually, it was a Stan's chocolate cake donut I wanted. But donuts always tasted better with coffee.

Regardless, I needed both. And a shower.

Last night, after returning home and our short—albeit uncomfortable—discussion on the front porch, he'd wordlessly unlocked the door and we'd both retreated to our separate spaces: me, upstairs to play the violin badly; him, wherever he went.

It was for the best. No other choice. Lisa would be arriving any day now, we would be switching places, and Abram could never know I'd been Lisa this week. Any like or regard or respect I had for my messy Adonis was as irrelevant as it was inconvenient.

Therefore, I put him firmly from my mind, played my violin badly for a few hours, went to sleep, and then woke up with an insatiable craving. For donuts.

Presently, checking the clock next to Lisa's bed and discovering it was still quite early, I decided to take my time getting ready while I waited for Abram to wake up and escort me to get donuts. The plan was: I would speak to him as little as possible on the way, and I would avoid him for the rest of the day.

In the meantime, I debated whether or not to take a bath, but ultimately decided against it. I already had that shower helmet. Plus, I suspected a bath would just make me think of Abram, and I definitely didn't need to be thinking about Abram while taking a bath. BIG NO.

Retrieving the awesome helmet from my room, I took a shower. I then turned the showerhead off, sat on the edge of the tub, removed the helmet, and turned on the main faucet. Since I had plenty of time before Abram woke up—given his slackerish history of sleeping until whenever—I shaved everything that was appropriate to shave. Usually, I didn't. Fanatical grooming was pretty low on my priority list. But, given my present predicament, how else was I going to pass the time?

Once finished, I turned my attention to the dry shampoo Gabby left two days ago. I'd never used dry shampoo before, and I had plenty of doubts about its effectiveness. I was pleased to discover it worked superbly. *Huh.*

After brushing my teeth, toweling off, and dressing in Lisa's clothes—a flowy, silk pink tank top tunic, a brand-new white lace bra, and a pair of tight jeans—applying makeup, and checking my appearance a few times, I was disheartened to discover that a mere forty minutes had passed since I'd woken up. And yet, the hunger had only intensified. For donuts.

7:53 AM.

Slowly, I descended the back stairs, strolled into the kitchen, sauntered to a stool, and sat. Sadly.

Sigh.

Man. I really wanted it (a donut). One of those colossal cravings held me in its grip, where you can almost taste the thing you want, your mouth waters just thinking about the coveted item, and you get this sense of restless injustice, like the world is conspiring against you, keeping you from the object of your desire . . . which was a donut.

Tapping my fingers on the quartz countertop, I glanced at the clock over the double ovens.

7:57 AM.

That's it.

Standing, I speed-walked to the pantry, pulled my wallet from my bag, pulled a twenty from my wallet, pushed the wallet and the bag back in their hiding place, and tiptoed to the front door. I couldn't wait. Abram was probably going to sleep until after noon, and I refused to be denied (A DONUT!)

Slipping on Lisa's Vera Wang comfy sandals, I crept to the door, opened it as quietly as possible, and closed it just as quietly.

The walk to the Stan's Donuts was speedy and uneventful, and the ordering process was efficient and swift. I was more than halfway home when I realized, in my rush, I'd forgotten to order coffee.

No matter. *I can just brew a cup when I- when I . . .*

Yikes!

I stiffened, stopped, and sucked in a breath.

There he was. Abram. Sitting on the outside steps, his elbows on his knees, his hands clasped in front of him. Glaring at me like I'd just deleted his LHC simulation data without making a backup.

Releasing the air in my lungs, I bit my bottom lip and approached the gate with caution. I shouldn't have been noticing how crazy attractive he was when he glared, but I did. How could I not? He glared at me as I punched in the code. He glared at me as I opened the gate and shut it firmly behind me. He glared at me as I approached. By the time I made it to the bottom step, I wasn't sure if the warm blush heating my cheeks was remorseful embarrassment at having been caught, or merely a reaction to the stern severity in his gorgeous dark eyes.

Either way, I tried to ignore both, and smiled. "Want a donut?"

His glare flickered to the bag I held, and then back to me. "You left." Abram's voice was cold steel, had cold steel been able to speak and was alarmingly good-looking when it glared.

I shifted my weight from one foot to the other. "Yes. Yes, I did. And I'm sorry."

"You broke your promise."

"I needed coffee, but I forgot to get coffee, because what I really wanted was a donut. And here, see?" I lifted up the bag. "I got enough for you too."

Nothing about his expression altered, which caused a thrilling little shiver to race down my spine. *My goodness.* Was it hot outside? It was hot outside, right?

He blinked just once. "What kind of donuts?"

"Uh, all kinds. A virtual cornucopia of donuts, if you will. They usually give people a box for this many, but I asked for a bag." Peering into the paper sack, I began listing all the options.

But as I rattled off the list, Abram stood, descended the steps until less than five decimeters separated us, and used his finger to hook the top of the bag open further, peeking inside. He was so close, I could smell him, his fragrance, and it had that melting effect on me as usual. But I also smelled the donuts, which meant I was now melting and trying not to drool.

Abram glanced between me and the interior of the paper bag. "Which one is your favorite?" he asked quietly, an edge of something treacherous in his tone, maybe even sinister.

I blinked up at him. "Why?"

"Because I want it." The softness of his response only served to underscore the meanness.

My mouth dropped open. "Why don't you just take the one you actually want and leave my preferences out of it?"

He lifted his eyebrows, giving me a pointed look, but otherwise didn't respond. It was response enough.

"You're unconscionable."

"Which one?"

"Fine. It's the chocolate cake donut. Happy?"

"Yessss." The flash of a grin also meant a flash of his dimples, the combination momentarily discombobulated me, just long enough for him to snatch the bag from my hand.

"Hey!"

"There are two chocolate cake donuts in here." He turned away and walked up the stairs.

"Yes. One for me and one for—hey!"

He'd extracted both chocolate cake donuts and carelessly handed off the bag to me, as though discarding it, walking through the front door. I chased him into the house and to the kitchen, gasping in horror when I saw he'd already finished one of the donuts and had just taken a bite out of the other.

I don't know what made me do it, but I tossed the bag full of inferior donuts onto the kitchen island and grabbed his wrist. Actually, I do know what made me do it: fury and hunger. I wasn't hangry, I was *furngry*.

Before he could react and holding his eyes, I guided his hand to my lips and took a giant bite, shoving a full half of the remaining chocolate cake deliciousness into my mouth.

His eyes grew round with shock even as he laughed. "You're going to pay for that."

I didn't respond. I was too busy chewing, giving him my dirtiest look, holding his wrist in place with a death grip, and ignoring the excited, hot, electric shiver dancing down my spine. He flexed his arm, as though to raise his fingers and finish off my precious. I couldn't let that happen. Plus, I wanted to see his arm flex again.

Grabbing his forearm, I shoved it down with all my might, and I swallowed. He chased his hand, his mouth open and ready to bite. So did I. A brief struggle ensued, during which our foreheads knocked together as we both reached the shared target.

"Ow!" I said, but I didn't back down. I refused to cede my grip on his arm, because doing so would mean surrendering my breakfast, and the loss of watching him strain, and listening to him grunt. Twisting and trying to jump, it was no use. He was bigger and stronger and taller, so much taller, and he smelled so, so, so good. *Olfaction satisfaction.*

Momentarily distracted by (what else?) Abram-fragrance, his forearm slipped from my fingers and he held the remainder of the donut above us both, turning his face toward mine.

"Give it to me." I clawed at his raised bicep, breathing hard, headless of how this pressed my body more completely against him. Or how every time I jumped for his arm, my chest bumped into his and I slid down his front.

I am so hot right now.

"What? Give you what?" he whispered, tilting his head to the side, liquid brown eyes shaded beneath those dark lashes.

No matter how I pushed against him, he held firm. So firm. So very, *very* firm.

Out of breath, I ignored the swirling butterfly field in my stomach, determined to reach the donut, no matter what it took. *Mine! Mine mine MINE!*

"You know what I want, *Ahab.*" I lunged against him. I didn't know what made me do it—

Actually, I do know what made me do it: fury and hunger and horniness. I was no longer *furngry*, I was *frunghorngry*.

Despite my lunging, he didn't even rock back on his heels.

Ugh. Damn him. Why was he so immoveable? He was in my way, keeping me from what I wanted, and—in that moment—my throat burned with how much I despised him. SO MUCH!

But Abram did lower his arm at the last minute, holding the donut behind his back. As I reached around him blindly, my lips accidentally grazed his jaw, our bodies sliding together, the friction causing an immediate straining and awakening within my own. Flinching as though burned, I retreated, working to subdue this destructive awareness fragmenting my composure as his arms came around me, the donut now behind my back.

"Too bad, *Liza.* I didn't get what I wanted either." He was breathing hard. *Good.*

"Oh yeah? What's that?" I ground out, also breathing hard.

"You . . ." he said, his voice a gruff whisper, his mesmerizing gaze darting between my eyes and mouth.

I sucked in a short, surprised breath, blinking furiously as pinpricks of heat pulsed just beneath my skin. But before I could connect too many fantasy-fulfillment imaginary dots, he leaned even closer.

I felt his breath on my lips as he finished the thought, "You . . . are not allowed to leave the house without me."

"You were asleep."

"You know the rules."

"You can't lock me up."

He nudged my nose with his, the barest of touches, a gentle slide, whispering darkly, "But I can *tie* you up."

Oh.

My.

GOD.

I held perfectly still despite being out of breath, my eyes on his, my heart in my throat; the sensation of being launched into the air and falling all at once; my lower abdomen a swirling, twisting, universe of activity. Because I wanted it.

I wanted it.

I wanted it.

I want it. So. Bad.

His eyes held me transfixed, turning impossibly darker, hotter, half-lidded monsters, mirrors of my darkest desires, and they lowered slowly—so slowly—to my lips. He licked his bottom lip, also slowly. And he leaned. And I exhaled an incomplete, hitching breath of sweet anticipation. And I let my eyes flutter close. And—

"Hey! Why is the front door open?"

The sound of Gabby's voice followed by the front door closing had the same effect as a gunshot.

We jumped apart. I scrambled around the kitchen island, placing it between us. He backed up to the kitchen table. Our eyes met—his dark and piercing, mine probably frantic and disoriented—and crashing cymbals sounded between my ears just as Gabby walked into the kitchen.

"Hey you . . . two." She'd started her greeting with a smile, but ended it with a frown, glancing between us. "What's wrong? What happened?"

Abram, the muscle at his jaw jumping, pushed his fingers into his hair, his eyes sliding to the side and giving the full weight of his glare to Gabby. "What are you doing here?"

Holy hadron collider, he sounded pissed.

She retreated a step, visibly alarmed. "I left a note. Yesterday? On the doorstep?" When he continued glaring at her without speaking, she lifted her palms. "Jeez, Abram. What the hell? You look like you want to murder me."

Abram's glare flickered to me for the briefest of instants, and then dropped to the floor. He lifted his hands to his hips, but he still held the partially eaten donut, a fact he didn't seem to realize immediately. Giving his fingers a stern double take, he studied the donut for several seconds before taking a deep breath and placing it on the kitchen table behind him.

During this odd moment, Gabby sent me a wide-eyed look. I knew it was supposed to impart something to me, but I had no idea what. I wasn't yet thinking clearly, still recovering from my *franghorngry* moment of madness.

Make no mistake, it was madness. Gabby had saved me—saved us both—from making a colossal and intractable error in judgment.

"Gabby," I said, my voice breathless and quiet because my thoughts were too loud. I gestured to the bag on the island. "I picked up some, um, donuts, if you want any."

"She's not staying." Abram said this firmly, his hands now fully on his hips, shifting his scowl from her frown to my face.

I stared at him, working hard to catch my breath and keep my eyeballs from broadcasting how badly I still wanted . . . I still *wanted.*

He stared back. He blinked. Aggravation dissipated, becoming something else entirely—conflict, concentration, fervor—and I experienced that bizarre tunnel vision again.

Eventually, Abram took a deep breath. He closed his eyes. He shook his head.

"Fine. She can stay for an hour, and that's it. And she has to leave her cell phone on the kitchen table." Eyes still closed, he rubbed his forehead like he had a headache.

Gabby's mouth dropped open, and she seemed to be on the precipice of saying something—likely cheeky and inappropriate—so I shook my head furiously, making my eyes as large as I could, hoping to impart to *her* that saying anything at this moment would likely result in her being expelled from the premises.

She started, rolled her lips between her teeth, and shifted her eyes back and forth between Abram and me. Clearly a struggle for her to keep quiet, she appeared to be almost bursting with the need to speak her mind. Come to think of it, I'd never known her to hold her tongue. Ever.

It must've been a real character-building experience, not getting what she most wanted in that moment; even if it felt like a compulsion; even if it would have been a terrible, terrible mistake.

I know how she feels.

* * *

If someone had asked me for one word to describe myself prior to Lisa's phone call earlier in the week, I would have replied, *rational.*

But no person is just one thing, one label, one facet of their personality or single characteristic or decision they've made. This was a fact that could sometimes be super inconvenient. Like now.

"What's going on?"

My eyes cut to Gabby's. Held. I couldn't believe she'd been quiet for so long. It must've been a full five minutes since she left her phone on the kitchen table and we climbed the stairs to Lisa's room.

Gabby sat on the low bookshelf at one end of the room, her legs extended in front of her, her ankles crossed, her false fingernails tapping on the wood. I sat on the bed, my feet flat on the floor, my arms crossed over my stomach. I'd been slouching and staring at nothing since entering the room.

When I didn't respond, because I was still debating what to say, she whispered, "Does he suspect?"

"Suspect what?" I whispered back.

Her lips formed a flat, frustrated line and she crossed to the bed, sitting next to me and leaning her head toward mine. She smelled like sweetness and flowers. "Does he suspect you're you?"

"No. Of course not."

"Well, that's a relief. Because, man, he looked pissed when I got here." She breathed out. Now she was slouching too. Her gaze turned assessing as it moved over me. "So, what's going on then? What did I interrupt? And don't say nothing, because I definitely interrupted something. Were you two fighting?"

I stared at her, wondering where I'd placed those prunes.

"Mona!" she whisper-hissed.

I stood, waving my hands around my face, feeling harassed. "I don't want to talk about it."

I didn't even want to think about it. That person in the kitchen? That wasn't me. I wasn't her. She wasn't rational. And I didn't know how to be rational about it. Or rationalize it.

Gabby breathed out again, a huff this time. "You're so frustrating." She stood and shadowed me around the room. "Just tell me what happened. I will die of curiosity if you don't. Do you want me to die? Don't answer that!"

Upon reaching the corner of the room, I spun, my hand nearly knocking over the pile of CDs I'd yet to put away. "Gabby. I don't want to talk about it."

Her nose scrunched and her lips became impossibly small. "Fine."

"Fine." My arms were crossed again, but I didn't remember crossing them. "Now, tell me—"

"If you tell me what's going on between you guys, I'll tell you what happened with Lisa and Abram last year."

I laughed, it was a tired sound, and I shook my head at her. "You already promised to tell me about Lisa and Abram if I told you that stupid story about my TA." *Blarg!* Rocks of emotion in my throat. *Ignore!* "And besides, Abram already told me what Lisa did."

Gabby flinched and stepped back. "He did?"

"Yes, he did," I said through clenched teeth, feeling angry all over again on Abram's behalf. "How could Lisa do that? What the hell was she thinking?"

Gabby exhaled loudly a third time, closing her eyes. "Okay, well, first of all, she was drunk."

"Not a good excuse."

"And she was angry at Tyler." Gabby paced away, her tone resigned. "And Abram—I mean, you would've had to be there—was just the most delicious thing, so hot. And during his set? Talent is such a turn-on, you know? And that voice . . ." her tone held a dreamy quality and she was staring at nothing, clearly thinking about my messy Adonis.

So, I snapped my fingers in front of her face. "Snap out of it!"

She flinched, coming out of her daze, and glared at me. "What was that for?"

"You've already expressed how happy he makes your hoo-hah. I don't need to hear it again. Tell me what happened—from your perspective—with Lisa that night." I fought to suppress an irrational flare of jealousy. Some primal part of myself wanted to claw her eyes out for thinking thoughts about Abram.

NO THINKING THOUGHTS ALLOWED!

Placing a hand on her hip and waving the other through the air, she continued. "Fine. After his set, I'm trying to get her upstairs, so she can sleep it off, and she gives me the slip. I freak out, because—you know, she's shit-faced and *somewhere*—so I call Leo. He and I start searching the house, calling everyone, and then Abram calls Leo, says she's with him." Gabby paused here to wince and peek at me. "Naked."

The flare of irrational jealousy was now more of a campfire, every word out of her mouth building it higher. "What happened next?"

"We race to his room and"—Gabby's wince intensified—"he'd put a shirt on her, but she was all over him. And instead of laughing it off, or keeping her occupied—which is what would have made sense to me —he looks *pissed* and is pushing her away. I mean, he looked like he was about to lose his cool." She stopped here to give me a look like, *can you believe this guy?*

I couldn't believe her.

"Leo was all, like, apologizing. But I didn't appreciate how Abram was kind of rough, you know? Pushing her away."

That had me straightening my spine. "He was rough with her?"

Gabby's eyes lost focus and moved to the wall behind me. "He wasn't, like, rough *physically*. He wasn't pushing her, he was pushing her hands away. But his words were totally disrespectful *and* he threatened to file charges."

"File charges. Wow." Good. "What did he say?"

"I don't even remember. Something like, *Don't fucking touch me!* And he kept telling her to get away from him."

I was so confused. How was Abram telling Lisa to back off disrespectful?

"Did he call her names?"

"Well. No. Just like I said, *Get out of here!* That kind of thing. Like I told you before, he was a dick to her. She wasn't herself. She was drunk, and he wasn't cool. And threatening her with calling the police, also not cool."

"Gabby." I waited until I had her attention. I erased all emotion from my voice, because otherwise I was going to scream. "How would you have felt if you woke up and a strange guy was naked in your bed? And then he began touching you, *groping you*, and no matter what you said, he wouldn't stop? Wouldn't you want to file charges? And isn't that what you said I should have done? Even though what happened to me, which was nothing, didn't include—"

"It's not at all the same thing! You can't compare the two." Her lips flattened and a frown pulled her eyebrows together. "Firstly, it's not like she could've hurt him, Mona! Or made him do anything he didn't want to. Abram is three times her size."

I shook my head, wanting to scream, and instead closed my eyes. "I can't believe you don't think what Lisa did was wrong."

"Of course it was wrong!" Gabby's voice lowered, now laced with an edge of seriousness. "Lisa felt like an asshole the next day, okay? And she wanted to apologize, but he was already gone, not to mention it was so embarrassing, alright? She regretted it immediately. The two situations are completely different! You can't treat all these kinds of things like they're the same. That's stupid. She made a mistake. And I hate to break it to you, Mary Sue: people—other than you, obviously—make mistakes."

Leaning my shoulder against the wall, I rubbed the back of my neck and opened my eyes, a picture on the shelf snagging my attention, a moment in time forgotten until now. A shot of the three of us—of me, Gabby, and Lisa—from when we were eight leaned against a collection of dusty magazines. Gabby, in the middle, wore a dark brown wig to cover her red hair.

"I make mistakes," I mumbled, studying the photo, feeling strangely lethargic and heavy as well as a powerful sense of loss.

Gabby didn't respond at first, merely studied my profile. But then she came to stand next to me, presumably to peer at the shelf.

"Ha," she said, the smile in her voice drawing my attention. "I remember that day. I wanted to look like you and Lisa, so Leo got me that wig as a joke." She turned her face to mine. We were standing so close, I could make out the dark blue flecks in her moss green eyes. "I wore it every day for a year," she added softly.

"I remember." My lips curved into a small smile, some—most—of my anger dissolving as nostalgia took its place, and I remembered how she'd cried when Leo told her she couldn't take the wig home. I'd hugged her then, comforting her, and telling her she would always be my second twin.

As I gazed at Gabby now, I tried to chase the anger, to hold a new grudge, to judge her for excusing Lisa's shoddy treatment of Abram so easily. But I couldn't.

What did I expect? This was Gabby. Gabby made mistakes. Gabby walked through life with blinders on either side of her face and a mirror in front. Gabby wouldn't understand because she couldn't. Did I expect anything differently? No. There was nothing to learn from Gabby other than how not to behave. *That's just how she is.*

And yet, did nostalgia mean I'd made excuses for her because I'd known her all my life? Definitely. Behold the power of nostalgia.

Cursed nostalgia!

What was it about nostalgia? I despised it even as I longed for it, often suspecting it was the most powerful emotion, eclipsing even grief and fear. Nostalgia seemed to make everything, no matter how large the offense, forgivable.

Clearing my throat, I returned my attention to the photo. "What happened to the wig?"

"I think my mom burned it after I tried to wear it to that movie premiere." Gabby chuckled.

But then she grew silent so suddenly I looked at her again. Her lips were pulled down at the corners and she seemed to be trying to swallow.

"What? What is it?"

She glanced at me and smiled. It didn't reach her eyes. "Nothing."

"Nothing?"

"Nothing my therapist hasn't already heard." She turned and strolled away, stuffing her hands in her back pockets. "Speaking of which, I could give you her name. If you want."

Pushing away from the wall, I straightened the stack of CDs I'd almost knocked over. "What for?"

"You know I've been going to therapy for—like—ever, right? Well —" Gabby sat on the low bookshelf again "—I think maybe you should go to therapy and figure some shit out."

I couldn't help but screw up my face and give her the side-eye. "I do not need therapy." I rejected the mere notion on a visceral level and repeated words that Dr. Steward had said to me on any number of occasions: "We—all of us—are extremely privileged and lucky, and I recognize my privilege. I've been given every opportunity to succeed, and I recognize that I've grown up with virtually no hardship in my life."

My sister's best friend watched me with wide eyes, her mouth hanging open, her eyebrows high on her forehead. "Wow. I—*wooow.*" Gabby leaned back, her gaze moving over my face as though she were seeing me for the first time.

"Therapy would be a misuse of time and energy that could be spent attending to others who are actually in need of help." This last statement hadn't been one of Dr. Steward's frequent reminders, but I could extrapolate. My discomforts were *nothing* in comparison to what other people lived on a daily basis, and I wouldn't waste my time—or a therapist's time—with my small concerns.

Gabby and I stared at each other for several long seconds, during which she appeared to be stunned. It was clear she didn't know what to say, but she had an abundance of thoughts on the subject. Conversely, I didn't need to give the issue any additional consideration. I knew my thoughts, and therefore I knew what actions to take and how to behave.

Eventually, the lack of conversation or action made me antsy. I turned from Gabby's stare and reacquainted myself with our surroundings. Picking up the violin I'd left on Lisa's desk, I carefully returned it to its case.

"You are . . ." Gabby paused, and I looked at her. Her expression was free of judgment. "You are . . ." Again, she didn't finish her thought. This time her mouth opened and closed, as though she were hunting for the most-accurate descriptive phrase possible, her eyes narrowing as her focus seemed to turn inward.

Closing the violin case, I secured the latches and leaned it against the wall near where Gabby sat conducting her mental word search.

I'd just straightened when Gabby asked, "Are you a virgin?"

[12]
NEWTON'S SECOND LAW OF MOTION: CONCEPT OF A SYSTEM

I froze, shifting my eyes to her face. She'd asked the question evenly, thoughtfully, as though merely questioning whether I'd ever baked a turkey in the spatchcock position, and did I recommend it or have a good recipe.

I shook my head. "I'm not answering that."

"Come on. Tell me. I'm seriously trying to help you."

"Oh yeah?"

"Yes."

"Gabby," I leveled her with a glare, "You don't even like me."

"That's not true. I like you, but you are also so freaking irritating."

"Which means you don't like me."

"Because you became a Mary Sue. But I love you."

I snorted, shaking my head, and returned to Lisa's desk. Picking up the first half of the music books stacked there, I walked to the closet.

"If you search your coldly rational soul, you will see that I am telling the truth." She watched me for a few minutes as I ignored her and piled the sheet music neatly in the corner of Lisa's closet. Eventually she added, "Mona, we've known each other almost our whole lives. I will always want what I think is best for you."

"You want what's best for me? Which is what?" I returned to the desk, grabbing more music books.

"First and foremost, a life of fulfillment. Secondarily, security, peace of mind, comfort, and companionship."

Her response surprised me to such an extent, I lost my grip on the second stack of music as I knelt, and they fell to the floor in a haphazard pile.

"Did I *surprise* you?" She asked this feigning a British accent.

I huffed a laugh, but said, "Yes. I find your answer surprising."

"You can thank my therapist. So—" she sauntered over and shoved my shoulder again with her fingers "—are you a virgin?"

"No," I ground out reluctantly, rearranging the pile.

"And I assume you lost your virginity to a boyfriend?"

I shook my head. "No. I've never had a boyfriend."

"Really? Now you've surprised me."

"How so?"

Gabby was quiet for a bit. I heard her take a deep breath. Release it. Take another. Meanwhile, finished stacking the music, I stood and returned to the bed, reclaiming my seat at the end of it.

Finally, she said, "But, I guess, it does kind of make sense."

"What makes sense?"

"You've never had a boyfriend, and that makes sense. It would require you asking someone to put you first."

I gritted my teeth. "Gabby—"

"But how does that work? I mean, you yank away when I touch your arm and you've known me forever."

I tried to hide my wince by studying Lisa's bedspread for lint. "So?"

"*Soooo*, you don't like to be touched. At all. How does sex work if you don't like touching?"

"I don't like uninvited touching, when it's a surprise." I believed these words when I said them. But after they were out of my mouth, I discovered they weren't entirely accurate—not recently, not with Abram—and worked to suppress a blooming yet distressing warmth low in my stomach.

"I don't get it. What do you do when you have sex? Announce what you're going to do before you do it?"

"Not all sex requires a lot of touching. I'm extremely clear regarding my expectations before sex, what I want out of the experience, what we will and will not do, what I hope to achieve. I ask my partner for the same information. If the guy does anything unexpected, I simply end it."

"*Reeeeeeally?*" Gabby plopped down next to me on the bed, the intensity of her gaze told me she was absolutely fascinated. "Like, you talk about the sex before you have it? What you're going to do? What's going to happen?"

"Exactly." How else was I supposed to determine whether or not sex with a partner was necessary? The scientific method existed for a reason.

"That's so interesting!"

I squinted at her. "You don't?"

She shook her head.

"Not at all?"

She shook her head again.

I scrunched my nose. "If you don't talk about it, about the plan, then how do you give consent?"

She scrunched her nose in return but also laughed. "Uh, through my actions."

I turned away and stood before she could see my expression, walking to the desk. Consent through actions? Like people expected each other to read their minds and know what each person liked without talking about it first? And that assumed the other person would be mindful enough to ensure climax was reached? What about boundaries? Limits?

Sure. Right. Okay. NOPE! Not for me.

"I have more questions about your pre-sex discussions. But first, how many partners have you had?" Her voice adopted a tone I associated with academic discussions. For some reason, it helped me relax a bit, made the conversation feel less personal.

Sitting on the edge of the desk, I crossed my arms. "Seven."

"Seven?" She stared at me, her eyebrows arched high on her fore-head. "Oh. Okay. Wow. Also surprising."

"Why? How many have you had?"

"One," she said quietly, giving me the impression that her *one* had been meaningful. Clearing her throat, she continued, "Was any of the sex enjoyable?"

I paused to mentally thumb through all relevant encounters. "Some."

"Were they all one-night stands?"

"No."

"Some were multiple-night stands?"

"Yes."

"But none became a boyfriend?" A renewed hint of curiosity edged into her voice.

"No."

"Why not?" she asked.

"It wasn't necessary," I said with a sigh, tired of this discussion.

"Necessary?"

How could I explain this to Gabby in a way she'd understand? I'd sought to answer a question. The question had been answered. Case closed.

Eventually, I decided on, "I don't have time for that."

"That? What is 'that'?"

"You know—" I waved my hand in the air "—calling, texting, having conversations about mundane things, making plans. That." Not when I could achieve more satisfaction on my own than with a partner. It was simple math.

Gabby blinked at me several times. "It's like I don't even know you, Mona."

My chuckle caught me off guard, so did my lingering smile as Gabby and I looked at each other. Her eyes were intent as they moved over my face, like she was trying to solve a puzzle.

"You need help," Gabby said at last, causing my smile to vanish.

I frowned at the floor. "Help with what?"

"You have a distorted view of reality, and what you deserve," she said softly.

"No. I just don't believe romantic relationships are necessary."

"You think you deserve less."

"It's not about what people deserve, Gabby." I sighed. Again. Hadn't it been an hour yet? Shouldn't she be leaving soon? "It's about what people need. I don't need—or want—a relationship."

"Because you don't have time?"

That wasn't precisely true, but—as Lisa would say—whatever. "Sure."

"Because you're so busy being a genius and doing the math, you don't have time for people?"

"I have time for people, just not a boyfriend."

"Even if that boyfriend was awesome? Even if he built you up, supported you, loved you, adored you, and made it his life's mission to ensure you knew—every day—how amazing and special you are?"

"That's not a boyfriend. That's a dog."

She waved away my sarcasm. "You don't need love? Companionship?"

I hesitated, searching the air around her head for the right words.

"Fine," she said before I could assemble a response. "Then you think you *need* less than other people."

I shot her a questioning glance, but before I could respond, she snapped her fingers.

"I have an idea!" Gabby scooched to the end of the bed closest to me and leveled me with an intent and wide stare. "Abram."

I returned her stare, giving nothing of my thoughts, or my feelings, or my body's betraying, quantum reaction at the mention of his name. "What about him?"

"He's hot, right?"

I shrugged and confessed to the understatement of the century, "His exterior is attractive."

"Yeah, but what do you think of him so far? You two were flirting up a storm the other day. Is he a guy you might want to get to know better? If you know what I mean."

"I don't know him very well," was what I said, but my thoughts on the subject were: *I LIKE HIM SO MUCH!*

"Ah ha!" She pointed at me. "You didn't say no, which means you've pictured him naked."

I sighed for the hundredth time. Speaking of, where the heck was Abram? Shouldn't he be kicking Gabby out?

She grinned, wagging her eyebrows. "You should let him touch you."

I choked. "Pardon?"

"Let him touch you. I'm not saying—you know—let him do whatever he wants or anything. I'm just saying, *if* he touches you, and *if* you like it, you should let him. And also, you shouldn't interrupt the touching with discussions of consent and expectations or whatever."

I looked at her askance. "You're kidding."

"I'm not. You should just—you know—give a guy the opportunity to read you, see if he can figure out what you like without giving him printed directions. And a map. And a contract to sign in triplicate. See if you can enjoy not knowing what will happen."

I was already shaking my head before she finished, planning to tell her how ludicrous of an idea this was.

First, no.

Second, also no.

Third, what happens when Lisa arrives?

And fourth, an encounter without explicitly communicating expectations, hard limits, and goals? What was the point? The data wouldn't be generalizable!

Except . . . the times Abram has touched you without asking, you've liked it. Mucho.

My pulse jumped. *Just the thought of all that—all that touching me without . . .* I rubbed my chest, at a hot tightness there, and tore my stare away to scowl at the wall. Gabby's suggestion was on repeat in my head, and it wasn't just anxiety or fear I was feeling.

"You're thinking about it!" Gabby jumped up from the bed and crossed to the desk, standing directly in front of me.

"Gabby, you're mentally disturbed."

"Don't deny it, you're definitely thinking about it. You should make the Mona-moves on him."

I gave that suggestion a firm mental shove. "And what happens when Lisa gets back? Would she pick up where I left off with Abram? Pretend to be me pretending to be her? Gross and cosmically wrong on so many levels."

She sighed impatiently. "You think too much. She'll just call things off."

"Just like that?" I snapped my fingers. "And he won't care?"

Gabby shrugged. "I mean, probably not? Look at him. He's a hot commodity in this town. If he wants some, he doesn't usually have to work too hard to get it. He's a goodtime guy."

I shook my head lightly, squinting at her, a flare of something uncomfortable in my chest. "A goodtime guy? What does that mean?"

"It means he's experienced, and he'll show you a good time, but you don't have to worry about him getting clingy." When I continued to stare at her she huffed and lifted her eyes to the ceiling, exasperated. "Let me put it this way: I've never seen him with a girlfriend, but he's always surrounded by girls."

"And you know for a fact that he has relations with all these girls?"

"You sound like a lawyer, Mona. This isn't a trial." She studied her nails. "Guys like him always have—"

"Guys like him? Guys like what?"

"You know, insanely hot, talented, always single and keeping his options open. He's not going to care when Lisa calls it off."

I could feel myself making my about-to-sneeze face. What Gabby was saying was diametrically opposed to the Abram I was coming to know, especially after talking to his mother and sister. He just didn't seem like that kind of person—

Wait. What kind of person? You mean someone like you?

I flinched, frowning, not liking this thought. And it wouldn't be the same, would it? Yes, I'd had relations with several men without any intention of making any of those men my long-term partner, but that was all in the interest of testing a hypothesis. Totally different.

Okay. Whatever you need to tell yourself to sleep at night.

"Why are you making that angry face?" Gabby lifted an eyebrow, her gaze moving over my features. "Don't get mad at me for Abram being easy. I'm trying to do you a favor here. Get in there and use him to have a good time."

Pinching the bridge of my nose, I took a deep breath, irrationally offended on Abram's behalf at him being labeled a 'goodtime guy.' That wasn't Abram. It just wasn't. Don't ask me why, but I knew this was an unfair estimation of his character.

Anyway! I couldn't think about this now. Therefore, I ignored this discordant assertion.

"Whatever. It doesn't matter, because nothing is going to happen between us. I can't ignore that Abram is in a position of authority over me, over Lisa." I said this mostly as a reminder to myself. After our donut encounter this morning, I couldn't and shouldn't forget that *nothing* was ever going to happen between us. He and I weren't even friends. Lisa's well-being was his responsibility. "He's been tasked with ensuring my safety. How inappropriate would it be for me to, as you say, make moves on him? I would never put him in that position."

"Oh, come on. I'm sure he wouldn't mind being put in *any* position with you if—"

I interrupted her mid-eye roll. "No. I think he's already been through enough. Lisa did enough damage last year, don't you think?"

"It's not like being with either of you would be a hardship." Her hands fell to her legs, smacking her thighs as she completed the eye roll. "See? This is what I'm talking about. Why can't you understand how beautiful you are? Anyone, including Abram, would be lucky to—"

"He's not an object! Even if he's been with the entire female half of Chicago, he's still not an object!" I whispered harshly, straightening from the desk, causing her to rock back on her heels. "People are so much more than what they look like, what is wrong with you? He's not disposable. He's not here to use and amuse. He is more than 'like, super hot.' He is a *person*, with thoughts and feelings and a family who loves him, who he also loves. He is funny and sweet, and irritating and witty, and doesn't like to show his smile. He writes music and sleeps at crazy hours, he eats pizza cold—who does that? So gross—and knows too much about whales, and steals donuts, and should really invest in a new razor . . .”

I stopped there because Gabby was giving me a sideways look, the rest of her face frozen, the fire of suspicion behind her eyes.

“What?” I asked sharply. “What is it?”

“I don’t get it. You’ve slept with like, seven guys, right? And never wanted a relationship with any of them.”

“We didn’t sleep together, we had sex as a means to determine specific aims. And that doesn’t mean I’ve treated them like objects.” I hadn’t. I really hadn’t. It had been a mutually beneficial arrangement, where we’d both used each other’s bodies to answer—*You know what? Never mind.*

“You . . .” Her eyes narrowed. “You’re into Abram,” she said and nodded, slowly at first, but then faster after a second. “Like, way, way, *waaaaay* into him.”

I pinched my nose with my thumb and forefinger again, closing my eyes. “Just because I recognize that Abram isn’t an object, doesn’t mean I’m into him.”

But, for the record, she was totally right. I was into him. Way, way, *waaaaay* into him. And now I had a headache.

“Oh girl, you know what? I take back my suggestion. Avoid him. You don’t want this goodtime guy as your first crush. He’s the caviar of goodtime guys. Avoid him at all costs.”

Peeking at her, I frowned, because she was contradicting herself and her expression looked so entirely earnest. “You make no sense. A minute ago, you’re telling me to use him for his body. But now that you think I like him, you’re telling me to run the other way?”

“Yes.” She nodded, her eyes large and sympathetic. “Lisa will be back in a few days, and Abram can *never ever know* that you impersonated her this week. He will totally *flip out* and tell the world about it. His sister is a journalist, you know? It’ll be everywhere.”

I studied her, her words, her expression. Clearly, she believed what she said, but I couldn’t help offering a counterpoint. “Really? I don’t know. What about Leo? Wouldn’t that make things awkward between them? And when I apologized on behalf of Lisa for what happened last year, he accepted the apology, no problem."

"You have to trust me on this. He has mad respect for Leo, but this guy is ridiculous about lies. I know him much, much, much better than you do. Remember? I hang with him and your brother and their group when Leo is in town, so I know Abram. When I say he's uptight, I mean it."

"But—"

"He hates lies. Hates them."

It was a struggle not to roll my eyes. "Everyone hates lies."

"He has ended friendships, both long-term and with powerful people who could help him in his music career—like, a lot—because they told a stupid lie and he found out about it. Ask Leo, you don't lie to Abram. And knowing Leo, how laid back he is, he probably wouldn't be surprised if Abram ratted you both out to the press. Now, I'm not saying Leo would forgive him for it, but he wouldn't be surprised."

"Hmm." She looked so serious, I decided to stop pushing the issue. For now.

"So, yeah. If you like him—like, if you like *him,* as a person—if you're crushing on him at all, pretend he doesn't exist and push him from your mind. Avoid him like the plague or whatever. Even if you weren't already lying to him, I'd say the same thing. He is definitely *not* someone you want to have feelings for."

Giving me one more nod, she stepped back, glanced around the room, and sauntered to the door. "I'll be back tomorrow to check on you."

"Gabby," I called to her as her hand touched the doorknob. "You confuse me."

"I know." She shrugged, a flat smile on her lips. "But honestly, babe, I'm just looking out for your heart. Learn from your sister's mistakes: don't go chasing musicians or windmills."

I stared at her, unable to believe my ears.

Windmills? Had Gabby just made a Don Quixote reference? *Did that just happen?*

Before I could ask or clarify, she opened the door and strolled out of it.

* * *

I'd wanted to ask Gabby about the drugs and whether Lisa had been selling them to teenagers. I'd wanted to uncover why my sister had been arrested and what the deal was with Tyler. But I hadn't. I'd been too distracted by Abram, and talking about Abram, and thinking about Abram.

What is happening to me?

Taking a pain reliever for the headache, I lay on the bed, staring at the ceiling for approximately twenty minutes, and gave myself a pep talk.

FACT: He can never know you are Mona. Ever.

FACT: You must avoid him for the REST of your LIFE.

FACT: Your interactions serve no purpose. They have to end.

FACT ACCORDING TO GABBY: He's a goodtime guy.

And, most importantly, stop noticing the way he chews. It's not okay.

But traitorous little objections searched for cracks, issuing rebuttals and trying to bargain—

Why can't he know you're Mona? Maybe Gabby was overexaggerating about his loathing of liars. Once you explain the situation, he'll understand. What if he'll keep it a secret too? What if he helps you?

If I have to avoid him for the rest of my life, why avoid him now? Shouldn't I make the most out of the time we have left?

All interactions serve a purpose, even if they're not immediately apparent. Right? What if Abram has something to teach you? What if not knowing him puts you on a path of inexorable ignorance?

And what's the harm in watching him chew? It's not hurting anyone. I can hide and watch him chew, right? He won't even see me.

And, I'm sorry, but he just doesn't seem like a goodtime guy. He just doesn't. Being surrounded by women doesn't mean he's a goodtime guy, it just means women like him. And I don't blame them!

—and this was concerning because: why?

Why was my heart doing this to me? Why was I arguing with myself? I'd never allowed a crush. I'd been tempted once or twice, but the most logical path forward had never included time for a relationship. Therefore, crushes were (are!) irrelevant.

So why him? Why now? Why? Why? Why? WHY?!

What a mess.

Going in circles, and growing increasingly frustrated, I decided there was no point in continuing this discussion with myself. Facts were facts. What I needed was a distraction. So I snuck down to the kitchen. All was quiet, and Abram was nowhere in sight. But because I was a loony bird, I also sniffed before taking another step, searching for smells. The aroma of donuts permeated the air, but I detected no trace of Abram-fragrance.

Heaving a large sigh, I meandered to the kitchen table, hoping against hope that the remainder of my chocolate donut was still there. It wasn't. Instead, I found a plate in the center of the table with—*one, two, three, four, five . . . –*thirteen chocolate cake donuts.

!!!!!!

I stared at them, not understanding how it was possible to have so many emotions at once.

He went out and bought me donuts.

I was rubbing my chest, massaging the warm, tight ache there, before I realized what I was doing.

He bought me donuts. My favorite donuts. Thirteen. A prime number. A baker's dozen.

As I stared at the pile, I was distressed to discover that my mouth was now dry, which ultimately necessitated a swallow. My mouth should have been watering at the sight of all that deliciousness, but it wasn't. And, worse, I suddenly had no appetite. It's hard to think about eating when you're panicking.

However, the panic did help me close the door on my traitorous thoughts. I didn't want messy, and the only way to avoid more messy was to put all dissenting opinions on lockdown. I would focus on the facts, as they were, and stay the course.

I made myself tea, crept to the mudroom, and found my old dog-eared copy of Moby Dick waiting for me. It felt familiar, and paired with the aroma of peppermint tea, it felt like an oasis.

But my brain was not quiet and would not allow me to absorb the story when I opened to the bookmarked paragraph where I'd left off a few days ago. Taking several calming deep breaths, I flipped open a random page and forced my eyes to read the words,

Whenever I find myself growing grim about the mouth; whenever it is a damp, drizzly November in my soul; whenever I find myself involuntarily pausing before coffin warehouses, and bringing up the rear of every funeral I meet; and especially whenever my hypos get such an upper hand of me, that it requires a strong moral principle to prevent me from deliberately stepping into the street, and methodically knocking people's hats off - then, I account it high time to get to sea as soon as I can.

A little huff of wonder slipped past my lips and I blinked at the black ink. What were the chances? *This!* This was what I needed to read. It was a sign. It was magic. It was the universe telling me—

But wait.

My eyes drifted to the top of the page and I was no longer surprised or convinced the universe was telling me anything at all. Opening to this very page was no accident. I'd triple folded the corner, because it was my favorite passage. Like all mysteries investigated thoroughly, there was a perfectly reasonable explanation.

Mystery solved, I took Melville's advice in any case.

Closing my eyes, I went to space. I visited the safety and calm of my brain-planetarium—my own version of Melville's sea—and distracted my mind from small cares with the complexity of creation. From the Sloan Great Wall to a single quark, the whole and the individual pieces, working within the constraints of laws, of beautiful order.

No wonder I was frazzled and confused. Since starting undergrad, I'd never taken such a long break from academic pursuits or my research interests. I'd traded order for chaos, knowns for unknowns, equations for unsolvable conundrums.

This wasn't my world. I didn't belong here. Here was Lisa's reality, not mine. Here were decisions based on desires, not facts and risk/benefit ratios.

Also here, footsteps approaching.

My eyes flew open just as Abram rounded the corner. Acting on some crazed instinct, I shoved Moby Dick between my legs (ha! . . . *that's what she said)* and picked up my mug, holding it over my lap to obscure the book from view.

My ruckusy and flustered movements immediately drew his attention, his handsome face turning toward me, his eyes scanning over my form as his thumbs hooked into his pockets.

"Hey," he said, sounding and looking totally normal, where normal for us was now apparently defined as friendly and interested. "There you are."

"Yes. Here I am." I was attempting to hold the mug *just so,* which made my elbows feel awkward.

His eyes dropped to my lap. "Is that a book? What are you reading?"

I clenched my thighs around the novel, my voice higher pitched than I would have liked as I said, "Nothing."

"Come on." A faint smile on his lips, a delightful little crooking of his eyebrow, he wandered closer, making no attempt to hide his blatant inspection of my lap. "What's the title?"

His voice dropped a half-octave. It had a flustering effect on me. *Why must he be this way? Where are his flaws?!*

"Hair removal for dummies," I sputtered stupidly, moving the tea to the side so as not to spill it on me and Moby.

But before I could manage settling the tea on the seat, he reached between my knees and withdrew the book. CURSES!

Instinct told me to launch myself at him, like I'd done this morning, and take it back by force.

I didn't. I balled my hands into fists, threw my legs over the side of the bench seat, and crossed my arms to keep from reaching for him or the book. Another tussle with Abram would lead nowhere good—depending on one's definition of the word *good*—and there'd definitely be no interruption just in the nick of time.

Tossing me a triumphant side-eye and a smirk, he lifted the book and read the title. And then his head shifted back on his neck and the smirk disappeared. He blinked. He frowned. He squinted.

"Moby Dick?"

I cleared my throat, searching for a plausible lie. "After our discussion about whales, it looked interesting." As I said this, I stared at my feet, but then I peeked at him to see if he bought my untruth.

He gave his head a subtle shake. "You're lying."

Lifting my chin, I kept my mouth shut. *See?* Lying was at the bottom of my failure pile, along with matching my socks and telling the difference between Taylor Swift and Katy Perry and Lorde; they all looked identical to me, but then I'd never been good with faces.

"You're lying," he said again, like this discovery was fascinating rather than worrying. "You didn't pick this book up because of our discussion about whales. You've read this book before."

"Fine. Yes. Guilty." I glared at his chin and the ever-present potential for a wizard beard. *I hope he never buys a new razor.*

Abram laughed like I was strange, coming to stand directly in front of me and holding out the book. "Why would you lie about reading Moby Dick?"

I accepted it, careful not to touch his fingers, and asked a question instead of answering his, "Have you read it?"

"No," he said softly, tilting his head to the side as though to ensure I didn't break eye contact.

"Really? And after all your whale facts, I'm a little disappointed." Goodness, he had pretty eyes. So pretty. So very pretty . . . *I bet he uses those eyes on all the girls.*

Bah.

Once again internal monologue, STFU.

It was a struggle to keep my face free of revealing expression, but I managed it. Not that I thought he was, but what did I care if Abram was a goodtime guy? It wasn't my business. And if it was true—which my subconscious seemed to be pondering—good for him.

To the point: Abram's goodtime-guy status was irrelevant to me.

Okay. Good. That's settled. Now all I had to do was leave. *Time to go. Get up, get up, get up!*

I didn't get up. I couldn't seem to make myself move. What I needed was an exit strategy. Brain-tussling with Abram about my favorite book was likely to be just as dangerous as body-tussling with him over a donut.

"I only know that stuff about whales because of my sister's friend, Janie. She knows a ton of random facts."

Perking up at the mention of Marie, I wanted to say, *Tell me more!*

Instead, I tried to think of something Lisa might say while searching for a way to extract myself from this assuredly captivating conversation. "She sounds boring."

"She's not." A hint of irritation entered his tone. "She's awesome."

"Awesome?" I asked before I could catch the question, knowing I sounded interested. Marie had been just the best person ever, of course I was curious about her friends. Specifically, how would one go about being friends with Marie?

One of his reluctant smiles made an appearance, his eyes dancing, like he knew how curious I was. They were so very bright and engaging as they moved between mine. "Yes. Amazing. Brilliant. Surprising. Funny. Fascinating. Beautiful. She reminds me of you, actually. She—"

ALERT! COMPLIMENT ALERT!

I jumped up, bumping into his chest before maneuvering around him. It couldn't be avoided. He was standing so close and I had to leave. Now.

"Okay. Well. See you later." I tucked Moby under my arm and darted for the back door, a wave of warm pleasure rushing up my cheeks.

He thinks you're beautiful and fascinating and surprising and— Wait, why was beauty the first thing I was happy about? Shouldn't I be focusing on brilliance? And funniness? Beauty was irrelevant, *irrelevant I say!*

"Wait, where are you going?" He caught my arm.

I spun, my eyes going to where his hand encircled my wrist. He immediately let me go.

"I thought I might practice the violin again," I said while rubbing my wrist. An arm grab had never felt so good.

His attention flickered to the door behind me. "You're going to practice outside?"

Bah! My overthinking about his indirect compliments had me all turned around.

"No, uh, obviously not. I'm going upstairs. To my room." Taking a pivoting step, I aimed in the direction of the back stairs, and said, "Fare thee well."

And then I grimaced at having said *fare thee well* while endeavoring to keep my pace unhurried.

He shadowed my steps all the way down the hall and into the kitchen before calling suddenly, "I guess you don't want to go to Anderson's with me then."

If I'd been making tracks, I would have stopped in them. Anderson's? The bookstore?

But if I go, I'll be spending time with Abram, which is a bad idea.

I swatted away good intentions and sense and I turned completely around. "Anderson's? As in the bookstore?" I asked, doing nothing to mask the naked hope of my expression or in my voice.

I couldn't hide them. No one was that good at lying.

"Yeah." He sighed, sounding regretful even though his brown eyes were glittering mischievously. His lips remained flat, but that left dimple winked at me, a slight indent in his cheek. *No wonder he covers his mouth when he smiles, that dimple is his tell.*

But I didn't care if he thought it was funny to dangle a bookstore visit as a carrot, I didn't care if he was inwardly laughing at me. I wanted to go. I wanted to go very, very badly.

"I was going to drive over, and then grab some food"—he shrugged —"but if you want to practice violin instead, then—"

"Let's go!"

[13]
NEWTON'S THIRD LAW OF MOTION: SYMMETRY IN FORCES

Unsurprisingly, Abram insisted on driving to Anderson's Bookshop.

On the way, we discussed options for a post-shopping meal. What he didn't know was that I planned to spend as much time at the bookstore as possible, so most of the lunch places he suggested wouldn't be open by the time we left. I didn't correct him. Let him believe what he wanted, we wouldn't be leaving that bookstore until after closing if I could help it.

Upon arriving, I made a beeline for the nearest display, not caring about the genre. I planned to go through every single section, every shelf, every book. When I went back to being Mona, I would never take for granted the ability to go where I wanted, when I wanted, ever again.

Abram and I stuck together most of the time, him pointing out books he thought were interesting, or ones he thought I might like, or asking me what I thought about a title or a cover or a blurb. Eventually, I began doing the same with him.

It was . . . fun. I was having a great time, the comradery, the quiet, the whispers, and the inevitable snickering when we made it to the romance section. (My snickering, not his).

"What are you laughing at?" he whispered, trying to get a good look at the cover of the book I was holding.

I pressed the cover to my chest. "Nothing." It was the most ridiculous cover—a cross-stitched beard—with the dumbest title I'd ever seen—*Grin and Beard It*.

Abram glanced between me and the back of the novel. "You read romance?"

"Um, no," I said, tucking the book back where it belonged. Serious people with serious thoughts didn't read romance novels.

"Why not?"

I gave him a look. "Why would I?"

"You like to read, right?"

"Uh, yes. But—"

"You should try this." Abram selected a novel from a nearby shelf and showed me the cover.

I scanned the title, glanced at Abram, and then placed it back on the shelf. "No, thank you. I don't read that kind of stuff."

"What kind of stuff?" He grabbed it again, leaning a shoulder against the shelf, giving me the sense of being caged in (but not in a bad way).

I made a face as I inspected him, unable to discern whether he was poking fun at me, or the author, or what, so I said, "I'll read it if you read it."

"Deal." He handed it to me again. "I like this author."

I reared back, shocked, stunned, shocked again. "You read romance?"

"Yes."

I blinked at him several times; apparently my eyes couldn't believe my ears. "No, you don't."

"Yes. I do." He leaned closer, smiling down at me like he thought I was cute, or my disbelief was cute, or something like that.

"Prove it. What else has this author written? And no looking at the shelf or the book I'm holding." I hid the novel by twisting away, but my attention remained on Abram's face, enthralled. I still couldn't tell if he was joking.

"Let's see, uh, *Devil In Winter*—that was a really good one—and the other book I really liked was *Love in the Afternoon.* The main character was obsessed with animals." His smile grew as his eyes drifted over my shoulder. "She cracked me up."

Captivated, I stared at him. I didn't know what other books this author had written, so I couldn't fact-check his statements. Nevertheless, I was now convinced Abram read romance.

His gaze returned to mine. "What?"

"I'm so confused."

"Why?"

"When would you have come across romance novels? Did your mom read them?"

"No." He wrinkled his nose—just a little—at this question. "My mom reads gardening books and science fiction. But my sister reads everything." He tapped at the cover of the book I clutched. "I read whatever she recommends, and she recommended this author, highly."

"Your sister is so . . ." I was in love with Marie. No use denying it. *Teach me your ways, Marie-Wan Kenobi.*

"What?"

"Amazing," I said on a sigh.

His grin was as quick as it was massive, but then he dropped his chin—as though to hide his smile again—and cleared his throat. "She is, but don't tell her I said so."

"Why wouldn't you tell her yourself?"

"You know how it is between siblings."

My eyebrows inched upwards. "How is it?"

"They live to torture each other."

"They do?"

"Of course." His eyes moved between mine and he looked truly confused by my confusion. "Come off it, Lisa. Leo doesn't talk about you and your sister much, but he's told me a few stories about you. You love to piss him off."

Oh! . . . *yeah.* I'd forgotten for a moment who I was supposed to be. Okay, I'd forgotten for longer than a moment. Actually, I'd been Mona all day.

"Ah! Hahaha. Yes. That is true." I turned and promptly winced.

He was not finished. "The time you texted Meghan using his phone, but called her Melissa? Classic."

I glanced at Abram, who now walked at my shoulder, and gave him a noncommittal shrug. I didn't know anything about a Meghan, or a Melissa, so it was probably best neither to confirm nor deny his statements.

"Actually, I should thank you for that one."

I stopped. "You should thank me?"

"Oh yeah." He nodded, looking serious. "Did you ever see them together? She wasn't good for him."

Frowning, I nodded—again vaguely—making a mental note to ask Leo about this Meghan person the next time we spoke. And then I'd ask him why he'd never told me about this Meghan person.

"Well, see? That wasn't torture. I was helping Leo make good life decisions."

"Sure." He gave me another little smile, now squinting. "And what you did to your sister before her graduation? With the newspaper? What was that?"

Staring at Abram, I became very, very still. *How did . . . ?*

"How do you know about that?" I whispered the question. My hands suddenly felt clammy, my throat hurt, and my heart was beating like mad.

"Leo told me. He thought it was hilarious." Abram had picked up a book and was browsing the back cover, apparently not noticing the shift in my demeanor.

Leo thought it was hilarious?

Coming to myself just enough to realize it probably wasn't a good idea to continue staring as though shell-shocked, I turned. Nodding faintly, I grabbed the first book I found and pretending to read the cover, I worked to regain my composure.

Upon arriving two days before my graduation, she'd given an interview to the university's newspaper pretending to be me. Luckily, the student reporter called to double-check one of my statements and I'd discovered the "prank" before they'd published the story.

It wasn't that big of a deal to anyone but me. And—I reasoned—from the outside looking in, I could see how it might be funny. She'd told the reporter I planned to give up physics for a career in performance art, that I'd discovered my true passion and that passion was nude interpretive dance.

Hilarious.

Except not. Not when you've spent four years struggling to be taken seriously.

"It's a small world." Abram's statement brought me back to the present, and I worried for a moment that he'd been speaking and I'd missed some of it.

But then he said, "What are the chances that you go to boarding school with this girl, and then she goes on to the same university as your sister, and she's on the newspaper the same year your sister graduated."

I blinked, processing his words, and asking before I could catch myself, "Sorry, what?"

He glanced at me, his lips curved to the left. "Leo said Mona freaked out, thinking the whole thing was real, thinking you actually gave the interview." His gaze moved over my features and warmed, softened, his mouth gave in to a real smile. "Your sister must not know you very well, to think you'd do something so mean." ***

"What are you doing?" Abram's attention flickered between me and the book I'd just opened. "Are you starting? Now?"

"Yes." I flipped to the page that read *Chapter One*.

My plan to remain at the bookstore until closing didn't come to fruition, mostly due to a Julius-and-Ethel-Rosenberg-level betrayal by my stomach. It had growled so loudly, Abram gave me the side-eye, paid for our purchases directly, and pushed me out of the shop.

Silly with starvation, I had a fantastical thought: had I not been so hungry, I would've liked the afternoon to last forever.

I'd had the best time. The BEST time. *THE BEST TIME!*

Other than that one minor uncomfortable reminder of Lisa's practical joke and his bizarre statements that followed, good feelings reigned. I hadn't been able to figure out how to ask him about the prank without blowing my cover—was he saying that Lisa hadn't actually given the interview? That the interviewer/reporter had been in on the joke? Or what?—so, I ultimately decided to let it go. For now. *Something to ask Lisa or Gabby about later.*

It had been somewhat difficult to push it from my mind. But my continued proximity to Abram while browsing at the bookstore meant his mysterious man-scent had been easily accessible. Loose and wonderfully fuzzy headed, anytime I thought of Lisa's prank, trying to parse through what he'd meant by "Your sister must not know you very well, to think you'd do something so mean," all I had to do was move closer to Abram. I'd pretend to reach around him for a book, or brush past him when the space between aisles grew tight—and take a big sniff.

Instant olfactory sensory relaxation.

Presently, we were sitting in a booth at a small Italian place not far from Anderson's. We'd just ordered—lasagna for me, steak of some sort for him—and then I'd opened the romance novel he'd bought me.

"I thought you were hungry?" He poked at the book with a breadstick.

"I am. But my brain is also hungry. For stimulation."

"What? My conversation isn't stimulating enough?"

I smirked, because he was just so darn cute sometimes and it made me smile.

"I didn't say that." I cleared my throat in an effort to erase the smile from my face, lifting the book higher to hide the persistent grin as I mumbled, "But you said it and you're very perceptive."

A surprised-sounding laugh emanated from his side of the table.

Impulsively, I lowered the book and peeked at him, anticipating he would do something to hide his happy expression. Like clockwork, he covered the bottom half of his face with his hand. My heart gave a little tug at the sight. For a big, strong, tall, dark and manly musician, he sure was super adorable sometimes.

"Fine." Abram shook his head, turning it away from me and pulling out the book he'd bought for himself. Setting it on the table, he opened it. "Go ahead and read."

Lifting my book, I grinned secretly, and read.

I had doubts that I'd be able to concentrate, which were initially well-founded. A few times, struck by a bizarre compulsion, I snuck a glance at Abram. He would either: a) already be watching me, which would cause us both to hastily return our eyes to our books, or b) I'd steal several seconds of watching him before he caught me, which would cause us both to hastily return our eyes to our books.

After a few minutes of this unfathomable behavior, we both settled, reading quietly, absorbed in our books.

Sometime later, the arrival of our food surprised me, and I blinked dazedly at our server when he set my dinner down. Despite being hungry, I found the sudden presence of our food inconvenient. Setting the novel aside with a sigh, I placed the napkin on my lap. Apparently, for a moment there I'd forgotten I wasn't in nineteenth-century England.

"How's the book?"

"It's really good. Really good," I said distractedly, picking up my fork and knife, cutting into the steaming plate of lasagna and adding, "She paints a vivid picture."

"I have some more suggestions, if you want—"

"Yes. You should write them down."

"Even if they're romance novels?" Abram leaned forward to cut his steak, sparing me a quick, amused look.

"But is it really a romance novel?" I lifted my chin towards the book. "It reads more like fiction."

"Romance is fiction." He punctuated this statement by taking a bite of steak, and then chewing.

"But it's- it's-" Interesting? Well researched? Engaging? Well written? *All of the above.*

"Not what you expected?" he supplied, smirking around his bite. "What did you expect?"

Shrugging, I lifted a small rectangle of lasagna on my fork and blew at the steam. "I guess something brainless." I didn't add that I followed the New York Times Book Review and they'd had more than their fair share of articles calling the romance genre "fluffy."

If you couldn't trust the New York Times Book Review, who could you trust?

"Why? Because it's about love and has a happy ending? And only stories of unhappiness with tragic endings are important? Because a struggle that leads to something good isn't worthwhile?"

Taking a bite and avoiding eye contact, I shrugged again because he'd just hit the nail on the head. His questions challenged my preconceived notions and made me sound like an idiot. I wasn't used to feeling like an idiot. Or being challenged. *Then again, I usually never deviate from my appointed lane . . .*

It was both an uncomfortable and exhilarating experience.

I felt his stare linger for a moment before he spoke. "Glad you like it."

Grateful he'd decided to let the subject drop, I said quietly, "I do. Thank you for recommending it to me."

"No problem." I heard a smile in his voice. "Is it better than Moby Dick?"

"I don't know. I just started." I gave the cover a wistful glance before giving Abram my eyes. "But Moby Dick is one of my favorites."

"Really?" His face screwed up. "Why?"

"It's about dealing with disappointment and putting things into perspective. Everyone should read it."

His weird look persisted, like my words made no sense.

So I laughed. "I know, not a very modern concept."

"You like reading books about disappointment?"

I nodded, agreeing before thinking too much about it.

"Why?"

I hypothesized out loud. "It's comforting."

This earned me a single-eyebrow lift. "How so?"

Again, speaking without considering my words, I said, "Think about it. Stories of expectations, hopes, and dreams not being met are confirmation that life is—fundamentally—a . . ." *Disappointment.*

Staring at him, and realizing what I was just about to say, my chest tightened. I was officially unnerved. Did I really think that? Did I really think that life was a disappointment?

I guess I did.

Abram lifted both eyebrows. "A what?"

"Um," I stalled.

How could I possibly think life was a disappointment? I lived a charmed life, right? I'd never wanted for anything. I'd been given every advantage. I had the use of all my limbs. I had my health. I'd been told by many people, many times how beautiful I was (if I'd only make an effort). I'd traveled extensively. I'd worked hard to be recognized as a content expert in my field, to be taken seriously, and now I was being courted by all the top research programs in the world. I had everything I'd ever wanted. *Everything.*

Right?

My gaze moved over Abram, his artfully messy hair, his scruffy beard, the twinkle in his amber eyes, the dimple at his left cheek, the curve of his generous lips. I'd almost kissed those lips earlier in the day.

Or maybe, suggested a mutinous little voice, *I have everything I've allowed myself to want.*

"Life is a what? A series of unfortunate events?" he prompted, snapping me out of my contemplations. "A whale hunting trip?"

There was no way I was going to tell the truth of my thoughts, but I had to say something. I decided on, "A challenge."

"Hmm." Abram's eyes narrowed. That paired with the small smile still on his lips gave me the sense he suspected I wasn't being honest.

We stared at each other for a long moment until he speared a bite of steak with his fork. "You should get a new one."

"New what?" New perspective on life?

"New copy. Of Moby Dick. Yours is all torn up." He placed the bite in his mouth.

I averted my attention before I could indulge in my weirdo desire to watch him chew. "Then what would I do with the old one?"

"I don't know, give it away?"

"What?" I reared back. "Absolutely not!"

"Why not?"

"Books are friends. You don't just- just- just give away friends!"

Abram, his elbow propped on the table, covered the lower half of his face with his hand, but his shaking shoulders gave him away.

Squinting at him accusingly, I crossed my arms. "You're laughing at me."

"Yes. I am."

"How would you like it if someone gave you away?" I muttered, indignant.

"Well, since the question infers that I would've had to give myself to that person before it would be possible for her to give me away, I wouldn't like it."

The temptation to ask *Have you?* And, if so, what happened? And who is this stupid woman who gave you away? was nearly overwhelming. If anything was true in the universe, it was that anyone who could willingly give Abram away was stupid (and also Newton's Laws of Motion).

Locking eyes with Abram, the questions were at the forefront of my brain, that mutinous little voice pushing them to the tip of my tongue, but the server chose that moment to swing by to refill our waters, saving me from making a critical error in judgment.

After ascertaining all was delicious and well, the server left. I did my utmost to ignore the curiosity pressing uncomfortably against my skull, and instead took a bite of lasagna.

I felt Abram's attention move over me, and eventually he said, "So, you read a lot," giving me the impression he was trying to get me talking again.

Since this was a benign, previously established fact, I confirmed it.

"Every night before bed, for about an hour. If I don't have a busy day the next day, I'll read for an hour and a half."

"Oh. Really busy day? Like what? Getting a blowout from someone named George?"

I was about to ask him who George was when my slow brain

finally caught up. *Double yikes.* Again, I'd forgotten who I was supposed to be. *I blame Lisa Kleypas's excellent novel.*

"Well . . ." I worked for a moment to identify an appropriate response to his teasing. Luckily, I was able to stall by taking a bite of my food. Once I finished chewing, I said, "Who is to say how I spend my time isn't any more or less important than how you spend your time?"

"Good point." He nodded eagerly, like he'd been hoping I would respond this way. "So, tell me, how do you spend your time?"

Taking another bite, I chewed for longer than was necessary, my eyes moving up and to the left, because—since I was not in fact Lisa— this was a tricky question. I had no idea how my sister spent her time. Furthermore, I couldn't help but feel I'd just fallen into a verbal trap of some sort.

Unable to delay responding forever, I eventually decided on, "I sleep." This was true for Lisa, me, and humanity.

"You sleep." His voice was deadpan.

"Yep. Speaking of which, did you, uh, sleep well last night?"

Abram's gaze flickered over me, as though he thought I might be leading him into a trap of my own. Little did he know, I was just trying to change the subject.

"Yes," he said reluctantly, "I slept fine. Why?"

"It's just, you were up early." His sleep patterns were so sporadic, and this facet of his personality fascinated me.

Abram finished chewing a bite of steak before responding. "You were expecting to make it to the donut shop and back before I woke up?"

I shrugged, but also shot him a guilty look.

He chuckled. "I came down the stairs just as you walked out the front door."

"Why didn't you try to stop me?"

He ignored my question and asked one of his own, "Any regrets?" The speculation behind his eyes made me think maybe the question had a double meaning, but I was too distracted by the memory of this morning's tussle to parse through what the double meaning might be.

The grabbing, the teasing, the friction of our bodies as I jumped and slid down his, the touching, the staring, his scent . . .

Instead of answering directly, I cleared my throat and said, "It's important to live in the present." I said this mostly to remind myself, but also, due to the limits of the space-time continuum, living in the present was the only option. Wishing for a different past or an impossible future was pointless. "So, uh, did you write any music last night?"

"No, but I did get some lyrics written earlier today. You're playing the violin again?"

"Yes. I can almost play "*Twinkle Twinkle Little Star,*" which means "*Old MacDonald*" is next, and that's my favorite, with all the *bock, bock, bocking,* and *moo, moo, mooing,* and then the wolves came, as the prophesy foretold, in this economy." I forced myself to take a deep breath here so I would stop talking. Something about the way he was looking at me with those intense, deep brown eyes made me feel fidgety.

But Abram grinned, and the flash of dimples made my knees happy I was sitting instead of standing. "Why do you do that?"

"Do what?"

"You say weird stuff sometimes. Like, 'and then the wolves came.' What is that?"

"It's just a thing I do . . . when I don't know what to say." I'd been caught without prunes and my lasagna was finished. Might as well tell the truth.

"So you speak nonsense?"

"It's not nonsense. These phrases, they're special. They're special phrases that work for almost any occasion. They're evergreen."

"If you say so." During dinner, his left dimple had become a permanent fixture on his face and it was hugely distracting.

"They are." I rubbed my forehead, feeling somewhat harassed by his attractiveness. "Here, say something and I'll use one of my phrases."

"Fine. Let's see. Um—" Abram's gaze moved beyond me. "Okay. Want to go see a movie?"

"In this economy?"

A short, surprised laugh shook his shoulders and lit his eyes. "You're nuts."

"So let it be written, so let it be done."

"Oh no. You're not going to stop, are you?"

"Be that as it may, still may it be as it may be."

He was fighting a massive grin. "Please stop."

"There's no escape from destiny."

"What can I say to make you stop?"

"Wise words by wise men write wise deeds in wise pen."

"You are so fucking weird sometimes." He shook his head, his shoulders also shaking, losing the fight.

"As the prophesy foretold."

"Oh my God—" he clutched his stomach, tossing his head back to laugh "—I love you."

I sucked in a breath, my heart doing a strange, twisting thing. I kept my eyes affixed to the table so he wouldn't see my illogical and sudden turmoil, because it was illogical and it was turmoil. I told myself that his words had been an expression, nothing more.

Abram is a goodtime guy, he probably loves everyone.

Yes. Exactly.

. . . Wait! No. No, he is not a goodtime guy! Stop thinking of him that way.

The explanation was much simpler: he didn't *love* love me. It had been a figure of speech.

I lifted my gaze—just for a single second—to peek at him. But then I couldn't look away because something distressing happened.

The laughter and resultant smile lit up his face, casting everything else in the room in bleak shadow, and he wasn't hiding either this time. However, it wasn't just the smile that was distressing—I'd seen him smile several times at this point—but rather my new and completely involuntary physical reaction to it. The sight hit me in the stomach, an unexpected blow, jarring my teeth, a little painful and a lot uncomfortable. At first.

And then the pain dissipated, became an expanding warmth, a hum of kinetic energy—even though I was sitting perfectly still—radiating outward to my fingertips and toes, clouding my brain, and wrapping my whole person in a lovely, tight, cozy cloud.

Holy shit.

What the hell was that?

A microcosm of the big bang *but in my body!*

Disoriented and mesmerized, I couldn't take my eyes from his face where the effects of his laughter still lingered, giving his features an attractiveness that was four-dimensional. More than physical, it was an allure that permeated both space and time.

"What?" Abram's laughter had tapered while I'd been having a mini freak-out. "No more phrases left?"

I pretended like I needed to scratch the back of my neck as I quickly sifted through the possible anytime-phrases remaining:

Just like in my dream.

But at what cost?

And thus, I die.

They all felt a little too . . . accurate.

So I shrugged, glancing at him quickly and offering a tight smile, murmuring, "And then the wolves came."

[14]

NORMAL, TENSION, AND OTHER EXAMPLES OF FORCES

Recovering from the mini big bang took some serious concentration. Luckily, Abram's mood had turned contemplative on the drive home and neither of us spoke.

Although, halfway through the drive, while we were stuck at a stoplight, he turned to me and said, "Thank you for coming with me. I had a great time."

I was trapped in the sincerity of his stare, caught in the velvety cadence of his voice, only able to nod dumbly and mutter stupidly, "Great time. I had . . . also."

He grinned, his features softened by the glow of nearby streetlamps and the red light of the traffic signal, his four-dimensional attractiveness growing to ten dimensions, where the tenth were those pesky infinite possibilities and I was suffocating in the tenderness of his big, gorgeous, ten-dimensional brown eyes.

Oh my heart.

But then the light changed and he gave the road his attention, leaving me to my entropy. Thank goodness we still had several blocks before the house. I required both the dark and the quiet to order my thoughts.

Closing my eyes, I frantically tried imagining the vastness of space.

Like earlier in the day, I worked to put facts first and events into perspective. I reminded myself that I didn't belong here, that this was Lisa's reality and not mine. That Helped.

I reminded myself of Gabby's advice, that he wasn't the type of person I wanted to have feelings for. That also helped even if I didn't 100 percent believe it.

The crack had widened, the mutinous bargaining voice had grown more persistent, leaving me with an undercurrent of agitation instead of peace, and wishing instead of acceptance.

As soon as Abram pulled into the street parking outside our house, I was out of the car, walking to the gate and punching in the code. By the time he'd sauntered to where I stood holding the gate open, I had a plan. Once we made it inside, I was going upstairs and going to bed. I hadn't been sleeping well, and lack of sleep could lead to poor decisions.

Abram said nothing as we walked up the stairs to the front door, and I kept my eyes firmly fixed forward, my jaw clenched, my hands fisted at my sides. *No matter what, you will go upstairs and go to bed. By yourself.*

He withdrew the keys and unlocked the door; I felt his eyes move over me just before opening the door. "You want to watch a movie?"

I waited until we were inside and I'd slipped my shoes off before answering. "Um, no thanks." Without turning, I added, "I think I might go to sleep."

I sensed that this answer seemed to take him aback, as though it had been exactly the opposite of what he'd been expecting. I took advantage of his momentary confusion and turned for the kitchen, my brain telling me to *go, go, go!*

Even so, my movements were sluggish. The logical path was forward, I knew that. Nothing could ever happen between us, I knew that too. Watching a movie with Abram would undoubtedly lead to *not* watching the movie while still *being* with Abram.

But to what end? The way he'd been teasing me all day, the easy banter, how I caught him looking at me in the bookstore and over dinner, how I'd undeniably been looking at him in the same way. I wasn't stupid. All the variables plugged into an equation that equaled mutual attraction.

This wasn't a crush, this was requited desire and reciprocated like. Kissing, unscripted touching, gazing, whispers. . . I was near dizzy at the thought. But in this specific case, that also totaled certain disaster.

He's not a person you want to have feelings for.

And yet, I wanted.

Something is wrong with me.

"You're tired?" he asked, following me into the kitchen and to the back stairs.

Offering just my profile, I shrugged noncommittally, because I wasn't tired enough to sleep and I didn't want to lie to him anymore, not even a white lie. Placing my hand on the banister, a twisting in my stomach made me pause just for a moment as I prepared to launch myself up the first flight.

But before I could climb the first step, he covered my hand, stopping me. A warm, electric current traveled up my arm, weaving itself into my bloodstream and brain. I glanced at his hand on top of mine, and the mutinous whispers returned. Another something terrible had happened: I officially liked it when Abram touched me.

Meanwhile, he hesitated for the span of a breath, and then stepped close. So close, I felt his chest against my back, his thighs against my backside. Abram pulled my hair to the side and the fall of hot breath against my neck caused the most potent and delectable involuntary shiver of my life.

Holy hadron collider.

I was a solution, he was a solute, and total saturation was on my mind.

"Care for company?" he whispered before I'd recovered, his lips just barely against the shell of my ear.

Holy hadron collider, indeed.

The fragrance of him invaded my good sense and for a moment I lost my breath. My breasts swelled, heavy and needy and hot, my nipples tightening into little beads, pressing against the lace bra. I felt the silk of the shirt everywhere it met my skin. He was close, so close, touching, right there and my eyelids fluttered under the weight of such heavenly sensory overload.

And yet, even under attack, my good sense held firm, buffered by a grim sense of certainty: I didn't believe Gabby, that Abram would be fine with a fling. I didn't. He liked me. This was as real for him as it was for me. What was happening between us wasn't something Lisa would be able to just call off when she took my place.

And that meant I would not be able to live with myself if I allowed him to believe *anything* between us was a possibility. That would be the same as leading him on, as using him.

My foolish heart, however, thought his idea was great. In fact, it had decided to hatch an escape plan and was currently attempting to beat itself out of my chest. *Oh please oh please oh please say yes!*

I cleared my throat, concentrating on the grim resolve. "Company?" The question was just above a whisper, because I couldn't manage much else. Gravity had seemed to reverse, or become centripetal in nature, pulling me in all directions at once.

"I could read you a bedtime story, from your new book." Knuckles brushed softly against the skin of my neck, the silk of my shirt, and then down my bare arm, raising goose bumps in their path. "Or I could sing you a song."

Oh no. *Do not want!* If Gabby was to be believed, I wouldn't be able to withstand an Abram talent-assault in addition to the rest of what I knew about him. Usually, musicians held no allure for me. But Abram was breaking the mold on all my *usuallys*.

Grasping that grim resolve, I slid my hand from beneath his on the banister, folded my arms over my chest (to conceal *that* situation), and turned to face him.

Swallowing the rocks in my throat, I asked, "Are you flirting with me?"

Two dimples, an unhidden smile given freely, gorgeous brown eyes caressing my face.

This is hard. So hard.

"You have to ask?" he said. Flirtatiously.

Despite the disobedient—and therefore destructive—thrill his nonadmission elicited, I cleared my throat and forced myself to say, "Do you think that's appropriate?"

He blinked, his grin faltering, but only a little. "Appropriate?"

"Yes." Crowbarring indignation into my voice I didn't feel, I narrowed my eyes. "Aren't you supposed to be the adult here? Ensuring I don't get into trouble or harm myself? For all intents and purposes, you're in charge of me, reporting back to my parents about my behavior. They trust you with my well-being. Leo *trusts* you. Therefore, let me ask you again: do you think flirting with someone you're in charge of is appropriate?"

Abram flinched back, taking two shuffling steps away as I spoke. At first, his eyebrows lifted, but then they lowered into a severe line over his darkening eyes.

"Are you . . . are you kidding?"

I glared at him, saying nothing, because I didn't trust myself to speak. *This is so hard.*

He shook his head, just slightly, as though to clear it, his eyes searching. "Or are you serious?"

"Serious," I parroted immediately, grasping at the word. Then I swallowed. Because I had to. *This is the hardest.*

Abram flinched, his lips parting, giving me the impression that a very loud objection was on the tip of his tongue. But then he snapped his mouth shut, staring at me for several seconds, perhaps expecting me to say *just kidding!* When I continued glaring in silence, he glanced at the ceiling. He then glanced at the wall to his left. His hands came to his hips. He exhaled a light laugh, shaking his head and covering his mouth.

He'd gone back to hiding his smiles, even the bitter ones.

I waited, watching him, feeling . . . horrible. And enormously uneasy. Also, immensely remorseful, wishing I could take the words back, but knowing it was for the best.

By the time his eyes had traveled around the kitchen and returned to mine, they were shuttered, dim, remote, and hit me with a force that felt physical.

"Yes. Absolutely. You're right." His tone matched his expression, and the combination made me wonder if my heart had just sustained a serious injury somehow. It would've explained why it was suddenly so hard to breathe.

I think it's hard to breathe because this is hard.

"I, uh, that's okay." My voice wavered along with my resolve and I took a step toward him. Apparently, at some point over the last several days, I'd become magnetized to Abram.

Or maybe it's gravity, he is quite big.

Or maybe it's one of the four fundamental forces, working on an atomic level: weak, strong, electromagnetic, gravitational.

Or maybe—

But he held up his hand, staying me. "No. It's not okay. Please accept my apology. I . . ." A flicker of something ignited behind his eyes, a vulnerability that crippled my brain, there and hidden in an instant. He dropped his gaze to the floor, and gave his head another shake before adding quietly, "No excuses. It won't happen again."

PROBLEM-SOLVING STRATEGIES

The potency of my self-doubt and regret was a new experience. When Abram left me at the bottom of the stairs with a polite departing head nod after my duplicitous speech about the appropriateness of his actions, I felt a large part of myself go with him. It felt like a physical separation, being split into two distinctly different versions of myself—one followed the logical path, and one followed him—and that was nonsensical.

The one that followed him wanted to tackle him to the ground and spill my guts. I almost did.

The rest of me retrieved my dirty cup from earlier in the day and made a new cup of tea, blinking away tears. I was the worst kind of hypocrite, acting like I had all this moral authority. Meanwhile, I was a lying liar of lies, sitting on a throne of lies, eating lie soup and liar cake.

Try as I might to be rational, I couldn't shake the sense that something was very, very wrong with me. This sense was only heightened by the near constant ache in my stomach and heart, both of which felt like an overreaction.

I never overreacted. Underreaction was where I lived my life.

You cannot deny he was behaving inappropriately, given what he knows to be true of the situation, a shrill little voice reminded me, one that sounded suspiciously like Dr. Steward.

Unable to navigate this strange labyrinth of emotional upheaval, I spotted the bag from the bookstore on the counter, grabbed my new book, left my new cup of tea in the sink, and went upstairs to play the violin. Unpacking it, I tried to play. I couldn't play. My fingers weren't working right. Setting the instrument on the desk, I picked up my new book. I set the book down. I didn't want to read.

Making a split decision, I changed into the bikini from the other day. I then marched down to the back door, intent on the pool—my hairdo and Gabby and George-the-stylist be damned.

But before I opened the back door, I spotted movement. It was now dark outside, but the pool light illuminated the water. Abram was swimming laps. I didn't press my face against the glass, but I did watch him without meaning to, tracking him, unable to look away, admiring how he paired gracefulness and power. He wasn't a perfect swimmer, his technique could use some help, but he was strong and fast and clearly determined to swim forever.

I must've watched him for a half hour, probably longer. My feet grew tired of standing in the same place, necessitating that I shift my weight and flex my calves. Still, he swam. It wasn't until he stopped and straightened, breathing hard and wiping away excess water with his hands, his eyes seeming to move directly to the window where I stood, that I tore my gaze away and stepped back.

Spooked—because clearly I was still overreacting—I sprinted to the back stairs. But then, a thought occurred to me. Pivoting, I jogged to the pantry, grabbed my backpack, and hastily climbed to the second floor, running into Lisa's room after a short moment of hesitation, closing and locking the door.

Eureka!

I had my laptop and research notes. Yes. Yes, yes, yes!

Why I'd neglected to retrieve my backpack prior to now, I couldn't fathom. I'd had opportunity and means—plenty of both—and yet I'd left everything there, hidden in the pantry, out of sight and out of mind.

There is something wrong with me. Why did I wait so long? This behavior isn't normal.

Powering up my laptop, I took a deep breath, some of the earlier ache dissipating as I entered my password and navigated to connect to the Wi-Fi. That's when another disaster struck.

"What? What's this?" I asked the little yellow exclamation point next to our Wi-Fi network.

It's not working.

The Wi-Fi was down. I plugged my phone in and unlocked it to double-check. Sure enough, my phone couldn't connect either.

"Shoooooot!" I made a fist and shook it at the sky. And then I sighed, letting my hand drop.

Using the cellular hotspot, I could connect my laptop to the internet. Sadly, it wasn't fast enough for me to run my analyses, or access my data in any meaningful way. But I could check my email and browse the internet.

So I called Lisa's lawyer, left another voice message noting that she'd never called me back, and connected my laptop to the substandard hotspot.

I searched for any news of Lisa's arrest. I came up empty on *arrest,* but I did find recent links pairing her name with Tyler's. Bracing myself against the sliminess, I clicked on a story from TMZ, timestamp three hours ago.

Front man from Pirate Orgy spotted getting cozy with an unnamed female who was definitely not his longtime ladylove, Lisa DaVinci, DJ Tang and Exotica's wild-child youngest daughter. The pair were making out at a . . . and then blah blah blah.

I clicked through a few gossip sites, all telling the same story: Tyler had been photographed and filmed at a club with someone who was not Lisa, though there was no word from Lisa and no sightings of her. Neither my sister or Tyler were considered big names or newsmakers. She and I seemed to exist on the outer rim of celebrity culture—me because I actively rejected it, her because (I hypothesized) she tried too hard to be a part of it.

After I tired of searching for news on Lisa, I clicked through several of my bookmarks, checking to see if the latest editions of my favorite peer-reviewed publications had been published. They had not. So I busied myself by reading random news stories until doing so made me want to stab someone. I closed my laptop.

And then, debating and dismissing all my non-Abram-related options, I realized I was officially bored.

* * *

It was 6:03 AM and I was awake.

Despite falling asleep after midnight—after spending the remainder of the evening wandering around a silent house, in a boredom funk, eventually watching slowly loading, low res YouTube videos on how to do makeup and hair—I could not go back to sleep.

As dawn gave way to day, I lay in bed, wondering what the last Hawaiian tree snail was up to these days as well as how I could arrange things such that Abram was told the truth about me, about Lisa, without everything going to Venus (hell).

By 7:00 AM I accepted the fact that I had just as much insight into the thoughts of the last Hawaiian tree snail as I had into fixing my present predicament. Therefore, best not to think about either.

The next hour was spent taking a meticulous shower. I—gasp!—washed my hair. And then I tried to give myself a blowout. I did okay, but more practice was needed, and more understanding of what product to use, how much, and at what stage. I added this knowledge deficiency to my list of videos to watch for the day.

Once the hair was done-ish, I (quietly and clandestinely) followed the tutorial I'd saved to my phone for how to do "day eyeliner." Apparently, there was a difference between day and night eyeliner, as well as occasion eyeliner and non-occasion eyeliner (aka everyday eyeliner). Basically, there was an eyeliner strategy for all possible situations.

Are you meeting your boyfriend's parents? There's an eyeliner for that.

Are you going to an office party, during the holidays, but not a Christmas event? There's an eyeliner for that.

Are you flying to Hawaii to view the last Hawaiian tree snail? . . . there was no eyeliner for that. But, should I survive the remainder of this week, I was tempted to record a tutorial for it.

A full hour and a half later, I was dressed and 100 percent ready to do absolutely nothing productive all day. Giving my laptop's new hiding place one last longing look and mentally cursing the lack of high-speed internet, I meandered downstairs. I hadn't appreciated how much I would miss having meaningful tasks to occupy my mind until they were no longer an option.

Striding into the kitchen, I didn't even sniff the air. Honestly, I was sorta kinda hoping to run into Abram. I hadn't seen him since spying on him from the window yesterday. The house had been quiet, like I was completely alone, its sole occupant. I'd been tempted to venture into the basement last night, where the recording studio was housed, or to the third floor, where he was occupying a guest bedroom. I didn't.

This morning, however, the temptation felt more like an incessantly prodding urge and I used food to justify it, arguing with no one about the fact that I was hungry. I'd noticed he'd cleared away the chocolate cake donuts at some point, so I couldn't even eat those. There'd been no decent food in the fridge for days, so of course I must find him and force him to go out with me for food. And if, incidentally, we had to share a meal and talk to each other . . .

But then I opened the fridge, as though to prove what I already knew to be true, and discovered it was now stocked with essentials: eggs, butter, cheese, a variety of vegetables, hummus and several kinds of healthy-ish dips, both raw and cooked chicken breasts. I could easily make a healthy and hearty breakfast, lunch, and dinner. No problem.

Stupid food.

I made myself eggs and toast. I ate them. They were delicious. My stomach was happy with the best breakfast I'd had since arriving in Chicago, but my heart still felt sick and my brain still felt bored.

The discombobulation persisted throughout the day as I wandered the empty main and second floors, checking the clock, wondering when Gabby would arrive. Eventually, I watched a few more tutorials on hair product usage. One of my bookmarked peer-reviewed journals uploaded their monthly publication; I read it from start to finish, jotting down a few thoughts in the composition book that held my current research notes.

I made a big salad for lunch and used all the cooked chicken. I also made four cups of peppermint tea which necessitated four trips to the bathroom. After my late lunch, I managed to read a few chapters of Moby Dick. If ever there was a time to remind myself of life's disappointments, now was that time.

All the while brain-bored and heart-sick. *Or maybe I'm heart-bored and brain-sick?*

Afternoon finally, *finally* crept into evening with no sign of Gabby. Okay. Yes. I was actually looking forward to her visit, and not just because I'd be grilling her for answers about Lisa's arrest. I . . . liked talking to her. *I know!* It was like I didn't even know myself anymore!

The light in the mudroom had dimmed to a soft yellow and then the orangey-pink indicative of sunsets. Staring at the evocative color, I realized it had been a while since I saw a sunset. Several months at least.

Placing my book on the bench seat, I dragged myself to the elevator and punched the call button several times. Yes, I could have taken the stairs, but apparently a by-product of being discombobulated was a general sense of lethargy. I didn't want to take the stairs. I wanted to be sad and lazy.

Leaning a hand against the wall, I waited, twisting my lips to the side as I contemplated how best to view the sunset. My parents had a balcony that was more of a deck leading off my dad's office. It faced northwest.

My mind was on the sunset when the doors slid open, which was probably why I didn't immediately realize Abram was standing in the elevator. But when I did, I gasped. Cartoonishly. And then held perfectly still, staring at him with wide eyes.

Why I did this, I don't know. My body had officially become weird around him. I was on the verge of disowning it and all its crazy Abram-related flutterings.

Meanwhile, he leaned against the back of the elevator, his arms crossed, looking at me with bland indifference. He was wearing all black. Black T-shirt, black jeans, black boots. *Wait. Why is he wearing shoes?*

"Are you going up?" he asked. Eventually.

"Uh. . ." I twisted my fingers. Debating. Debating. My attention lowered to his shoes again. *Is he going somewhere?*

The doors started to slide shut and he made no move to stop them. So, of course I launched myself into the scant space at the last second. The thing about small, private elevators is that their safety measures aren't as responsive as the big, corporate building ones. Which meant I was knocked around a little by the closing doors.

Visibly alarmed, Abram reached out, one hand sliding around my waist, the other gripping my upper arm as he pulled me further into the small lift. This was presumably to either: a) save me from the jaws of death, or b) keep me from clumsily crashing into him.

With comical belatedness, the doors opened again, like, *Oh. Did you want to get on? Sorry about that, old chap.*

But I was already on the elevator, now pressed against the back wall by Abram; his back to the opening as though shielding me from any further door-related injuries; his eyes on mine, a mixture of concerned and confused.

"Are you okay?"

I nodded hurriedly, breathing in through my nose because I missed how he smelled. *Soak it up, buttercup. This might be your last opportunity.*

As usual, the fragrance of him had an inebriating, relaxing effect. But for some reason, this time it also made me want to . . . lick . . . something.

Abram continued to stare down at me. "Are you sure?"

"Yes. I'm fine." I took another breath through my nose. "How are you?"

Abram's grip loosened a little, like he planned to release me.

So my mutinous mouth lied, "But I think I banged up my shoulder a little. Oh. Oh, ouch." I lifted my right shoulder, making a wincing face, even though no part of me hurt. *Pathetic.*

"Is that where the door hit you?" His attention shifted to my offended shoulder and he inspected it, his eyebrows pulling together.

Huh. Clearly, he believed me, and I couldn't believe he'd fallen for that. *Perhaps I no longer require lying lessons.*

"This is where it hit, yes." I leaned forward a smidge, the doors behind him finally slid shut, and the elevator made a *whirring* sound as it slowly ascended.

I could only assume he'd pressed the button for the third floor when he'd originally stepped onto the elevator from the basement and that's why we were moving. I hadn't pressed the fourth-floor button yet, I'd been too busy liking how his body cocooned mine; liking how close he was and how that meant I could feel the warmth of him; liking how his hand slid up my arm to gently prod and smooth over my shoulder, checking for injury; liking how he hadn't seemed to notice that my hands were on his biceps, enjoying the solid strength and size. Or if he'd noticed my hand placement, he didn't seem to care.

Basically, continuing to gaze at Abram, I liked everything about the moment, and this was odd because he was—essentially—taking care of me. If you didn't count medical professionals, I'd never experienced *taking care* with anyone but a nanny, my sister, and Gabby, all incidences which had occurred many, many moons ago.

He frowned at my shoulder. "I think it's fine. But if it bothers you, we should ice it."

"Okay," I said softly, feeling inclined to agree with just about anything he suggested.

But then he stilled, his eyes cutting back to mine. Abram lifted an eyebrow, his gaze narrowing, assessing, examining.

He let me go. He removed himself to the adjacent wall. He crossed his arms.

Clearing his features of expression, his gaze dimming once more to disinterested and reserved, Abram stared forward and cleared his throat. A renewed pang of regret bounced around inside my ribcage as I watched this transformation, amazed at how much distance he was able to put between us in such a small space.

Clearing his throat again, he glanced at the digital floor readout, and then back to me. "Which floor?"

"The, uh, the fourth floor. The top floor." The pang of regret sunk to my stomach. Knowing why he'd stepped back and not at all blaming him for putting distance between us, I rubbed my shoulder.

Though it was my heart that felt injured.

[16]
FURTHER APPLICATIONS OF NEWTON'S LAWS OF MOTION

I watched the sunset. By myself. Wondering when Gabby would finally show up. Feeling like the personification of a bookmark.

Bookmark was the perfect descriptive word for this restless paralyzed state of being. I couldn't think. I couldn't do. I was a placeholder with no power or free will. My only utility was the fact that I existed. A bookmark.

No longer feeling lazy, I jogged down the stairs to the second floor and changed into the white bikini I'd worn twice but had never used. In record time, I was ready to move. I needed exercise so I could sleep. I needed sleep to set my brain in order. *I'll feel better, more myself, after a good night's sleep.*

Again, taking the stairs, I marched past the kitchen, down the hall, and to the mudroom, determined to expend some energy. Alas, just before opening the door, movement in the pool caught my attention.

Abram. In the pool. Swimming. Déjà vu.

Staring at his form, I was breathing harder than I should've been. But that was because I was truly torn. *What should I do?* My brain was getting a rare workout.

We had a gym in the basement. I could change—again—and use the treadmill.

He couldn't swim forever. I could wait until he was finished.

I didn't have to exercise at all. I could go upstairs and read my new book, or good old Moby Dick. A voice that sounded a little like Gabby's whispered between my ears, *It's the only dick you're getting any time soon.*

Growling at the window, I shoved the crass—albeit true—thought to the side. There were several logical paths available to me. But instead of taking any of them, I gathered a deep breath, squared my shoulders, and opened the door. No doubt I was being stubborn and stupid.

But I wanted to go swimming.

Abram using the pool was not a reason for me to avoid swimming. We could be friendly. We were adults, at least in the eyes of the US government. We would be able to manage a civil conversation. Why would he care if I went swimming? He wouldn't.

He won't. . .

Strangely, this thought did nothing to make me feel better.

Still breathing harder than I should've been, I opened the door and left the house. Making a short detour to the little pool shed tucked against the façade of the brownstone my parents had torn down, I grabbed a pair of goggles and a towel. And then I approached the pool, my eyes following Abram as he continued his laps, ignorant of my arrival.

Setting the towel on one of the nearby lounge chairs, I cleared my mind of all dissent and stepped into the pool, hustling to the side he wasn't using. But he must've seen my legs or sensed a shift in the force, because he stopped swimming mid-lap and stood, wiping his eyes and frowning at me.

He was also breathing hard, which was to be expected given the fact that he'd been swimming for an eternity.

Giving him a tight smile and a head nod, but no eye contact, I dipped the googles into the pool and ignored the frantic beating of my heart. Goodness, I'd forgotten how perfectly formed he was up close with no shirt, and this time rivulets of water were dripping from his perfectly formed . . . form.

"Lisa." He moved a step closer.

"Abram." The end of his name caught in the back of my throat, necessitating a thorough throat clearing.

He waited until I'd finished clearing my throat before asking, "What are you doing?"

"Uh, well, you see, if you get the goggles used to the temperature of the water before you wear them, they won't fog as much." I rubbed the lenses with my fingers, staring at the action of my hands with an intensity of concentration more befitting rocket science. *I would know.*

"Not the goggles." He moved again, the ripples of water caused by his body now meeting mine. "What are you doing?" he asked, slower this time.

"I'm going to swim some laps." Finished acclimating the goggles, I pulled them on, correcting the suction around my eye sockets.

I felt his eyes on me. I felt them as assuredly as if he'd touched where he looked. That meant I had the urge to lower myself into the water up to my neck before he spied what my nipples thought about being the subject of his attention.

Spoiler alert: They liked it.

But I didn't lower myself, even though they'd tightened into traitorous stiff beads. Given historical data, everything about this situation and my body's reaction to it should have alarmed me.

First, I wasn't usually scantily clad while around another person.

Second, if I was, it occurred in near or complete darkness, and only after a great deal of discussion surrounding expectations. On the off chance that it wasn't dark, my nipples didn't typically have an opinion about being gazed upon one way or the other.

However, as Abram drifted closer, I discovered my well of wary was running distressingly low. Some reckless part of myself encouraged the rest of me to remain standing, betraying boobs be damned. Abram wanted an eyeful? Fine with me.

Actually, great.

Fantastic!

My irrational thoughts were as follows: I liked him looking. I *wanted* him to look. I wanted him to like what he saw and think about me later. I couldn't talk to him; I couldn't kiss him; I couldn't touch him. But I could stand here, in this bikini, and give him a memory. Hopefully a nice one.

And inexplicably, if I were being honest with myself, Abram looking at my body made me feel absolutelyfuckingfabulous.

See? Clearly, I was sleep-deprived and veering into Gabby's mentally unhinged lane.

"You're going to swim laps in a bikini?" he asked, his voice a little rough.

"Yep." I adjusted my hair so the rubber strap of the goggles didn't tug uncomfortably.

"In a string bikini?"

"Yep." The pool was cool, my cheeks were hot. I dipped my head all the way underwater, getting my hair and face wet while sneaking a glance at Abram's glorious torso, illuminated to perfection by the pool light, and made a nice memory of my own.

I am an Objectifying Olivia. I am Hypocritical Helen. I am a Lying Lisa. I am Winnifred the Worst.

Breaking the surface, I wiped my nose and lips of water, and backed up to the edge of the pool. Freely accepting that I was behaving irrationally, I smoothed my hair away from my face with both hands, the action probably doing great things for my chest headlights.

Abram made a huffing sound, which morphed into a low growl. "You can't wait until I'm finished?"

"You don't need the whole pool." I glanced at him from behind my goggles. And then I stared at him from behind my goggles. And then I ogled him from behind my goggles, which felt most appropriate because goggles were probably designed for ogles, hence the name.

"I'm almost done." He said this through his teeth, his dark glare continuing to blatantly travel over my body. He needed goggles.

"No. You're not." I set my hand on my waist. "Yesterday you were in here for an hour or more."

His eyes narrowed. "How do you know that?"

Stiffening, my hand dropped from my waist. I took a deep breath as a stalling tactic, perversely pleased when his eyes dropped to my chest—as though compelled—before he closed them. The muscle at his jaw jumped. His nostrils flared. He looked pissed. Or frustrated. Or both.

"I wanted to go swimming yesterday," I finally admitted, seeing nothing wrong with telling the truth. "I waited for you to finish. It took forever. I'm not waiting today."

Now he gathered a deep breath and my eyes dropped to his chest and stomach, the sparse smattering of hair and definition of his muscles were hypnotic. Once again, I had that urge to lick . . . something.

Shaking his head, he opened his eyes. They were focused on a spot behind me and to the right, giving me the impression he was purposefully averting his attention.

"Fine. I'll leave." Abram began wading through the water, aiming for the pool steps.

"Fine." I frowned, not liking this development and tearing my ogling eyes from his body. Focusing on the far end of the pool, I muttered childishly, "Good idea. I don't want to embarrass you."

That stopped him. "What?"

"I mean, when I lap you," I said matter-of-factly. "I don't want to embarrass you by how much faster of a swimmer I am. Than you."

Abram's eyelids lowered, a spark of irritation—but also something else—seemed to change them, turn the typically light brown irises the color of smoldering embers. Even in the pale, cyan illumination of the pool light, and from behind the lenses of my goggles, I saw the transformation.

"You think so?" His jaw worked and his words sounded like a dare. Both made my skin erupt in goose bumps of anticipation.

If I thought his glare had been sexy, this look paired with his bare chest and ticking-time-bomb jaw was cosmically erotic. *Another nice memory.*

"I know so," I said, just as darkly, lying. I wasn't certain I could beat him, but I was certainly up for giving it a try.

"Fine." He spat the word, moving his big body through the water and to the edge of the pool. Placing himself three feet from where I stood, he didn't glance at me as he barked, "Here's the deal: two laps—there and back two times—winner stays, loser leaves."

Oh jeez. Okay. Hmm . . .

I'd previously promised myself never to enter into a bet with Abram. *You promised the universe. You promised—*

"Five laps. There and back five times," I said, ignoring the recollection of my promise even though doing so gave me a niggle of discomfort.

I'd suggested five laps partially to be contrary. But also, partially because five laps were more than two. If he won, at least I'd get *some* exercise. And also, partially because I wanted to see him wet, angry, and breathing hard up close again.

"Okay." He drew out the word, still not looking at me. "Five."

"Good. Ready?" I lifted my hands to the edge behind me, gripping it and bracing my feet against the wall.

He did likewise. "On the count of three."

"One," I said.

I felt him glance at me, but all he said was, "Two."

"Thr—"

He pushed forward, BEFORE I'D FINISHED SAYING THREE!! UGH!!!!

Furious and, yes, turned on, I launched forward, pumping my arms and legs as though my life depended on winning, which it kind of did.

Since I'd promised I wouldn't make a bet with Abram, I decided to change it into a bet with the universe, in my heart, a secret bet. If I won, I would tell him the truth, about Lisa, about me, about how I felt —even though I didn't have complete clarity on that subject—but if I lost, I'd keep my mouth shut.

Lactic acid burned my muscles, my quads ached, my lungs felt like they might explode, but I made it to the far side of the pool and back in record time, narrowing Abram's cheating lead. After the second lap we were neck and neck, after the third I was slightly ahead.

But as we pushed off against the deep-side wall, marking the middle of the fourth lap, Abram surged forward. His hips were next to my face, which meant he was a half body length—a half *Abram* body length—ahead, and I was swimming as fast as I could. There was no way I would catch up. No way.

Despair and frustration gripped my throat and heart and lungs. I felt like crying. I think I did cry because I couldn't see out of my goggles anymore. Heading into the fifth lap blind, I gritted my teeth, telling myself this was it. This last lap was it. Even though I didn't believe in such things, I told myself, if I lost, it would be the universe communicating with me. I'd made a binding and irrevocable bet: I could never tell him the truth and there would always be lies between us.

I turned at the far wall just a second after he did. Head down, eyes closed, I put every joule of energy, every milligram of mass, every newton of force in my entire being into propelling myself to first.

Lungs on fire, my hand touched the wall and I immediately popped up, ripping off my goggles and looking to my right, to where Abram should have been. For a second, for a single, solitary moment in the eternity of time, my heart swelled with so much happiness and relief, I thought I might die. He was not there. He hadn't yet finished. *YES!*

But then, after two more seconds and no Abram, I frowned. Glancing around, searching for him, I found him treading water in the middle of the pool.

I blinked. Shocked. Stunned. Horrified. "What- why?" I didn't know what I wanted to ask first, and I was still struggling to catch my breath.

He was also breathing hard, also working to catch his, watching me with veiled eyes, too far away for me to search his face for answers.

"What are you doing?" I asked, my voice pitched high and slightly hysterical.

He shook his head. "I forfeit."

"You- you- you what?" Unthinkingly, I waded toward him, my dismayed stare transfixed on his extremely cool one.

"You win, I'll leave." Shrugging, he gave the water a languid stroke, bringing him closer, but only incidentally. I could see now that his destination was the pool steps, not me.

"No!" I darted to the side, putting myself in his path, forcing him to backtrack so as not to collide with me. "No, I don't win! It's not winning if you give up."

"What's the problem? You win." His glare had returned, his dark eyebrows descending over equally dark eyes.

"You forfeit, that's giving up. Not the same as me winning!" My voice was now a frantic, enraged whisper. I slammed the water with my hands, splashing it everywhere. I didn't care, angry tears were making it impossible for me to see.

God, I just . . . *I just* . . . I couldn't remember ever being so angry before.

"What the hell is your problem?" Once again, Abram was speaking through his teeth.

"You're my problem." I shoved my face into his. "You don't forfeit —i.e. *give up*—in the last leg of the last lap. That's a shitty thing to do."

"Oh? Really? Was that shitty of me?" Likewise, he shoved his face forward, not that he had much room to move.

"Yes. Very shitty," I whispered, but then swallowed the last word because the current of the water—waves caused by our race—pushed me forward. My front knocked into and then slid against his, the slippery friction like a KO punch to my good sense and a wake-up call to everything else.

Him. His eyes. His body. Just . . . *yesssss.* Yes. The texture, the warmth, the hard planes, the everything. My eyes fell to his lips, pink lusciousness framed by the black shadow of his scruff, a blushing rose among thorns, and I could not look away.

Abram sucked in a hissing breath, his hands immediately coming to my arms and separating us by gently—and firmly—moving me away. But he only moved me six or seven centimeters. We were still plenty close. *But not close enough.* But still plenty.

"What. Are. You. Doing?" he growled, sounding frustrated and furious. But the question also sounded like a plea.

Still transfixed by his mouth, I shook my head, blinking, breathing just as hard as I'd been when I'd finished the race.

Lie.

Walk away.
Say one of your anytime-phrases.
These were all signposts on the logical path forward. But I didn't do any of these. I couldn't. I was caught in some unknown field, propelled and shredded by an unidentified force, not contact, neither gravitational, magnetic, nor electrical.

Struggling against it made it worse. Ignoring it made it stronger. The only thing I hadn't tried was accepting it. *But I can't.*

"I can't . . ."

"You can't what?"

A wrinkle appeared between his eyebrows, something flaring behind his eyes as they drilled into mine. He released my arms, pushing his fingers through the fall of hair on his forehead, pushing it away with both hands, and then he waited. Glaring at me, his arms falling to his sides, standing still while his chest rose and fell with his slowing breaths.

He waited. He waited for me.

And I was such a mess, wanting to rage and laugh and cry; wanting him to pull me close, and dreading what would happen if he did; wanting to rewind time to the moment he'd stopped swimming so I could also stop and scream at him to finish, so I could win, so I could tell him the truth.

Now we were here and "by forfeit" was not how a bargain with the universe was won. This was not winning. This was neither winning nor losing, which meant I was back at square one. Which was losing.

I felt my chin wobble and I firmed it, pressing my lips together to stop the revealing involuntary waver, but it was too late. He'd seen it. I knew at once because he took a deep breath, the force of anger in his glare dwindling to merely mystified uncertainty.

"Lisa. What are you doing? Why are you doing this?" he asked with impossible tenderness. "You win. You don't want me. I'm done. I'm leaving."

"It doesn't feel like winning." My voice was unsteady and my words were unplanned, so were the hot tears that spilled over my cheeks. *I'm a mess!*

I hoped they'd be camouflaged by the residual pool water but knew at once this was not the case. Abram's gaze watched their progress, gliding down my face. His features were restive, betraying his indecision, his uncertainty. But the hesitation didn't last.

Lifting his hands to cup my face, his thumbs brushing away the tracks of saltwater, Abram's gaze softened. All contrary emotions dissolved, replaced by resolute concern.

"Don't cry." He pressed his forehead to mine. "Please don't cry."

"I'm not crying." I sniffled, closing my eyes, more tears leaking from beneath my lashes, my stupid chin wobbling. *Why did he have to forfeit?*

He chuckled. "Why are you crying?"

"Why did you forfeit?" I'd been aiming for accusatory, but the question came out sounding watery and just plain sad.

"You're crying because I forfeit?" His voice held humor and incredulity.

"No. That's not—" I sniffled again, taking several deep breaths, and then said firmly, "I'm not crying."

"Stubborn."

"I'm not—"

"Shh." Against my lips I felt his shushing breath, which made me hold mine. The ever present, simmering desire low in my belly twisted, but the paralyzing restlessness within me thawed. How my body could respond in this dichotomous way, at once relaxing and tightening when he touched me, I had no idea.

Abram's fingers pushed into my wet hair, curling around my neck, and his nose slid against mine, nuzzling.

"You have to tell me what you want," he whispered gruffly. "If you don't want me, tell me. But you have to know, you must know, I only want to make you happy."

ELASTICITY: STRESS AND STRAIN

S igh.
My heart.

I opened my eyes. Our gazes didn't clash, they mated. Instead of cymbals between my ears, I heard the gentle lapping of the pool against the tile, the sounds of the city, the hum of summer insects in our little garden oasis.

I breathed out, lifting my chin by a millimeter, licking my lips. *Kiss me.*

His gorgeous stare never wavered from mine, he didn't move, not to close the scant distance between our mouths, not to push me away. No.

He was waiting. Again. Waiting for me.

Please. Please kiss me.

I wanted him to end this torture because I couldn't be the one to end it. Telling him the truth was not an option because it would jeopardize my sister, and I refused to be another person who let her down. But kissing Abram without telling him the truth was also not an option, a line I absolutely couldn't cross.

However.

If he kisses me, I reasoned and bartered with the universe, searching for a new deal, *I'll have to tell him the truth, right? I wouldn't have a choice. The decision would be made.*

"Lisa," he said, a gentle whisper, the single-word reminder of reality breaking the spell so completely, it jarred me to my core. The seismic equivalent of telling a roomful of kindergarteners that they would never have candy again. And then following that devastation with a forty-five-minute lecture on taxes.

Stepping away, I dropped my head and closed my eyes, feeling the weight of air and dark matter and cosmic dust press down on my shoulders. I wanted to hit the water again. I wanted to throw a giant tantrum.

Instead I whispered, "Fuck."

A moment later, I heard Abram sigh. A moment after that, I heard the telltale sound of him moving through the water, leaving. My stomach sunk and I swallowed around the rocks in my throat, but I wouldn't cry. It was an unfair situation, of my own making, and he deserved better. So, so, so much better.

Let him go. And let this be the last time.

But then I felt his palm slide against mine, his fingers entwined my fingers, and he squeezed. My eyes flew open and, wide-eyed, I looked up at him. He wasn't looking at me. Jaw set, Abram's eyes were on the stairs leading out of the pool. Without pausing, he pulled me after him.

I found my voice as I crested the last step. "Where are we going?"

Releasing my hand, he passed me my towel, only glancing at me briefly. "Here. Dry off."

I accepted it, wrapping it around my body and reflexively folding the top over so it wouldn't unravel.

Abram wiped at his face, neck, and torso with forceful strokes, and then wrapped his around his hips. Reaching for and grabbing my hand again, we were on the move.

To the house, up the stairs, into the mudroom, down the hall. He stopped in the kitchen, turning to face me, but not releasing my hand.

"We should watch a movie. You like movies?" The words were abrupt, direct, and had an edge of impatience.

"Movies?" I parroted dumbly.

"Yes. Movies."

Inspecting him, I searched his face for some sign as to his thoughts, what he hoped to accomplish. He didn't look angry.

Disappointed? Yes.

Angry? Not at all.

But you know what? Of the two, the disappointment felt worse.

Gathering a deep breath, I couldn't help what expression my face was making, but I assumed it was something like dismayed remorse. "Abram, I am so sorry. I never—"

He waved away my apology. "Nope. No apologies. No explaining. No talking. No."

"No . . . ? No talk—"

"Go upstairs, change, shower, whatever. Come down when you're ready, to the basement. We'll watch a movie."

I shook my head, feeling my eyebrows pull together, not understanding what was happening. *He won't close the distance of three centimeters to kiss me, so he wants to watch a movie?*

He must've read the confused anguish in my eyes and on my face, especially since I was unable and disinclined to hide them, because his left dimple made an appearance. "Look—" he brought my hand up, pressing it flat between both of his "—I trust you, so trust me. I just want to spend time with you. We don't have to talk. You don't need to apologize for anything. We can sit together, watch a movie, share popcorn."

A little breath escaped me, one of wonder and distress. How was he so damn perfect all the damn time?

"There's nothing wrong with watching a movie, people do it all the time," he prodded gently, tilting his head, his hand coming to my hair, smoothing over the wet strands and down my back. "It doesn't have to mean anything."

* * *

It meant something.

Lying next to Abram on the big, red, plush love seat, tucked under his arm, my cheek on his chest, smelling his man-fragrance while we watched *The Blues Brothers* on the home theater screen, it definitely meant something.

But that didn't make him a liar, because it hadn't started out meaning anything.

After I went upstairs and showered, haphazardly blow-drying my hair and applying minimal makeup, I changed into a pair of yoga pants and a tank top. My brain on self-destruct autopilot, I didn't think about the logical path forward or fretting about my actions. I thought about popcorn.

We'd begun the movie in the chairs, with the popcorn between us on a buffer seat. He'd given me a polite smile, saying nothing, and motioned that I should take the chair on the other side of the popcorn. The theater seats were a good size, but Abram was taller than average. He shifted in his chair several times, crossing his legs at the knee when he couldn't stretch them out fully in front of him.

But ten minutes after the movie started, Abram sighed, picked up the popcorn and moved to the love seat at the front of the room, reclining on his back, a hand behind his head, his feet and legs stretched out toward the screen.

The love seat wasn't a typical love seat, which was a smaller version of a sofa. It was the width of a love seat with a pull-out ottoman piece extending towards the screen that turned it into a giant chaise lounge, basically a full-sized bed with sofa cushions at the back.

"Hey," I called out disgruntledly after he settled in, raising my voice over the action of the film.

He lifted on his elbow and twisted his neck to look at me. "What?"

"You took the popcorn."

He held out the bag with his other arm. "Come take it if you want it."

My frowning gaze flickered between the bag and his face. He'd made the popcorn. It didn't make sense for me to take the whole thing. I could go to the kitchen and get a bowl so the popcorn was split evenly, or I could take several trips (up to where he held the popcorn hostage) several times during the movie to grab handfuls, or I could—

"Or just sit up here with me. Whatever."

Well. Since he suggested it.

Clearly self-destruction autopilot was still engaged, because I crossed to the love seat, scooched back until I rested against the sofa cushions, my legs stretched out in front of me, and stuck my hand in the popcorn bag between us.

Around the halfway mark, my eyes glanced over at Abram. The popcorn was gone, so the bag wasn't between us. His ankles were crossed. He had a hand on the T-shirt covering his stomach and an arm behind his head. His eyes were on the screen and a smile was on his mouth. A sliver of skin where his T-shirt hem had lifted away from his jeans was visible, as was the gray-and-black waistband of his boxers (which might have been boxer briefs, more data were required before a definitive classification could be made).

He looked comfortable, relaxed, happy, and I felt an answering desire to an unasked question: I wanted to be as he was.

In his own way, but in a way that was entirely alien to me, Abram was stunningly pragmatic and rational. Here he was, in a state of disappointment, and yet also in a comfortable, relaxed, and happy state. How did he do that? How could one state follow the other so seamlessly? Or exist in tandem?

I formulated no hypothesis, because a second later, he caught me staring.

As usual, I quickly tore my eyes away, a blaze of self-consciousness rushing to my cheeks. His eyes were on me. I felt them, but I also confirmed this sense with a quick glance in his direction. His eyes were on me and it wasn't a quick scrutinizing. Now he was staring. Unabashedly.

"Hey," he said after a protracted moment, lifting his hand from his stomach and placing it on my back. His palm moved in a slow circle over the thin fabric of my tank top. "Are you comfortable? You wanna lie down?"

I wasn't comfortable only because I wanted to lie down. The logical path was to remain in my present position as lying down felt a little stupid and dangerous, like acknowledging the slipperiness of the slope and attempting the slope anyway.

Even so, self-destruct autopilot engaged, I nodded and lay down. His arm behind me didn't move as I readjusted myself, which meant my head rested on his bicep when I finally reclined. The butterflies in my stomach made concentrating on the film difficult, so when his arm came around me, squeezing me to his chest during a particularly funny part, I only knew it was funny because he was laughing so hard.

That was the moment my head ended up over his heart. Instead of listening to Dan Aykroyd and John Belushi tell me about their mission from God, I counted Abram's heartbeats, slowing my breathing to see if I could match his pulse to mine.

Tangentially, I realized that listening to Abram's heart had been a terrible idea, a critical error in judgment. Now—even with the tempo still filling my ear—I knew with absolute certainty I would never tire of the sound. In fact, I would crave it for the rest of my life, from this moment forward.

Our society warns us from an early age to eschew drugs that might be addictive, or habits and hobbies—like gambling or video games or fantasy worlds—that employ Skinner box tactics meant to target addiction-causing pleasure centers of the brain.

But no one tells you to avoid the sound of a heartbeat.

This was also *the* moment. Laying here with Abram was the memory I would keep, the one I would retrieve on rainy days, the one that would inspire wistful daydreams. And as beautiful as he'd been in the pool, as utterly perfect of an exterior he possessed, I wouldn't be thinking of his body when I missed him, I would be thinking of his heart.

By the final musical act, the entire length of me was pressed against Abram's body, one arm draped over his stomach, my other arm tucked between us, our feet tangled, his hand lazily moving up and down my side. When the end credits rolled, I didn't notice.

"Hey," he said eventually after the final credit had scrolled, the screen had faded to black. "The movie is over."

"Yep." I tightened my arm around his torso, holding on and squeezing my eyes shut. Maybe if I refused to acknowledge the existence of reality, reality would cease to exist. *All hypotheses are worth exploring! Even the crazy ones.*

He took a deep breath, his chest rising and lifting my head as he filled his lungs with air. I clung to him.

"Lisa." I felt him shift, his hand that had been supporting his head came to my forearm and he caressed the length of it with his palm. "Do you want to get up?"

"No."

He chuckled, and then sighed. "Okay. Do you want to talk?"

"No."

Seven. Eight. Nine. Ten . . . I was counting the beats of his heart between questions and noted with some interest that his pulse had just increased. His heart was beating faster, which meant mine—which had been in sync with his for the last quarter of the movie— also began beating faster.

"What do you want to do?" His voice deepened, and there was no mistaking the grumbly, suggestive quality to it.

"So many things," I whispered. My leg constricted over his thigh, my arm around his waist now squeezing, I scrunched my eyes tighter.

He waited, his breath becoming shallow.

Twenty-nine, thirty, thirty-one, thirty-two . . .

And then he waited, his breath returning to normal.

Forty-seven, forty-eight, forty-nine . . . Inexplicably, his heart rate slowed. Mine fell out of sync, because mine was still racing.

Abram took another deep breath, speaking as he exhaled, "Okay. We have time. When you're ready, I'll be here." His arm around me tightened briefly and then relaxed. He kissed my forehead. "I'll always be here."

As his words sunk in, a small, silent huff of bitter amusement escaped my lungs.

Time?

No. We had no time. Lisa was due back any day. There was no more time. Time was up.

Here?

Here he was. Here we were. Here was I. Experiencing the first and only time in my life where I didn't want someone to ask permission or for instructions prior to touching me, and that's exactly what he does.

Oh. The *IRONY!*

Hot tears of frustration pressed against the back of my eyelids, stinging my nose and throat. I rolled my lips between my teeth, firming my chin to keep it from wobbling. Meanwhile, Abram's heart had returned to its steady beat, his hand still smoothing languidly back and forth along my forearm, his breathing regular and even.

My mind worked to extinguish this reality and replace it with an alternate one, one where he knew I was Mona, but we'd still found ourselves at this singularity in time.

I wanted it so badly, *so badly.* If wanting were a means by which travel between dimensions was possible, surely my want would have carried us there. But the gulf between wanting and reality was just as vast as the chasm between wanting and action.

Not insurmountable, but well beyond my reach.

Unless . . .

Unless I actively made a choice to betray my sister by telling Abram the truth, or betrayed Abram by taking what I wanted with the lies between us. Those were my options. Neither were the logical path forward and both would fundamentally change who I was, thereby changing my reality.

These were the circular thoughts in my head as I fell asleep in Abram's arms. I didn't remember falling asleep. But I must have drifted off, because I was awoken from delightful dreams of alternate realities—where I told Abram the truth and he forgave me at once, offering to help with Lisa's plight just before removing my clothes— by someone holding my nose closed.

It was a peculiar thing, something Lisa and Gabby and I used to do to each other during sleepovers as children. As such, I wasn't able to incorporate it into my now deliciously dirty dream and it woke me at once.

Blinking scratchy eyes open, I squinted at the face above mine.

Gabby.

Her eyes were wide and she was mouthing something. I frowned, not understanding.

She huffed and then pressed her index finger to her lips, tilting her head to my right, her left while shifting her eyes meaningfully. Clearly, she was indicating to something on my right, so I glanced that way.

Abram. Asleep.

Oh. Oh yeah!

Understanding at once that she wanted me to be quiet so as not to wake my sleepy, messy Adonis, I nodded faintly, lifting the hand that rested on his stomach to gesture that I was getting up. This seemed to immediately relieve whatever anxiety she was feeling, because the crazy quality behind her stare ease and she nodded.

Rubbing my eyes, I scooched to the end of the couch as unobtrusively as possible, making careful movements so as not to disturb Abram. I met Gabby just outside the entrance to the theater, where—again—she pressed her index finger to her lips and waved me forward toward the hallway that led to the stairs.

Fuzzy headed, I followed, up the stairs, past the kitchen landing. It wasn't until the second flight that I spoke, asking and thinking at the same time, "How did you get in?"

Gabby glanced at me briefly over her shoulder. "Lisa has her keys."

I stopped.

Every cell, every atom, electron, neutron, positron, and quark within me stopped.

Time might also have stopped. The ability to see and hear certainly stopped, my brain and heart and body all aligning to become a void of absolute nothingness, which was accompanied by the strangest thought.

I no longer exist.

ABOUT THE AUTHOR

Penny Reid is the *New York Times*, *Wall Street Journal*, and *USA Today* Bestselling Author of the Winston Brothers, Knitting in the City, Rugby, Dear Professor, and Hypothesis series. She used to spend her days writing federal grant proposals as a biomedical researcher, but now she just writes books. She's also a full time mom to three diminutive adults, wife, daughter, knitter, crocheter, sewer, general crafter, and thought ninja.

Come find me -
Mailing List: http://pennyreid.ninja/newsletter/
Goodreads: http://www.goodreads.com/ReidRomance
Email: pennreid@gmail.com …hey, you! Email me ;-)

OTHER BOOKS BY PENNY REID

Knitting in the City Series

(Contemporary Romantic Comedy)

Neanderthal Seeks Human: A Smart Romance (#1)

Neanderthal Marries Human: A Smarter Romance (#1.5)

Friends without Benefits: An Unrequited Romance (#2)

Love Hacked: A Reluctant Romance (#3)

Beauty and the Mustache: A Philosophical Romance (#4)

Ninja at First Sight (#4.75)

Happily Ever Ninja: A Married Romance (#5)

Dating-ish: A Humanoid Romance (#6)

Marriage of Inconvenience: (#7)

Neanderthal Seeks Extra Yarns (#8)

Knitting in the City Coloring Book (#9)

Winston Brothers Series

(Contemporary Romantic Comedy, spinoff of *Beauty and the Mustache*)

Beauty and the Mustache (#0.5)

Truth or Beard (#1)

Grin and Beard It (#2)

Beard Science (#3)

Beard in Mind (#4)

Dr. Strange Beard (#5)

Beard with Me (#5.5, coming 2019)

Beard Necessities (#6, coming 2019)

Hypothesis Series

(New Adult Romantic Comedy)

Elements of Chemistry: ATTRACTION, HEAT, and CAPTURE (#1)

Laws of Physics: MOTION, SPACE, and TIME (#2, coming 2019)

Fundamentals of Biology: STRUCTURE, EVOLUTION, and GROWTH (#3, coming 2021)

Irish Players (Rugby) Series – by L.H. Cosway and Penny Reid

(Contemporary Sports Romance)

The Hooker and the Hermit (#1)

The Pixie and the Player (#2)

The Cad and the Co-ed (#3)

The Varlet and the Voyeur (#4)

Dear Professor Series

(New Adult Romantic Comedy)

Kissing Tolstoy (#1)

Kissing Galileo (#2, read for FREE in Penny's newsletter 2018-2019)

Ideal Man Series

(Contemporary Romance Series of Jane Austen Re-Tellings)

Pride and Dad Jokes (#1, coming 2019)

Man Buns and Sensibility (#2, TBD)

Sense and Manscaping (#3, TBD)

Persuasion and Man Hands (#4, TBD)

Mantuary Abbey (#5, TBD)

Mancave Park (#6, TBD)

Emmanuel (#7, TBD)

CPSIA information can be obtained
at www.ICGtesting.com
Printed in the USA
BVHW052119240119
538546BV00005B/11/P

9 781635 763393